# CHINA
# TRADE

BY

S. J. ROZAN

# CHINA
# TRADE

ST. MARTIN'S PRESS

NEW YORK

*Design by Judith A. Stagnitto*

LIBRARY OF CONGRESS CATALOGING-IN-PUBLICATION DATA

Rozan, S. J.
    China trade / S. J. Rozan.
        p.   cm.
    ISBN 0-312-11254-8
    I. Title.
PS3568.099C48   1994
813'.54—dc20                                    94-13083
                                                CIP

First Edition: October 1994
10 9 8 7 6 5 4 3 2 1

THIS ONE IS
AS IT ALWAYS WAS
FOR PRB

To

My sainted agent, Steve Axelrod
My genius editor, Keith Kahla
Sui-Ling and all the *Junggwok neuiyahn*, for examples
Becca, Carl, Deb, and Steve, for support
Betsy, Ellen, Ingrid, Jim, Lawton, and Royal, for criticism

and especially
Helen and Nancy, for everything

Thanks

# ONE

I jumped a pothole in Canal Street as I dashed between honking cars and double-parked ones. A cab driver trying to beat the light screeched on his brakes and cursed me, luckily in a language I don't speak. Pinballing along the sidewalk from fish seller to fruit merchant to sidewalk mah-jongg game, I charged up Canal and down Mulberry. I pushed my way through the throngs of shoppers, who're mostly local this time of year because Christmas is over but we're coming up on Chinese New Year. I hopped curbs, squirmed sideways, and tried not to elbow old ladies as I raced to the old school building on Mulberry opposite the park. When I finally got there I stopped. I drew in sharp, cold air until my heart slowed and my breathing was back to normal. Then I calmly climbed the stairs and rang the bell.

I hate to be late.

I especially would have hated to be late to a business meeting with one of my own brothers. Though given the way this all turned out, it's obvious to me I should never work for my family again.

In Chinatown, though, it's not that easy. They can't not ask you, and you can't say no.

Not that it was Tim who'd asked me. He hadn't been the one who called, and he hadn't been mentioned. That told me a lot: It told me he didn't approve of hiring me, though he hadn't stopped it. Well, he couldn't, could he? "Don't get my little sister, she'll screw up and I'll never live it down." No, he would have to pretend he thought I was the greatest private investigator since Magnum P.I. in order to save his own face; but I knew what he was thinking.

My family all thinks it.

The heavy wooden door, left over from when the building actually was a school, swung open. Well, maybe "swung" is too ambitious a word; it was more like it moved grudgingly aside. Nora Yin, one foot holding the grumpy door, stepped forward, took my arm, and steered me in.

"Hi, Lydia. Thanks for coming so fast." She gave me a real, if worried, smile. Nora was tall for a Chinese woman, and broad-shouldered. She'd been a year ahead of me in high school. Nora had never passed notes in math class and had been a volleyball star besides.

"Well, you said it was important, and I wasn't in the middle of anything."

And hadn't been for two weeks, I didn't add. Business was slow.

"We're in my office." Behind her, the door clicked sullenly shut. "Come on."

The building was the headquarters of Chinatown Pride, a group of community organizers, social-service deliverers, and general troublemakers. I liked them a lot. Their offices were on the third floor. The old gym and auditorium, which they used for public programs, were on the first floor, and their small museum was sandwiched between. They had bought the building from the city for a dollar. Now, looking at the peeling paint, listening to the stairs squeak, I wasn't sure who'd gotten the better deal.

"How's Matt?" I asked Nora as we climbed. I hadn't seen Nora's younger brother Matt for years now, but he'd been my first boyfriend. We'd had the sort of sweet, exhilarating romance that young teenagers carry on mostly in public, partly because you have no place to go, and partly because you're not sure, not really sure yet, that you want to go there.

"Okay, I suppose. He's still in California. I don't hear from him much."

Her voice had a chill in it that I was sorry to hear. They'd never been close; Matt was intense, impatient, a street-hockey player who'd scorned school. He'd sneered at Nora curled up in the Yins' cramped living room doing and redoing her homework, and at her weekend volunteer projects. Nora had despised Matt's cigarette-smoking friends and the hours wasted on street corners. After, to no one's surprise, Matt had gotten involved on the fringes of a now-defunct gang, he'd been shipped off to live with relatives in northern California.

They didn't think much of each other, I mused as we rounded the final landing, but family was family. I fight with my brothers all the time, especially Tim and Ted, but I'm not sure I'd like it any better if they just sort of pretended I didn't exist.

"Well," I said, "if you talk to him, tell him I said hi."

Nora shrugged at that, then put on her professional face to enter her office at the top of the stairs.

There were three people waiting for us there. The one nearest the door—a white, middle-aged man, stoop-shouldered, with thick gray hair—stood promptly as Nora and I came in, his eyes on Nora's worn vinyl floor like a little boy not entirely sure of what well-mannered behavior was but earnestly trying to remember. He held an earthenware teacup, the kind without a handle, and the air was fragrant with jasmine tea.

Nora stopped inside the doorway to do the introductions.

"Lydia, this is Dr. Mead Browning. Dr. Browning was on my thesis committee, from the Art History Department."

Nora's Ph.D. thesis subject was Images of Woman in Tang Dynasty Art, and her committee, I'd heard, was a triumph of her diplomatic skill.

Dr. Browning smiled bashfully when he shook my hand. He didn't meet my eyes, but probably that was my fault. My mother always says I stare.

Next to Dr. Browning a slim, sixtyish Asian woman remained seated as she extended her hand to me. She wore a soft, perfectly fitted black wool dress, small gold earrings with what looked like real pearls in them, and a single strand of what also looked like real pearls around her neck. I don't know anything about pearls; maybe they only looked real because of the air of grace and authority of the woman who wore them.

"And this is Mrs. Mei-li Blair," said Nora. "Mrs. Blair, this is Lydia Chin." Nora moved around her desk to sit in the old swivel chair behind it. The chair squeaked like the stairs. I shook Mrs. Blair's hand, thinking her name was probably supposed to mean something to me. Her hair had turned almost completely to silver and was cut into a satiny cap of exquisite precision. My hair, when it turns, will probably go messily gray, and my haircuts won't hold their organization any better when I'm sixty than they have since I was twelve.

The other person in the room was a man, Chinese, two years and two days older than me. He perched on the windowsill and fumed. That was Tim. I offered to shake hands with him, too, but that just seemed to annoy him. Nora hid a smile.

I stuffed my yellow hat into my jacket sleeve and hung the jacket on the back of my chair while Nora poured me tea. Then she got right down to business.

"We've had a robbery," she said. "We're hoping you can help."

"A robbery? When? Was anybody hurt? Why didn't you tell me?" Before I could stop myself my eyes flew to Tim, searching for bruises, cuts, signs of an armed struggle.

"We *are* telling you, Lydia." Tim's voice was exasperated. "And it wasn't a robbery, it was a burglary. No one was here and no one saw them. No one was hurt," he added, sort of extraneously. "People don't usually get hurt during the commission of a burglary."

"Sometimes they do," I said, before I could tell myself to shut up. "Violent criminal activity often happens in the course of the commission of non-violent crimes." I was suddenly appalled to realize I sounded as pompous as he did.

"I'm a lawyer, Lydia," Tim reminded me pointedly. "I know something about criminal behavior."

I squelched the obvious crack. "Well, tell me about your burglary." I looked back to Nora and smiled.

Nora picked up her cue. She shrugged at the semantic difference between "robbery" and "burglary." "Someone broke into the basement and stole some things," she said.

"What things?" I asked. "What do you guys keep in the basement?" So far as I knew, Chinatown Pride wasn't exactly rich in assets. I couldn't imagine anything from its basement being worth hiring a private investigator to find.

Nora looked at Tim, who looked out the window, frowning. "I have to tell you," Nora said, "that Tim doesn't approve of the way we're going about this."

"You don't actually have to tell me," I said. "I guessed."

"As CP's legal counsel he believes we should have called the police," Nora went on, before Tim could say anything. "The Board did meet and discuss doing that, but for what seem to us like good reasons we don't want to. We want to see what you can do first."

"Well, I'll be glad to help however I can," I said cooperatively, professionally, and maybe just a touch smarmily, for Tim's benefit. "What was stolen? And why aren't you telling the police?"

Nora's eyes, this time, went to Dr. Browning. He looked quickly down at his teacup. Nora turned back to me. "A month ago the museum got an unexpected gift. The Blair porcelains—do you know about them?"

I shook my head. Tim barely hid a frustrated sigh. Now

that wasn't fair, I thought. I can't be expected to know about everything there is. If he weren't CP's legal counsel I'll bet he wouldn't know about the Blair porcelains either.

"What are the Blair porcelains?" I asked Nora as though it were a natural question.

Nora turned to Mrs. Blair, who took up her silent offer to be the one to answer me.

"My husband, Hamilton," Mrs. Blair said, in a voice that was quiet but not weak, "was a collector of Chinese export porcelains. Upon his death three months ago, I was faced with a decision about the future of his collection." She stopped to sip her tea. She had a slight Chinese accent in her British-inflected speech: English was not her native language, but she had been speaking it, quite correctly, for a long time. "My husband, Miss Chin, was something of a recluse. He collected strictly for his own pleasure—and mine, insofar as I could appreciate the beauty of the objects he loved so. The main pleasure I took from the collection was watching Hamilton's excitement and joy as each new piece came to us."

She stopped again, and though she drank, I didn't think thirst was what had put the catch in her voice.

She lowered her cup and continued. "I didn't share Hamilton's passion for these porcelains, but he was devoted to them. After he died, it did not seem right to me that an aging woman in an empty house should be all the companionship the pieces he had loved so much would have."

I finished my tea and half-turned to put my cup down on the coffee table. As I did I noticed Dr. Browning smiling slightly, looking at his knees. There was a little color in his cheeks, too.

Mrs. Blair went on: "There were many options for the disposition of the collection, and I had no basis for a decision. I consulted Dr. Browning, whom I had not met but whom Hamilton had greatly respected. After discussions with him and with Nora, I had given the entire collection to the museum here, as a gift."

6

I was astounded. "To CP?" I bit my tongue to keep from asking, Something that valuable?

Mrs. Blair smiled. "My family is from Hong Kong, not Chinatown, but I am Chinese. My brother owns an import-export firm further up Mulberry Street, but until Dr. Browning told me about Chinatown Pride, I had no idea there was a museum of any sort in this neighborhood. I feel, and Nora confirms this, that my ignorance is not unusual. If my gift can help raise this museum's profile in Chinatown and in the city at large, I would consider it an honor."

Nora turned to me. "When we started the museum," she said, "we wanted people—kids, especially—to come here to learn about what an ancient civilization they come from. To start being proud of being Chinese, instead of ashamed of being different."

"And it works," I said, recalling giggling groups of third graders poking each other in awe at the Peking Opera costume exhibit the day I'd taken my oldest nephews there. "It's beginning to catch on."

Nora nodded. She gestured the teapot around, but Mrs. Blair and Dr. Browning didn't want any more and Tim only drinks Lipton's. "The museum's grown slowly," she said. "The Blair porcelains are the most important gift we've ever gotten. There were other museums that were hoping for this collection and consider themselves better equipped to display and protect it. The Blair collection has quite a reputation among porcelain experts, even though almost no one has actually seen it."

"They haven't seen it?"

"As I said," Mrs. Blair spoke in a voice that was used to not having to be raised to be heard, and that was also, it seemed to me, used to being understood the first time, "my husband was a recluse. He found most people tiresome, greedy, and hypocritical. Without honor, and full of secrets. His collection was his refuge. Porcelain, he often said, had no secrets: It is surface beauty applied over a perfect foundation. My husband did not invite other people to share his refuge."

Nora looked at me with a steady gaze. "Lydia, I don't know how much you know about the museum world, but if it gets around that we couldn't hold on to this gift it would mean a tremendous loss of face for us. We might never get another donor to consider us again."

I began to get the importance of this to Nora and CP. "That's what was stolen? The Blair porcelains?"

"Not the whole collection," Nora said. "Two crates."

"How much is that?"

"Nine pieces," Dr. Browning unexpectedly answered. His voice was thin and reedy, and almost apologetic. "A tenth of the whole."

"It's about as much as two people, or possibly one person, could carry away," Nora added.

"Crates?"

"About this big." Nora made a box the size of a small trunk with her hands.

"Where were they stolen from?"

"Our basement. We had an alarm system put in and iron grilles on the windows. The grilles were cut and the alarm system had been disabled. It never went off."

"Disabled? How?"

"A device that kept the signal transmitting even though the wire was cut. Apparently it's not hard to do."

"No, it's not," I said absently. I knew that was true, though I didn't, myself, know how to do it. "But it takes planning ahead. Who knew the porcelains were here?"

Nora glanced at Mrs. Blair. "As far as we know," Nora said, "only Tim, myself, Dr. Browning, and Mrs. Blair."

"What about the rest of the Board?"

"Since the theft everyone knows. But they didn't know when they were coming or when they got here. Those were the kind of details I dealt with, as museum director. No one asked. But," she added, "whoever took them doesn't have to be someone who knew what they were stealing."

"You mean, they might have been just regular old thieves, and they happened on the Blair porcelains?"

"Well, it seems to me if they had come because of them they'd have taken them all. Dr. Browning says the things in those boxes aren't even particularly special."

Dr. Browning shook his head. "Not any more than the rest of the collection. It's all very, very special, of course." He looked up suddenly, his gray eyes wide, as if he were afraid he'd be misunderstood.

"How did you discover the theft?" I asked Nora.

Dr. Browning, again unexpectedly, answered that one, too. "I discovered it." He blushed, as if that had been an improper thing to do, discovering a theft. "When I came in yesterday afternoon to continue my work."

"Your work?"

That had been enough for Dr. Browning. His eyes were back to examining the floor.

"Dr. Browning is inventorying and cataloging the collection for us," Nora told me.

Puzzled, I asked Mrs. Blair, "Don't people who have collections like this have inventories?"

"My husband had a list," Mrs. Blair answered, "but I'm not entirely sure it's complete. The new pieces he'd recently acquired had not, I believe, been added to it."

Dr. Browning shook his head, as though he didn't believe they had, either.

"I'm surprised," I said. "I mean, even just for insurance, you'd think someone would want to be up-to-date on his inventory."

Mrs. Blair's smile was indulgent and tinged with sadness. When he was alive, I was willing to bet, his casual attitude toward things like that probably drove her crazy. Now she missed it.

"That's what I thought about the inventory, too," said Nora. "But apparently this isn't unusual." She looked to Dr. Browning.

"No, it's not." Dr. Browning answered a second late, as though he wasn't sure he was the one being spoken to. He smiled the bashful smile again, but kept his eyes on his shoes.

"A true collector knows every piece in his collection. He doesn't need a list, any more than you need a list of your friends."

Something I had just said reminded me of a question I hadn't asked. "Were these pieces insured?"

"The collection is," Nora said, after a hesitation that was, I assumed, another invitation to Mrs. Blair. "But those particular crates were the new acquisitions. Because Mr. Blair hadn't gone through the process of adding them to the inventory list yet, those pieces weren't covered."

"Those were all the new acquisitions? They all happened to be together?"

"They didn't 'happen' to be together." For the first time I heard the kind of frost in Mrs. Blair's voice that I associate with upper-class Hong Kong women. "I had them packed that way, to make Dr. Browning's task easier."

"Strange," I mused. "That that's what was stolen and nothing else."

"Perhaps strange," Mrs. Blair answered. "And perhaps coincidental. Any two crates would have included only certain pieces, about which we could have said it was strange that they, and not others, were stolen."

"I suppose," I agreed, not sure I supposed any such thing. I turned my attention back to Nora. "Well, on principle I hate to agree with Tim, but the police have resources I don't have. Why aren't you going to them?"

Nora looked at Tim. His jaw was tight and his ears were crimson. Childhood memories of times when his ears were that color gave me a strong urge to hide under the desk.

Nora poured more tea for herself and for me. She warmed her hands around her teacup. "Dr. Browning tells me it's almost impossible to recover stolen art. And the police have other priorities. We decided that the damage it would do our reputation if we made this public would far outweigh whatever advantage the police would have over our doing this privately."

I looked over at Mrs. Blair, wondering how she felt about

10

the theft of Hamilton's porcelains being handled without benefit of law enforcement.

As if reading my mind, Mrs. Blair smiled. "I concur completely in this decision, Miss Chin. Nora consulted me on behalf of the Board before the decision was final. The police, as Nora said, have their own priorities and restrictions. As there is no possibility of an insurance recovery, I see no advantage in calling them in."

"Restrictions?" I looked from her to Nora.

"The police," Nora said, replacing a stray freshly-sharpened pencil into her freshly-sharpened-pencil cup, "are limited in the methods they're permitted to use. In the sense, I mean, that if a crime's been committed, they have to be as interested in catching and prosecuting the criminals as in recovering the property. We're not. We want the porcelains back first. We'd like to see the criminals caught if possible, but that's secondary."

"Do you mean," I said, "that you'd be willing to deal with whoever has them?"

Nora glanced at Tim, who scowled.

"We might," she told me.

"Can you afford to do that? Buy them back?"

"Not for their market value, absolutely not. But maybe we could . . . work something out."

"That's where I come in?"

"Well, we have to find them first. Someone on the Board suggested hiring a private detective, and of course you were the one we all thought of right away."

Of course, I thought. Even poor Tim must have thought of me right away and frantically tried to find some way to keep his busybody, embarrassing little sister out of his business.

"And I again concurred," Mrs. Blair assured me. "I understand that you're young and relatively inexperienced, but Nora gave you quite glowing notices. And being Chinese . . ."

She didn't finish that, and I wasn't sure what she hoped would come of my being Chinese.

I looked around the room. Dr. Browning was gazing at his shoelaces. Tim wouldn't look at me. Mrs. Blair was smiling gently. I turned to Nora. She looked at me with something like pleading in her eyes. Coming from her, that was startling, and I found myself feeling touched and suddenly protective.

"All right," I said, in my best client-relations voice. "Art's not my specialty, but I have a colleague who's experienced in art cases. I'll need particulars, and I'll do what I can."

After all, I thought directly at Tim, who seemed to find glowering out the window as fascinating as Dr. Browning found staring at his shoes, if I needed a lawyer, I'd go to you. That's what you do, this is what I do. I don't have an advanced degree and you don't have a gun.

And just because I'd never heard of the Blair porcelains didn't mean I couldn't find them.

TWO

**P**orcelain," I said, critically examining the blue willows on the fluted white cup in my hand, then lifting it to sip the ginger tea it held. "What do you know about it?"

"Nothing." Bill Smith, my sometimes-partner, put out his cigarette as the waitress came back to our table with his double espresso. "Except that you're going to spill your tea if you keep trying to read the bottom of that cup."

I'd just about come to the same conclusion, and was about to give up, but when he said that I raised the cup and ducked my head anyway, until I could see the "Royal Doulton" on the bottom. I didn't spill a drop. The cup matched my saucer, but it didn't match Bill's, or the flowered teapot on the table. In fact, nothing in this Greenwich Village cafe matched anything else. That was why I liked it here.

"People steal it," I offered.

"People steal anything. I had a client once who wanted me to steal his girlfriend's garbage."

"You're kidding. Did you?"

"I told him I'd steal it but he'd have to go through it himself. I figured he was looking for evidence she was seeing another guy."

"What did he say?"

"He didn't want to go through it, he just wanted to have it. Something she'd touched and been close to, he said. He wanted me to steal him a fresh batch every Friday."

"Yuck. What did you do?"

"I suddenly remembered I'd been called out to work on a case in Missoula, Montana. I suggested he get somebody else."

I sipped my tea and watched steam cloud up the cafe window. "I think that's what Tim was hoping I'd do," I said. "Suggest they get somebody else."

"Your brother Tim? He's the client here?"

"Well, sort of." He drank his espresso, I drank my ginger tea, and I told him about CP, the museum, and the missing Blair porcelains.

Bill's not really my partner. He's a solo p.i., a one-person shop with a varied caseload, just like me. Only he's older, taller, and tougher looking—oh, and a male white person—which means he doesn't go as long between cases as I sometimes do. But most cases are better if you work them in pairs, and he's usually who I call in when I need someone. Since we met I think he's pretty much stopped calling in anybody else, too, except when he needs big muscle. I'm a good bodyguard, I'm a great shot, and I can fight; but at five-one, a hundred and ten pounds, I'm not very intimidating.

When *I* need big muscle, I just call him.

"I really hate the idea of working for Tim," I finished up the story. "But I feel bad for Nora. She's always been one of those people who put other people first, ever since she was a kid, and the museum matters a whole lot to her. I guess maybe I feel a little guilty, too. I used to date her brother, and we

13

laughed at her a lot. Behind her back," I added, so he wouldn't think I'd been too awful.

"Her brother? That was that guy named Matt? Your first boyfriend?"

Even for Bill, that was surprising. "How did you remember that?"

"He's the one who threw you over because you were wild but not wild enough?"

"You're ignoring my question. And *I* broke up with *him*, in case it should happen to interest you."

"That's not how you told it the first time. And it interests me deeply. I remember with crystal clarity everything you ever told me about your love life. I search your words for clues, your memories for hints. I examine the smallest detail for the key that will unlock the door to your heart."

"Well, keep it up." I yawned. "Don't let me stop you."

"Well," he said, "in the meantime, if I'm going to have to work for your brother Tim, I think you're going to have to buy me a piece of pie."

"Don't pick on my brother," I said as he waved the waitress over.

"You always do. Want some apple pie?"

"No. That's because he's stuffy and patronizing and has no sense of humor."

"And because you always had to wear his hand-me-downs."

"No, it's because they wouldn't let me wear his hand-me-downs. They were a club I couldn't join, my brothers, and their club had all the fun. They played baseball while I learned to embroider."

"You embroider beautifully."

I glared. "And I'm a great shortstop." He knew it was true; we'd played together in a Central Park league last summer.

Bill grinned. "Hey, calm down. You can wear my hand-me-downs any time. I have this great ripped T-shirt—"

The waitress brought his pie just in time, so I didn't have

14

to sock him. She also brought two forks. The pie was warm, its trails of cinammon and nutmeg mingling with the ginger from my tea.

"I suggest we discuss this case," I primly suggested.

"Anything you want, boss." Bill, still grinning, moved the pie to the center of the table. "Who's CP's protection?"

I knew what he meant, and the answer wasn't Pinkerton.

"I asked Nora that," I said. "She said not to worry about it, that that had nothing to do with this."

"How does she know that?"

"She can't know that. I finally caught on that she didn't want to talk about gangs in front of the *low faan. Low faan*," I started to add, "that's—"

"Barbarians," Bill cut me off. "Guys who look like me. Isn't that what your mother calls me?"

"No, she has special words for you. Anyway, I think that's what it was. I'll go back to talk to her later, but it doesn't really matter. That's Golden Dragons territory, that corner, so it's bound to be them."

All of Chinatown, with very few exceptions, is divided among a small number of gangs who extort protection money from the shopkeepers, guard the gambling dens, deal drugs, and run whatever rackets there are to be run on their blocks. They're one of the worst facts of Chinatown life, but they are a fact, and I've never seen the point of pretending to outsiders that it doesn't happen like that.

"Have you talked to them yet?" Bill wanted to know.

"My mother would kill you if she heard you ask that. As if any decent young woman who respected her father's ghost would increase his sufferings in the spirit world by taking unnecessary chances, like for example speaking to a Golden Dragon." I squared my shoulders righteously. "Not yet," I added.

"Want me to come with you?"

"Oh, god, no. They may not talk to me, but they certainly won't talk to you."

"I could pretend I'm a bad guy."

"Unless you could pretend you were a Chinese bad guy it wouldn't help."

"I'll work on it."

"I'll be careful," I said, hearing in his tone what he wasn't saying. "I'm only promising that because you didn't tell me to."

"Oh, I know better than to do that."

"That's why I love you."

"Really? You love me?"

"No, but I appreciate you."

"Well," he sighed, "that's more than I deserve. Okay. Where do you want me to start?"

I wasn't sure, so I drank some tea and thought out loud. "What happens to stolen art?" I didn't really expect him to answer me, but he did.

"Depends who stole it. If they know what they're doing they'll find a fence who specializes."

"What does he do with it?"

"He launders it through shady galleries. Usually he'll have private customers of his own, too."

"What if the thieves don't know what they're doing?"

"It's a pain to unload if you don't have a fence. Porcelain may be different, but in general you don't get nearly as much for art on the black market as it's worth—if you can find a buyer at all. There's a provenance problem."

"There's a what kind of problem?"

"Provenance. Where the thing came from. Most people who collect are as interested in value as they are in beauty. Sometimes more. Having a clear provenance is like having a pedigree. Otherwise it's harder to be sure things aren't fake. Or stolen."

"That's why you have to launder them through galleries?" I sampled the crumbly topping on the pie.

"Uh-huh." Bill ate some pie himself and went on: "The other possibility about stolen art is that it can have been stolen on commission for someone in particular."

" 'Can have been'? Is that really English?"

16

"I'll look it up. There's a big lump of raisins over there."

I directed my fork to the big lump of raisins. "How often does that happen?"

"Raisin lumps?"

"Commissioned theft."

"I'll bet not often. Most people who could afford to do that could probably afford to buy the stuff they want outright."

"Except from a museum or something that refuses to sell it."

"Could that have been a problem here?"

"They hardly got the chance. People have to know you have something and then they have to offer to buy it from you before you can refuse to sell."

"Would they have, do you suppose?"

"Refused? I don't know. Why?"

"I'm just wondering if someone did know they were getting this gift, and knew that that meant he'd never get his hands on any of it."

"Mrs. Blair said she didn't tell anyone. And CP was keeping it secret until they were ready to unveil it to the public. They were planning a big opening. You don't like the coincidence theory? Break in to a place because it's there, grab whatever you can get your hands on, and leave?"

"I'm not nuts about it, but I've seen stranger things. Here, you finish." He slid the pie across the table to me.

"It's not my favorite theory either, but it's a place to start." I licked the last of the warm, spicy apple off my fork. "Anyway, once we find them, we can ask the bad guys why they took them."

I took a manila envelope out of my big black bag. "This is for you. It's Dr. Browning's descriptions of the stolen pieces, and some photographs. He hadn't gotten to photographing them all, yet."

Bill glanced through the list and the Xeroxed photos. "Well, you're right, it looks like porcelain. Where do you want me to start?"

17

"With the slime, funny man. The specialist fences and the shady galleries."

I gathered my things and went to pay the check.

Bill was lighting a cigarette in the late-day sun when I came out of the cafe. The air was so cold, after the cozy warmth we'd been sitting in, that the sharpness of it was like a slap in the face.

Bill's jacket was open and he wore no hat. Another hatless guy in another open jacket jumped back onto the curb so that a four-wheel-drive vehicle—so useful in the city—wouldn't hit him. Then he calmly ambled across the street and up the block.

"What is this, a man thing?" I asked, pulling my hat down around my ears and zipping my jacket up to my nose. "No hat is macho? That guy almost got killed probably because his brain is frozen."

"Or the driver's brain is fried. You want me to call you later? Where will you be?"

"Try me at home, this evening."

"Where are you going now?"

I fished in my pocket for a subway token. "Downtown," I said. "I've got to see a man about a dragon."

## THREE

**B**y the time I came out of the subway, back in Chinatown, it was dark. I hate that about winter. I pulled my collar up to keep the icy air off the back of my neck and headed along Pell Street.

Even in the dark and the cold Chinatown was crowded. It always is. Sometimes I get up at six on a Sunday morning just to go out onto streets I can have to myself. You can walk along the sidewalks then, at your own pace, without tripping over a guy who's stopped for a bogus Rolex at a storefront stand or being jostled along by a family of four in a hurry to get the fish home for dinner while it's still flopping and gasping in the plastic bag.

The sweatshop day had just ended. Women who'd been at their sewing machines since seven were haggling with vegetable sellers who'd been at their stands since eight. The women's high-pitched voices cut through the shrieking laughter of children and the short-tempered shouts of the merchants who were only interested in How many? and Next! In the street a car drifted by with a blasting radio, the driver drinking in the sights, oblivious to the honking behind him. A wind-up plastic bird swooped, cawing, out of a street vendor's hand and over the heads of the crowd, nosediving into a fire hydrant across the street.

By the time I reached the shop I was headed for, I was grateful for the soothing ring of a two-note chime as I opened the door, and even more grateful for the silence that followed when I closed it.

In the shop's dim interior dark wood cabinets, built in China a hundred years ago, glowed in the light of glass-shaded lamps. Tiny brass knobs gleamed on rows of small, square drawers that ran practically to the ceiling. The air was rich with quiet scents, ginger and ginseng, honey and lotus root. Ceramic urns of various sizes sat in corners, on counters, and on top of the low, lionfooted table where old Mr. Gao would sit and drink tea with his customers when business was slow.

The shop was an apothecary, and old Mr. Gao, at the moment, was behind the counter, pouring golden powder from a pewter scoop onto a white square of paper while an anxious woman watched. He was a tall, slow-moving man with sharp-knuckled, bony hands. Sparse threads of still-black hair ran straight back from his forehead over an age-spotted skull.

I stood a respectful distance away and listened to the quiet murmur of Mr. Gao's voice. His fingers, deliberate and precise, folded the paper while he spoke. His words and the movement of his hands came to an end at exactly the same moment, and he handed his worried customer a perfectly square, flat little package. Thanking him, she grasped her purchase and bustled out.

Mr. Gao, a small, satisfied smile on his thin face, watched her until the two-note chime rang behind her and the door clicked shut; only then did he turn to me.

"Ling Wan-ju, what a delight." He smiled. Speaking in Chinese, he used my Chinese name. Mr. Gao's voice was soft; I couldn't remember a time, no matter what was happening, that I'd ever heard him raise it. "Have you come for something to stop the young men from swarming around you like bees in the honeysuckle? Or are you here to bring me some New Year's luck?"

"Neither, Grandfather." I returned his smile. "I haven't had much trouble with swarming bees lately. And I'm sure your continued prosperity in the New Year will have little to do with me." Mr. Gao wasn't really my grandfather: All my grandparents' pictures have their places near the picture of my father at the little altar where my mother burns incense and spirit money to ease their lives in the next world. The title was one of respect.

"Well." Mr. Gao turned, reached for one of the drawers. "To encourage the bees, I have a tincture—"

"I'm sure my mother's already bought it, Grandfather. And I'm sure it would work, if the honeysuckle were willing."

Mr. Gao closed the drawer and smiled at me again. "The bees cannot smell the nectar until the blossoms open. But flowers find their own time to seek the sunlight. With what can I help you, Ling Wan-ju?"

"Grandfather, I have the temerity to come here to ask for a favor."

He nodded gravely. "I hope it is within my power to grant."

"I have a friend," I said carefully, "who would like to pay her respects to the *dai lo* of the Golden Dragons."

Mr. Gao's expression didn't change. "Do you think," he asked, "that that's wise—of your friend?"

"She feels that it's important," I answered. "She's trying to be wise, and also to be useful."

"Is it more important to her to be wise, or to be useful?"

"Probably," I said, "she'll never be wise."

Mr. Gao, pursing his lips, looked into the ancient shadows of his store. Beyond the clouded glass half-panel in the front door were the night streets of Chinatown. I could see shapes there, moving, blending, separating; beyond the silence I could hear muffled voices, like the dim moaning of long-forgotten ghosts.

"Wisdom comes only from experience," Mr. Gao finally spoke. "And then only to one capable of profiting by it." With a pencil, he stroked quick Chinese characters onto a sheet of paper, then folded it over. "The desire to be useful is a virtue, though who can tell what will come of it?" He handed the paper to me. "Tell your friend to come to this place tomorrow morning at ten. She must come alone. She will be safe."

"Thank you, Grandfather." I tucked the paper into my pocket. "My friend and I are in your debt."

Mr. Gao, our business concluded, formally offered his respects to my mother and brothers, and I offered mine to his sons and his many grandchildren. The two-note chime rang behind me as I stepped from the shadows and silence of Mr. Gao's shop into the icy scramble of Pell Street.


A cold wind was cheering on the scraps of paper that pounced on people's ankles as I made my way up the street. I was tempted to go home, but I'd skipped karate class yesterday, and I don't like to miss two days in a row. I subwayed up to the dojo in Tribeca and, after I'd stretched, was assigned by Sensei Chung to take the beginners through their exercises. Probably because I didn't come yesterday, I grumped to myself. I strode up and down the rows of uneven shoulders and marshmallow fists, practicing patience, one of the virtues I have a little trouble with. Finally it was time for black belt sparring, and I got in two good bouts, practicing virtues I'm better at.

Later, flushed and invigorated, I changed my clothes and called Bill.

"I'm in your neighborhood, at the dojo," I told him. "You have anything new?"

"At my age? But I'll buy you a drink."

We met at Shorty's, the bar Bill's lived over for sixteen years—since the days when I was sneaking off to a corner of the schoolyard with Matt Yin. Bill was there when I got there, in a battle-scarred booth with an amber drink in front of him. I waved to Shorty behind the bar and slipped in across the table.

"You look gorgeous," Bill told me. "Violence becomes you."

I thanked him politely, and ordered a club soda with three limes from the waitress who came by.

"I'm getting a burger," Bill said. "Are you interested in dinner?"

"No, thanks, my mother's cooking. Something to do with scallions and bean thread."

"Sounds great," said Bill wistfully. He's a big fan of Chinese cooking, but he doesn't get invited to my mother's meals.

"I'll tell you about it," I promised. I sipped my club soda, trying not, in that after-class thirst, to gulp it all down at once. "Did you come up with anything?"

"Maybe," he said. "Not even a lead. A suggestion. But it's better than nothing, because otherwise all I've got is nothing."

The waitress brought his burger, thick and juicy-looking, smelling of the grill. I had that after-class hunger, too.

"A guy I know," Bill began, fiddling with onions and ketchup, salt and pepper, "who, of course, doesn't handle stolen art himself, but knows a guy who might know a guy—"

"Of course," I agreed. I peeled the pulp out of a wedge of lime.

"This guy says that he hasn't—that is, as far as he knows, his friends haven't—been offered anything that might come

22

from the Blair collection. But if he were—well, of course, *now* he'd call me, since he knows I'm looking and he's eager to co-operate. But if I weren't looking, and he had a nice piece of Chinese export porcelain for sale—something legitimate, you understand—"

"He sounds like a pain in the neck, this guy," I interrupted, as Bill bit into the assembled burger. It was dark red inside, just this side of purple. That's the way I like it best.

"Just a little cautious," Bill said. "He's been in business a long time."

I finished the last of my lime. It was fresh and clean-tasting, but it didn't clear the salty scent of grilled meat from my head.

"Anyway, if he had something along those lines for sale, he himself—he didn't know what his friends would do—but he himself would offer it to the Kurtz Museum."

"The Kurtz? Up on Fifth Avenue? The little townhouse one?"

Bill nodded, put the burger down. "They seem to be known for an extensive collection of export porcelains. They don't display them all, but they're apparently still collecting. Their director is an export porcelain expert."

"An export expert? I like that."

"He's also, my friend says, a very aggressive acquisitor." I didn't think "acquisitor" was much of a word, but I didn't bring it up. "He makes periodic buying trips to Europe, and his collecting has singlehandedly brought the Kurtz into the museum world big-time."

"Does your friend—or his friends' friends—actually mean to imply that the Kurtz might have stolen the Blair collection?"

"No." Bill took up a knife and fork, cut a large chunk off the untouched side of his burger, and deposited it on my napkin. "He means that the thieves may know what *he* knows and that we should find out if the Kurtz has been offered any of the stolen pieces."

"You sure?" I pointed at the burger chunk.

"It's those almond-shaped waif eyes. I was getting a stomachache from the guilt. Besides, maybe you were starving to death and too polite to say so. Then your mother would be grateful to me for saving your life and invite me up for a ceremonial meal."

"In your dreams." I stuffed stray pieces of onion back inside the roll and chomped. The burger was tender, juicy, and completely satisfying. "Mmmmmm. Okay, we'll go up to the Kurtz tomorrow. Did your friend have a name there?"

"Roger Caldwell. He's the director. Make that noise again?"

"What noise?"

" 'Mmmmmm.' "

"Make it yourself."

"I don't speak Chinese."

I finished my piece of burger and Bill finished his. "I have a date with the Golden Dragons' *dai lo* tomorrow morning," I said.

" '*Dai lo*'? That's Chinese for 'godfather'?"

I shook my head. " 'Elder brother.' But I think the idea's the same."

"It's all set up?"

I nodded.

"My offer still stands. I'll go with you."

"Thanks," I said. "But I'm supposed to go alone."

"If they were involved—"

"If they were involved they'll just tell me to get lost and hint at dark things happening to me if I don't."

"Or do dark things right then and there."

"No, I'm going with a guarantee of safe passage, at least for this meeting." I told Bill about Mr. Gao. "It's if they *weren't* involved that their *dai lo* might help us out, if he feels like it. But I don't think he'd feel like it for a white guy."

Bill couldn't argue with me, although a tiny little piece of me wished he could.

"Why did you tell Mr. Gao it was a friend who wanted this favor, and not you?" he asked.

"Oh, Mr. Gao shouldn't be doing this, setting up a meeting between a respectable daughter of a respectable family and a gangster. If anything bad should happen to me—"

"—which of course it won't—"

"—which of course it won't, Mr. Gao would lose face in a big way. This gives him an out: He didn't know it was me. If I hadn't given him an out he would have turned me down."

"But he knew?" Bill lit a cigarette. The shadows on his face jumped in the flickering light of the match.

"Of course he knew. Everyone always knows. But those are the rules. Everyone knows those too."

And of course, everyone does. It's just that not everyone always plays by the rules.

## FOUR

The address Mr. Gao had given me was a Chinatown tea shop not far from CP's building. At two minutes to ten the next morning I was there, alone, as Mr. Gao had said I must be, and unarmed, as the phrase "She will be safe" implied I'd better be.

Except for the pudgy proprietor, the shop was empty when I walked in. He lumbered off his stool at the cash register and showed me to a table; then he shouldered aside a curtain into the back of the shop and disappeared.

I took off my hat and gloves, watching myself do that in mirrored walls that reflected endless Lydias, endless chrome chairs, dingy tablecloths, fluorescent lights. They made the small, square room seem, not larger, but confusing and distorted. A single crimson-and-gold New Year's banner hung unevenly above the door. Smudged handprints clouded a glass case displaying sweets: almond cookies, bean-paste jellies, mooncakes. I could hear the snapping of sizzling oil from the kitchen behind the curtain, ready to receive three-flavor dumplings, which a tattered sign claimed was the specialty of the chef.

The fresh cold air that had come in with me was absorbed into the damp, rancid smell of corners unscrubbed for too long. No New Year's cleaning had gone on in here, but four brand-new calendars featuring alluring Hong Kong actresses in uncomfortable-looking poses—and varying amounts of clothing—hung on the rear wall.

I waited, my heart idling slightly higher than usual, my skin prickling a little. Chinatown gangsters aren't cute, or courtly, like the Mafia you see in the movies. They're nasty. And the Golden Dragons had another drawback: They were independent. The tongs are the organized crime down here, and the gangs are their foot soldiers. The men in the tongs allow the boys in the gangs a certain amount of freedom of criminal activity—from which the tongs take a cut—as long as they're available for errands for their elders. Like murder, kidnapping, and the occasional (though rare because they scare the tourists) firebomb.

Some gangs, though, aren't related to any tong, and have carved out turf on their own. They're unorganized crime. Nobody controls them.

The Golden Dragons were one of those.

It had been bitterly cold on my way over, and my fingertips were still burning. I would have loved some tea, but no one came to offer me any, or to ask if I wanted something sweet to eat. The proprietor hadn't locked the door, but nobody came through it. Trying not to tap my foot on the floor, I waited some more.

Finally, the curtain moved. A tall, wavy-haired young man, his face decorated with a sneer and a sparse mustache, sauntered out. He stood and looked at me. I looked back, taking in his leather jacket, tight black jeans, loafers without socks.

Even in this weather, bare ankles. Maybe I could do a paper: Cross-Cultural Expressions of Macho.

The sneer on his upper lip grew; I guessed that made it a smile. Unhurriedly, he crossed to my table, dropped onto the chair opposite me.

"Hey." He arranged himself in the chair, one ankle on his knee, one arm on the table, letting the single syllable hang in the air between us. I didn't reach for it. He spoke again, with a predatory smile. "So, you pretty cute. Old Gao didn't told me that. You Chin Ling Wan-ju, huh?" From his Chinese pronunciation of my name, I could tell he was from someplace where the dialect was totally different from the Cantonese I was raised on. From his English I could tell he hadn't been here very long.

Keep it bland and neutral, Lydia, I told myself. Don't look scared and don't try to look tough. "Yes," I answered. "Or Lydia Chin. Are you the Golden Dragons' *dai lo?*"

"What, you think I don't looking like *dai lo?*"

"Are you him?"

He eyed me before he answered. "Why you want meet him?"

Before I could speak, the chubby proprietor pushed through the curtain with a pot of hot tea, two cups, and a plate of black bean cakes. He put them down on the grease-spotted tablecloth and shuffled out.

"So," the young man said after we were alone again. He poured himself tea, leaving me on my own. "What you want, Lydia Chin?"

Oh, well, why not? "I'm a private investigator. I—"

"What? No kidding!" He laughed. "You kidding. Private eye? Got no trenchcoat, got no gun—hey, you got gun?"

"No," I said quickly. "No, I'm unarmed."

"Maybe I better look." He stood, leaving the smile behind.

I stood too, took off my own black leather jacket, held out my arms while he patted me down from behind, including places I couldn't have been carrying a gun. I gritted my teeth and let him finish.

"All right!" I snapped hotly, when it seemed to me he was past finished. I pulled away and sat again. I caught a movement in the curtain and a derisive snort; the proprietor had treated himself to a peek. I poured some tea to give myself something to do while I got my temper under control. Mr. Macho Gangster sauntered back around the table, sat in his former chair.

"Got boyfriend?" he asked.

"You got a name?" I snapped that, too. Calm down, Lydia, I demanded. Or at least learn to fake it.

"Sure." He picked up the smile where he'd left it. "Trouble."

"Trouble?"

"Sure. You come looking for me, but I find you." He chuckled. It must have been an old joke.

"Okay," I said. "That's fine with me." I sipped some tea. It was oversteeped and bitter, and I didn't need to be warmed up anymore. I put the cup down.

"So," he said. "How come you looking for Trouble?"

I wanted to answer that I did it for a living. But even more, I wanted to ask what I'd come to ask and get out of there.

"I'm investigating a burglary that happened three nights ago. I want to find out if the Golden Dragons were involved."

He showed me all his teeth in a smile. "What make you think I say?"

"Maybe I'll be lucky."

"Maybe not. But sure, you ask."

"At the old school building on Mulberry Street. Where Chinatown Pride is now. Three nights ago, two crates of porcelains were stolen from their basement."

"Porcelains?" Derision crackled in the word. "You think I stealing porcelains? What the hell I do with porcelains?"

"Sell them?"

"Who buy? Why be stupid?" He bit into a black bean cake. Crumbs rained onto his leather jacket. "Look, I got car, got apartments. Got lots of money. Buying girlfriend jewelry,

28

fur coat. Plenty where that come from, plenty more. Porcelains? Don't be stupid. Trouble don't looking for trouble."

Oh, sure. Just another hard-working Chinatown guy. "If the Golden Dragons didn't do this, can you tell me who did?"

"Got no idea, of course not."

"That's a little hard for me to believe," I said.

"Why hard?"

"That's your territory. Are the Golden Dragons such idiots that someone can pull off a burglary right under your noses, and you don't even get a cut?"

My stomach clenched when it heard my mouth say that. Oh, well. The worst that could happen was he'd kill me for insulting him.

He didn't kill me, though. He laughed. "Boy, you some private eye. Pretty stupid."

"I always thought I was pretty smart," I said.

"You always wrong. Or maybe, you smart for ABC girl. But you pretty stupid."

ABC, that's American-Born Chinese. Girl, that's not me. Stupid, maybe. "I'm right, aren't I? This is the first you've heard about this. Someone did come into your territory and burglarized that place and you don't know a thing about it."

"You lucky you cute," Trouble told me, his face suddenly turning hard. "And you lucky for know Old Gao. Even you know him, I should blew your head off for talks like that. Talking like Golden Dragons losing face. Golden Dragons got big face around here, you don't forget! Except," he said, relaxing, brushing crumbs from his mouth, "except you also wrong, because you stupid."

"Wrong about what?" I let the rest go.

"Golden Dragons' territory. That corner not our territory now. You so smart, how come you don't know it?"

"What do you mean, it's not your territory? You lost it?" Gangs don't lose turf in Chinatown without a fight, and those fights are not carried on in secret. If there'd been a turf war over that corner I'd have heard about it.

29

"No, not lost it. Renting it out." Trouble grinned a huge grin, as though this was a very funny joke.

Maybe it was, but I didn't get it.

"Renting it out? What does that mean? To who?"

"Guys from Flushing. Main Street Boys."

Flushing, Queens, is the fastest-growing Asian community in the U.S., and lots of gangs are active there, but the Main Street Boys were new to me. "Who are they?"

He shrugged. "Some guys. They don't got Chinatown turf. Their *dai lo* come to me, says he want that corner, pay me rent plus percentage. I say, why not? Not much money that corner, telling the truth. Maybe I making more this way. Certainly, easier. Trouble, Big-Shot Landlord!" He smiled the smile with all the teeth in it.

"When?"

"When they start? Maybe six month, maybe more."

"So that's Main Street Boys' turf now?"

"Oh, little private eye getting smarter!"

I had a brief flash of the look he'd have on his face if I poured the tea in his lap, but it probably wasn't hot enough anymore to do any permanent damage. In which case, the hell with it. "How far?" I asked instead.

"Couple buildings each direction. Little piece, let them getting started. Some day soon, retire, just collecting rent!"

Well, why not? All over the city, middlemen make a fortune without doing much work. It has something to do with controlling the means of production.

"So you think the Main Street Boys did this?"

"Maybe did, maybe got cheated and someone else did. Not important to me. I get rent, plus any from extras going on." That, I assumed, meant the floating gambling parlors and any drug deals done on that corner.

"Who's the Main Street Boys' *dai lo?*"

He shrugged. "Guy call Bic."

"Bic?"

"Sure. Always got cigarette. Got burn, too. On face. He says from lighter, explode one day while light cigarette."

That would make it easier to know him if I found him. "How do I find him?"

Trouble grinned. Then, as though talking about Bic had reminded him of something macho he'd forgotten to do, he went through an elaborate cigarette ritual himself. He took out his pack—Camels—and drew a cigarette without haste. He tapped it on the pack, stuck it loosely on his lower lip, lit a match, cupped it with both hands, sucked on his cigarette until it glowed.

Then he shook out the match and dropped it in my tea.

"You need boyfriend." He grinned. "Maybe I let you talk one my boys. But now, you leave. Don't come back this place. Go be private eye somewhere else."

He stood, blew an unhurried cloud of smoke in my direction, and, turning, strolled behind the curtain.

I stood too, and put my jacket on, taking exactly as much time to do it as it usually takes. I tucked my hair carefully into my hat. I pulled on my gloves, making sure the cuff of each sleeve covered the wristlets. I zipped my collar up to my neck, and even snapped the snap I usually leave open up there. Then, when I was good and ready, I crossed the room, pulled open the glass door without looking back.

As they say in the Bronx: Later for you, my man.

## F I V E

I stomped home, changed my clothes in a storm of pants and shirts and sweaters and socks. My mother wasn't home, which was a good thing. She would have had something to say about how I could keep a better temper if I met a better class of people, which I would if I were in a better profession.

31

Then I would have snapped at her, which would have been un-daughterly of me and would have made me feel guilty, which would have made me even angrier.

I walked, very fast, north and west from Chinatown practically all the way to Bill's Tribeca apartment before I stopped and called him. "I'm a couple of blocks away, in a bad mood," I said.

"Sounds like a phone booth to me."

"Don't start."

"Not with you," he assured me. "What do you want to do?"

"Complain."

"Okay, go ahead."

"Are you kidding? It's freezing out here."

"You want to come up here?"

"Good guess."

"Well, come on," he said. "But give me time to find my asbestos jockey shorts."

I scurried as fast as I could past the loading docks and factories, which are increasingly, these days, interrupted by art galleries and restaurants. This part of town may never be fashionable, but there's the kind of cutting-edge glamour to it that Soho had in its early days. Or so they tell me.

Bill's lived here since long before that, and I don't think he thinks much of cutting-edge glamour.

"It's me, freezing," I said into the intercom at the bottom of Bill's stairs.

"Is it safe to let you up?"

"Did you hide everything I could throw and break?"

"Yes."

"Then open the door."

The buzzer buzzed, and I climbed the two flights of slanted wooden stairs to where he waited at the top, leaning in the open doorway to his apartment.

"It better be warm in here," I said as I pushed past him into the living room.

"It will be as soon as the steam coming out of your ears

heats the place up." He locked the door behind me and said calmly, "I made hot water, if you want tea."

I dropped my hat, gloves, and coat on the sofa, and went straight to the kitchen, which is just a sort of bulge off the living room anyway. I pawed through the cabinet until I found some Lapsang Souchong, which is smokey and dark and murky, just the way I felt.

I brewed a cup in silence. Bill took my coat and things to the closet. He folded some sheet music that was open on the piano and slipped it onto a pile; then he closed the piano, both the top and the keyboard, the way he always does when someone comes over. He poured himself a mug of coffee and settled on the sofa to wait.

I carried my tea to the big reading chair, curled my frosty toes under me, and sipped. About halfway through, my toes and fingers and mood began to thaw.

"Were you practicing when I called?" I asked Bill.

"Yes."

"What were you playing?"

"Bartok. Sonata."

"What does that sound like?"

"Like a mess. I just started learning it."

I was feeling a little more human. "I'm sorry I interrupted. I know you hate that."

He sipped his coffee. "Tell me what happened."

"You're a man. You won't get it."

"Probably not. But I'm here and I'll listen. Unless you want to go down to Shorty's and take your chances, I'm your best bet."

I put my cup down and told Bill about my interview with Trouble.

Bill lifted his eyebrows. "That's really his name?"

"Of course that's not his name. His name is probably Scholar Reaches the Peak or Rarest Bamboo Arrow or something. He thinks 'trouble' is a big mean western word. Macho jerk. He wouldn't have treated me that way if I were a man. He wouldn't have treated *you* that way. Damn you all!"

33

I got up and started to pace. Luckily it's a long thin apartment.

Bill lit a cigarette, sat and smoked it while I passed him going north and then going south. When I was headed north again he said, "Listen."

"I'm listening, but I'm not standing still." I paced to the window, turned around again.

"Okay, that's reasonable," Bill said. "Look, Lydia. He's a jerk. But it sounds to me as though it worked out pretty well."

"Why, just because he didn't try to kill me and I learned something?"

"There've been times I'd have settled for half that. Either half. But no. Because you accomplished something: You got him to underestimate you. That's the best thing that can happen to you in this business."

"Oh, yeah?"

"Oh yeah. You're right: He wouldn't have treated me that way. He probably wouldn't have talked to me at all. He talked to you because he doesn't think you're a threat. He won't be looking over his shoulder for you and he won't go around warning other tough guys about you. I don't know if he'll be any more use to us in this case, but you're in about as good a position as you could be, if he is."

I stopped pacing, hands in my pockets, and poked at the rug with my toe. "You think so?"

Bill stood and went to the closet for our coats. He tossed mine over to me, and my hat at the same time. I pulled them both out of the air, hardly stretching.

"Come on." Bill grinned. "Let's go uptown."


We took the subway up to the Upper East Side. Bill has a car, but within Manhattan nothing's faster than the subway, and you don't have to park it when you get there.

The usual crowd was on the train: boisterous high school kids who should have been in high school, standing though there were plenty of seats, swiping each other's baseball caps;

34

yuppies, male and female, with short hair, wool overcoats, and suits, checking their watches impatiently; tired-looking swing shift workers carrying plastic bags and the *Post*; and the unshaven homeless guy jingling a paper cup full of change, who pointed out that he did not steal, rob, or take drugs, and apologized for interrupting our evening. It was just past noon. Bill gave him a dollar.

The subway had been overheated, and when we came out onto Lexington a bitter wind ambushed us as though it knew we didn't belong there.

"Jesus," Bill muttered, hands deep in his pockets as we waited for a light to change. The steam from his breath was snatched away by a gust.

"I'm going to buy you a hat," I told him. My words were muffled by the collar of my coat, which was up to my nose.

"You know I won't wear it."

"It'll be a nice, manly, macho hat," I promised. I looked around for one, as an example. The only men in sight were wearing a ski jacket and stocking cap; a navy topcoat and fedora; and an open jacket and no hat at all. The stocking cap was striped, red and white, about four feet long with a pom-pom at the end. I pointed at it. "Like that."

The light changed. The stocking cap and fedora came east, Bill and I went west, and the hatless guy seemed to be having trouble making up his mind. Well, that's what he got. At the last possible moment he dashed west, too.

"Do we know anything about Roger Caldwell?" I asked Bill as we headed toward Roger Caldwell's museum.

"He's been at the Kurtz for eight years. He was a curator of decorative arts at the Met before that."

"What's his reputation?"

"Knowledgeable and ambitious. The Kurtz was small potatoes before he got there. Now it's world-class."

"But still small."

"Still small," Bill agreed.

"You have a personality profile?"

"Well-bred, polite, scores high on the social graces."

"How come you know so much?"

"How come you ask me if you don't think I know so much?"

"I wanted to see how far you could go."

"With you? All the way, in a minute."

"Be serious."

"I am."

I frowned. "Let's go back to 'How come you know so much?' "

"I figured you'd want to know, so I called around. Is that a better answer?"

"Much."

The Kurtz Museum was the second limestone mansion in from the corner on Fifth. It had a broad bay front, a marble staircase up from the sidewalk, and a tall front door painted an elegant dark green. It also had a huge, polished brass doorbell, which I wanted to ring, in case a butler would come open the door; but a sign said the museum was open, so we just walked in.

A thin, middle-aged woman in a blue wool suit sat in the marble-tiled entrance hall behind a spindly desk. Her graying blond hair had a nice wave to it, every one of those hairs seeming to know exactly where to go. She smiled a professional, impersonal smile without parting her lips.

"Hi," I said, glad I'd gone home and changed from my gangster-meeting clothes to an uptown outfit. "I'm Lydia Chin, and this is Bill Smith. We have an appointment with Mr. Caldwell." I knew that was true because I'd made it this morning before my date with Trouble.

"Just a moment." Her voice was pleasant, but I was disappointed that she couldn't speak without parting her lips, too. She said something into the discreet, flat phone on her desk, then thanked it graciously. "Go right up." She nodded toward a marble staircase that curved up from the entry hall. "Dr. Caldwell's office is on the third floor."

"Oh," I said to Bill, as we started our climb. "*Dr.* Caldwell."

"Isn't everybody?"

We passed a statue in a niche, a naked Greek person with a spear. Along the short hallway on the second floor cases holding dishes and teacups were centered nicely under still lifes in tones of brown and gold. The stairway to the third floor curved too, and instead of a niche there was a small stained glass window glowing intensely red and blue.

On the third floor the walls were cream colored and the doors were beautifully polished wood. One was open and the rest were closed. "How about," I suggested to Bill, "that one?"

We went in that one, and inside it looked like everyone else's office: file cabinets and computers and two desks and two young people, a man and a woman, with executive assistant written all over them.

The young man, who wore round tortoise-shell glasses and a great blue bow tie with electric green dots, seemed to have been waiting for us. "Hi," he said as we walked in. His greeting was so enthusiastic he practically made two syllables out of hi. "You're here to see Dr. Caldwell?"

"Yes," I agreed. I introduced us to him.

"And you're from . . . ?"

I gave him a card. His face bloomed into a grin as he read it. "Oh, no, really? Private investigators? Trish, look!" He passed the card to the young woman, then turned his grin back to me. "What's this about? Oh, no, wait, I know. You can't tell me." He lowered his voice. "It's confidential, right?"

"Yes," I said. "I'm sorry."

"Oh, no, I understand." He nodded conspiratorially, as though there were people who didn't understand but none of us here was one of them. "Just one second. I'll tell Dr. Caldwell you're here." He jumped up from behind his desk, snaked around it, and stuck his head through a door at the end of the room. The young woman, whose golden hair hung in a French braid down the back of her silk blouse, smiled in an appraising way and went back to her keyboard.

I suddenly became acutely aware of my short, asymmetrically cut, stick-straight, very Asian hair, my total lack of makeup and nail polish, and the fact that I look twelve when I'm insecure. I was working on not being insecure when the blue and green bow tie reappeared, followed by another bow tie in a muted blue plaid. This one was worn by a smiling, medium-height man with sandy hair and the kind of strong, straight profile it takes generations of playing squash and going to Harvard to produce.

"Hello, I'm Roger Caldwell. Come in, come in. Ms. Chin?" He shook my hand. "Mr. . . . Smith?" Bill gets that a lot. Smith is such a common name that nobody can ever believe anybody is really named that.

Roger Caldwell looked no more than thirty but given the résumé Bill had laid out for me, he had to be forty-five at least. I looked for it in his face as he took our coats to drape on the claw-footed coatrack in the corner of his office, then gestured to two fragile-looking, softly upholstered chairs and a small sofa. He waited until we were seated before he seated himself. There were tiny lines around his eyes and a loosening of the skin over his cheekbones that gave him away if you were looking for them, but he probably got taken for a younger man a lot.

Not for a twelve-year-old, though.

I sat in one of the chairs, and Bill chose the sofa. I thought I detected relief in Caldwell's eyes at that, though he was probably far too well-bred to have said anything if Bill, at six foot two, a hundred and ninety pounds, had risked one of the delicate chairs.

The office walls were the same dark green as the front door and hung with gilt-framed paintings and glass-covered prints. A heavy desk stood at the other end of the room, under the window, where the wall curved out. The window, surrounded by thick green drapes, was bright with the view of Central Park across the street.

"Well," said Caldwell expectantly, looking from Bill to me. "Do you know, I don't think I've ever met a real private investigator before?" His look ended up back on Bill, as though he were waiting for Bill to tell him what was going on.

That happens a lot when we're together. On Bill's cases it's reasonable, but this was my case.

"I don't think I've ever met a museum director," I said, smiling.

"Oh." Caldwell chuckled. "Well, we're not a very exciting breed to meet, I'm afraid. We lead pretty quiet lives."

"For the most part, so do we," I told him, probably bursting his fantasy balloon. "A lot of what we do is routine. That's why we're here now—just routine. We're hoping you can help us out on a case we're working on."

"I'll be glad to, if I can. What's it about?" He gave one more glance in Bill's direction. Bill just smiled and said nothing. I began to speak and Caldwell turned politely back to me.

"Some valuable porcelains—Chinese export porcelains," I added, as though I knew what I was talking about, "—were stolen recently. Our client's hired us to recover them. The Kurtz is known for its collection of export porcelains, and it's possible the thief may try to sell the stolen pieces to you. We wanted to ask if you've been offered anything recently that may be part of this theft, or if you've heard of any on the market."

Caldwell rubbed his square chin. "Nobody's offered us anything recently. I'd actually be surprised if anyone came directly to the Museum: Usually we work with dealers, unless we're negotiating with an owner for an entire collection." He smiled. "We prefer that sort of thing to be a gift, of course."

"Do you think a thief would necessarily know that? About the dealers?"

"Maybe not a common thief, but I'd expect that anyone sophisticated enough to know that we, in particular, would be interested in what they have would know that. From whom were these pieces stolen?"

"I'm sorry, Dr. Caldwell. The client's asked us to keep that confidential."

"Of course." He grinned confidentially. "Theft is so embarrassing." He waved that away. "When did it happen?"

"Three days ago."

"Oh. Well, it's probably too soon to expect any of the

pieces to surface, but I'll keep an eye out. Without embarrassing the owner, can you tell me what I'm looking for?"

I took out the envelope of photographs I'd gotten from Nora. At first she'd been reluctant to let me show them around. But I'd convinced her that our chances of finding the pieces without photos were close to zero, and that, since almost no one had seen the Blair collection anyway, it wasn't likely anyone would recognize the pieces or where they came from. Or know where they'd gone to and from whom they'd been stolen.

"There were others," I said. "But they hadn't been photographed yet."

"Yet?" Caldwell, leafing through the photos, didn't look up. "This is a newly acquired collection?"

"It was in the process of being comprehensively catalogued." Neat recovery, Lydia, I thought. And alliterative, too.

Dr. Caldwell didn't seem to notice. "Well, these are some extraordinary pieces. I don't think I'll have any trouble recognizing them if they come our way." He handed the photographs back to me.

"Dr. Caldwell, I hate to show my ignorance, but can you tell me what things like this are worth?"

He gestured toward the photos. "That would depend very much on two things: their condition and their rarity. I don't know these pieces, so I can't speak to their condition, but they do look out of the ordinary, as I said." He shifted in his chair, tugged the crisp pleat in his trouser over his knee. "Export porcelain has a limited market, although people who collect it are devoted to it." He smiled an indulgent smile. "Some of them are a little dotty on the subject, actually. But most collectors are, about whatever obsession they've chosen. It's my own original field, you know. It's not as glamorous as some other things—silver, say, or even some of that hideous Americana that has to do with one-dimensional painted figures and hooked rugs—but it's quite subtle, and the best pieces display a truly impressive technical proficiency. You'll never find export pieces in the six-figure range, but some trade quite comfortably in the mid-five-figures."

As I digested that, Bill spoke for the first time. "The dealers you say you generally work with," he said to Caldwell, who turned with a look of surprise, as though he'd decided Bill didn't talk and was startled to find he was wrong. "Who are they?"

Caldwell missed half a beat; then he said, "There are three, here in New York. Shall I give you a list?"

"Please."

Caldwell went to his desk, flipped his Rolodex, and wrote a list with a black-and-gold fountain pen on a piece of creamy stationery. He came back and handed the paper to Bill, who looked it over and nodded before he slipped it into his wallet.

"Do you know them?" There was a tinge of disbelief in Caldwell's voice. Bill was in a suit and tie, but that didn't make him look any more like a man who'd know an art dealer if he tripped over one. The truth is different, but Bill doesn't advertise that.

"Two of them," Bill said diffidently.

"Well." Caldwell readjusted his assessment of Bill without much obvious difficulty. "I'm sure they'll be glad to help. Tell them I sent you, if you want, but I think you'll find everyone cooperative. Theft is a problem for everyone in our field." He looked at his watch. "I'm sorry, but I have another appointment. I'm just back from Europe; I was on a buying trip. And now there's so much to catch up on." He smiled apologetically. "Is there any other way I can help you?" Now that Bill was part of the conversation, Caldwell's eyes went again from him to me and back, settling on him.

"We'd like to have a look at your porcelain collection, while we're here," I said, as much to leave him with the idea that I was not just decoration as because I wanted to see what they had at the Kurtz.

"Oh, of course. Come, I'll ask Trish to show you around."

Trish, as it turned out, had gone to lunch by the time we emerged from the dark green of Caldwell's office into the light of fluorescent day.

"It's okay, Dr. Caldwell," the young man with the bright bow tie said. The tie's green dots seemed to glow brighter as his eyes lit up. "I'm not really busy right now. I'll do it."

"Well . . ." Caldwell looked at his watch again. "Yes, all right, Steve. Why don't you go ahead?" He offered his hand to me, then Bill. "It was a pleasure to meet you. I'll call you if I hear of anything that might help."

I thanked him, and Bill smiled, and we turned to follow the luminous Steve down the curving stairs.

## Six

**B**ack out in the freezing cold, our tour of the Kurtz completed, Bill and I considered our options.

"Coffee," Bill enumerated, lighting a cigarette. "Coffee, coffee, or coffee."

"That's what I like about you," I told him. "Flexibility."

"Coffee," he said.

"Quick? At the counter?"

He shrugged, breathing out a stream of cigarette smoke. "I see you and raise: to go."

We compromised on the counter of a Greek diner on Madison Avenue. The windows were clouded with steam and the plants hanging in them looked incredibly lush and healthy.

"They're really interesting, porcelains," I said, stuffing my gloves in my hat and trying to balance my hat on my lap. "I never really thought about them before."

The energetic Steve had taken us on a top-to-bottom trip

through the Kurtz Museum, formerly, we found out, the Kurtz mansion, home of Peter Kurtz and his Victorian-era family.

"The core of our collections is Kurtz's own collection," Steve had begun enthusiastically, looking back over his shoulder at us as we trotted down the marble staircase. "As far as porcelains—that's what you're interested in, right?—he collected mostly pieces made for the English and Dutch markets. The Museum has added American pieces."

"Made in America?" I'd asked, confused.

"Oh, no, no. Made in China for the American market. They made export porcelain to order in China in the seventeenth through the nineteenth centuries so pieces for the American market had eagles and things on them, and ones made for Great Britain had, oh, you know, Union Jacks and stuff. The truth is," he confided, "I'm not really a porcelain expert. I guess that's why the Director wanted Trish to take you around. My field is textiles. We have some wonderful carpets." His eyes widened hopefully.

"I'm sure you do, and we'd love to see them," I said quickly. "But we don't have a lot of time right now. Just a fast look."

"Sure. Well, all our best display pieces are on the first floor. I'll try to get it close to right."

He took us down to the first floor and, stopping at case after case, pointed out the cups and saucers, bowls, plates, and tureens; told us about *famille verte* and *famille rose* (that had to do with colors); showed us the armorials (the ones with coats of arms on them—bigger with the British than the Dutch or Americans, which I probably could have figured out if anyone had asked me); picked out the Chinese motifs, the Chinese interpretations of European motifs, the European orders for particular items painted with screwed-up European interpretations of Chinese motifs.

Steve spoke not as an expert but as an enamored amateur, fast sentences sometimes broken in the middle by the next thought pushing its way through. He started in the middle and jumped around, giving no introduction to lines like, "Of course it's not at *all* true that the export porcelains were lower quality than the *kuan yao*," when I didn't know that anyone ever said they were. "*Kuan yao*, that's 'official ware.' For the court. You know, internal use only," he added helpfully, for Bill, although Bill's chances of knowing what *kuan yao* was were actually better than mine. "See, for example?" He pointed to a large platter gleaming in the sun that poured in the tall windows. "That was made for export. Can you think of anything more wonderful?"

I had to agree with him. The springtime scene—little boys running with kites on a hillside, a sparkling sea behind—was so vivid I could practically smell the peach blossoms on the soft breeze.

I leaned forward to inspect the platter, and to read the card next to it, as though any information on the card would make sense to me.

Surprisingly, one thing did: the donor's name. "Dr. Mead Browning? He gave you this plate?"

"You know Dr. Browning?" Steve asked eagerly. "He's a big expert. One of the top people on export porcelains. He's been here a couple of times to study our collection. How do you know him?"

"Oh, I just met him through a friend. I don't really know him, I was just surprised to see his name. You know, to see anyone's name I've met as a donor at a museum."

"Oh, don't I know," Steve agreed. "Kind of makes you wonder what circles you travel in, doesn't it?"

Our tour went on, Steve picking out for us motifs, shapes, colors, differences in brushstroke and firing temperature. Stopping in front of a particularly intricate blue and white plate ("Nanking ware"), he said, "They made hundreds and hundreds of sets, and individual pieces by the thousands, of course, but porcelain, you know, breaks." He smiled an engaging, embarrassed smile, as if porcelain's breaking was a bad habit of his own that he'd tried to correct. "That's why complete sets are rare even in collections like ours. We actually only have one. That big tureen over there, and the tea set with it? They're from it."

"Why don't you display the whole thing?" I asked, inspecting the duck and drake swimming peacefully in the center of the huge bowl.

"Oh, the set is gigantic. I mean, hundreds of pieces. Nobody displays full sets, I don't think. You keep most of them in storage. Most of your porcelain is always in storage."

"Really? You mean you have a lot more pieces than this?"

Steve nodded earnestly. "In the basement, in the storage rooms. You want to see?"

We did, so he showed us. What he called the basement was what had been the kitchen, larder, pantries, and all those other rooms you see on *Upstairs, Downstairs*. Some of the rooms had iron-barred windows up near the ceiling where you could see people's feet walking by on Fifth.

All the rooms were storage rooms now. Rows and mounds and stacks of boxes and crates and locked lockers with arcane red crayon markings stood silently, dustily, in dim spaces lit by bare bulbs Steve turned on and off as we wandered. Everything down here seemed brown or gray and the shadows were deep. Inside these rectangular, non-committal containers, according to Steve, were porcelains, carpets, statuary; enamel pillboxes, carved wooden bookends, clocks; lace tablecloths, silver carafes, and a set of jewelled dueling pistols. I imagined the crates and lockers throwing their doors and tops open, and glowing colors, rounded shapes, sensuous textures tumbling out and flooding the room. It made me a little sad to think of all those colors, shapes, and textures locked up in these strict, uncommunicative cells.

"This is a lot of things," I said, a little lamely. "It seems like there's more down here than on display."

"Oh, absolutely," Steve confirmed. "That's true in any museum. The size of your collection is always much bigger than your exhibit space."

"I guess that makes sense. I just never thought about it

before." I was still feeling a little melancholy when we left the basement, and when Steve shook hands with us at the huge green door.

My tea arrived, pulling me out of my thoughts and back to the diner.

"What's up?" Bill asked.

The tea was chamomile; I squeezed some lemon into it. "Oh, I don't know. I was just thinking how sad it must be for all those things, locked up in a basement all the time."

"They're things," Bill said. "They don't get sad."

"Narrow-minded Western rationalism." I sipped my tea. "Actually, that's only one thing I was thinking. The other was: the mid-five-figures? For a soup bowl? When families are sleeping on the street?"

Bill's eyes met mine, and what I saw in them was what I was feeling. He didn't say anything, just drank his coffee.

"Well," I said, "but it's the case we have, right?"

"Right."

"Right. Okay, what's the plan?"

"Hey, you're the boss." He held up his hands innocently.

"Just wanted to see if you were paying attention. Okay. I'm going to see if I can catch Mary before she goes on duty. She's on the night shift this week."

Mary Kee is my oldest friend. We went to kindergarten, grade school, Chinese school, and high school together. Then I went to college and she went to the police academy. My mother was horrified when Mary chose to do that, and took every opportunity to console Mrs. Kee over her ill fortune in not having a daughter as exemplary as me.

She had no idea what was in store for her. Now Mrs. Kee consoles her, at every opportunity.

"You want to see if Mary can give you a lead on Bic?" Bill asked.

"Is my strategy that obvious?"

"Only to another brilliant detective."

"Oh. Okay." I finished my tea. "What are you going to do?"

"I thought I'd go see these dealers." He patted his jacket pocket, where Dr. Caldwell's list was. "Unless, as boss, you have another idea."

"No, I like that idea. We'll talk around dinnertime?"

He smiled over his coffee cup. "Warn your mother I might call."

"If she expects you she'll unplug the phone."

He sighed. "I'm not so bad, you know. I mean, I'm big, white, clumsy, ugly, and I don't speak Chinese, but otherwise I'm not so bad."

"You're a private eye," I reminded him. "My mother doesn't like private eyes."

"You're a private eye."

"And she considers that your fault." I left money on the counter, climbed down off my stool.

"That's completely unfair," Bill protested. He zipped his jacket and followed me out onto the sidewalk. "I didn't even know you when you started in this profession."

"What do you want, logic? She thinks if I hadn't ever met you I'd have gotten over this detective nonsense and found a respectable job. She's my mother. She's got to blame someone besides me."

"So you can still be innocent?"

"No, more because it's not *possible* that I would go on deliberately doing something she doesn't want me to do all on my own. There must be a stronger influence than hers at work, and the only influence stronger than a Chinese mother is an evil-intentioned man."

"Tell her my intentions are good."

"It's actually better if I mention you as little as possible. I'm freezing out here. Talk to you later, okay?"

We kissed goodbye lightly, the way we always do. We've talked it out a couple of times, what I want him to be—my partner—and what he wants me to be—more than that—and, though he teases, he doesn't push it. We make a great team, and it's all really good.

47

It's just that sometimes I feel a little lonely when he walks one way, and I turn and walk the other.

## SEVEN

I found Mary Kee at her mother's apartment on Madison Street, which is miles away, and miles away, from Madison Avenue. It's at the edge of Chinatown, although when the projects where Mary was raised were built, they were outside Chinatown by blocks and blocks. Chinatown, in the last ten years, has spread like a stain, grown like a weed, metastasized like a cancer, or expanded like a culturally vibrant, economically vital, hard-working immigrant neighborhood. It depends on your point of view.

When I'd called her mother's, on the chance she'd drop by there on her way to work, Mary had told me to come on over. The Fifth Precinct station house is a quick walk from Madison Street—one of the reasons Mary had requested assignment there. Sometimes, she told me, it's hard for cops to get the precinct assignment they want, but the NYPD is so desperate for Asian cops in Chinatown, Flushing, and now, Sunset Park, that they sent her here right out of the academy. She made detective here, and she's planning to stay.

Nice for me. And I try not to be too annoying.

I crossed Madison Street from the subway as the wind, pushing its way up the hill from the East River, draped plastic bags on the bare trees and redistributed cigarette butts and candy wrappers around the desolate lawns. The downstairs door to the boring slab of brick building where Mary's mother lives is always locked, but I've always had a key. I had it out, but I didn't need it; Mary was waiting, sheltered in the doorway, when I got there.

We greeted each other with a quick hug. "Hi," Mary said. "I'm running late. I didn't want my mother to start trying to feed you and all that."

"Late? You don't have to be in until four, do you?"

"I'm heading in early to finish some paperwork. Also," she admitted, "I get the feeling this is business." She didn't elaborate, but I knew what she meant: She also didn't want her mother to hear us talking investigating. Unlike my mother, Mrs. Kee speaks English. Just like my mother, she has this idea that if everyone totally ignores this detective foolishness her daughter will get tired of it and find something respectable to do.

"Except," I said, because it had just occurred to me, "I'm hungry. I'll walk you part way to work if we can go along Henry by the turnip-cake man."

"Sure. So," she said, tucking her arm into mine as we started into the wind, "I understand you have a favor to ask me that will involve risking my badge, my career, and possibly my life."

"Absolutely not," I said indignantly. "Who told you that?"

"You said 'favor' on the phone, Lydia."

"Maybe I want your mother's recipe for sticky rice balls."

"Take two pounds of rice—"

"Oh, never mind. Do you know a Flushing gang called the Main Street Boys?"

She cut me a sideways look from beneath her flat-brimmed toreador hat. A hat like that won't keep your ears warm, but I guess it's better than nothing. "I've heard of them. Why?"

"What have you heard?"

She sighed. "They're new, probably less than a year. It's all still shifting out there, the territories, not like Chinatown, but the Main Street Boys seem to be established. I think their *dai lo* is from somewhere out west, but I don't know if they're connected to a West Coast gang. Why?"

She'd answered my question, in a cop sort of way, so I had

to answer hers. "I need to talk to their *dai lo*. A guy called Bic. Bic," I added, "like the lighter."

That was a p.i. sort of answer.

Mary's reply wasn't unexpected. "Don't do that, Lydia."

"Why not?"

"Every time you get near a gang member I get ulcers. If a gang is involved it's a police matter. Tell us and we'll deal with it."

I avoided the question of why, if the police could deal with it, there were so many gangs running their brutal operations in this small neighborhood. I knew the answer: That will continue as long as honest citizens like me refuse to come forward to talk to the police.

I also avoided telling her I'd had tea with one *dai lo* this week already.

"They may not be involved, Mary. That's why I want to talk to them. To find out."

"We can find things out."

"This is for a client."

"Oh, no kidding. Who?"

"I can't tell you."

We had reached the turnip-cake man's stand on Henry Street. Our conversation stopped while I bought two of the soft, salty, chewy squares he had sizzling on the wok. He slipped them into a wax-paper envelope for me. I offered a bite to Mary, who nibbled on a corner of one; then, as I was munching, she said, "So you can't tell me who the client is, and he doesn't want to report the crime, but he wants it solved anyway. So you have to mess with a gang. Do I have that right?"

"The client has a good reason for—"

"They always do, Lydia. The gangs and the tongs count on that."

"I don't think this is that kind of crime. I really don't know. If I could talk to this Bic I'd have a better idea."

We both stopped, without discussion, at the corner of the next block. It isn't good for either of us to be seen together in the heart of Chinatown, except at family association banquets or other social events where we might be expected to appear, regardless of what we do for a living.

Mary looked at me closely for a long time, long enough for me to finish both my turnip cakes. "Well," she finally said, "I can't run him, because nothing I'm working on could remotely involve him, and someone would pick it up." I understood that. The NYPD frowns on cops using the computer system for personal reasons, and helping out a p.i. who won't even tell you what the case is about is definitely a personal reason. "But I'll ask around."

"Thanks," I said.

"I still think you shouldn't go near him, or any of them. But if I don't check him out for you you'll probably go over to Flushing with a sandwich board that says, 'For a good time call Lydia Chin but only if your name is Bic.' "

"Not a good time. A hot time."

"Matchless."

"He could be my new flame."

"You could carry a torch for him."

"Have a torrid affair."

We both collapsed in giggles. Mary recovered first.

"Will you promise me," she asked, "that if it looks like trouble, you'll call me? Before, not from the hospital?"

"I've never ended up in the hospital," I said, my professional dignity affronted.

"Upstate, that time—"

"That wasn't my case! That was Bill's case, so it was his fault."

"Oh. If it's somebody else's fault it doesn't count? What if this time it's Bic's fault?"

I winced. "I see what you mean. I'll be careful, Mary. I really will."

"That's not what I asked you. But I guess it'll have to do. I've got to go. If I get anything I'll call you."

"Thanks."

She turned, walked a few steps, turned back. "I don't suppose it ever occurred to you to do something less dangerous and more respectable for a living?"

"Sure." I grinned. "But police work is so boring."

Mary made a face, turned again. I watched her toreador hat and her long swinging braid disappear into the currents of people flowing through Chinatown.


There were a couple of things I could profitably do now. I could go over to Mulberry Street and talk to Nora, or I could go uptown and try to catch Dr. Mead Browning, who was, as it were, the last person to see the Blair porcelains alive.

Nora was closer. Besides, my head was about as full of talk about porcelain as I could take for one day.

I called CP from the phone on the corner, the one in the little enclosure that replaced the pagoda-shaped booth that stood there for years and years. I always found that booth sort of offensive, but my mother liked it, so maybe I'm just touchy.

Nora was there and said she'd be glad to see me.

"Is Tim there, by any chance?" I asked her.

"No, I think he's at his office. Do you want to talk to him?"

"No, I want to *not* talk to him. Unless you think he knows something I should know about, in which case I would reluctantly interview him. As a hostile witness."

"I don't suppose he does. What is it between you two, Lydia? Tim's a good guy, just a little stiff. You never give him a chance."

"What is it between you and Matt? And Tim's the one who never gives *me* a chance. Nora, I'm freezing. I'm going to hang up and come over, okay?"

She said okay, so I hung up.

The streetcorner astrologer was squatting, in five layers of jackets, in his usual spot as I rounded the corner at Mulberry Street. His hand-lettered charts—magic marker on squares of cardboard box—waited patiently, like him, for customers. His sticks and coins in their little silk pouches were just ready, I could tell, to jump out and reveal to some anxious soul the nature of the luck he could expect in the coming year. Or she could expect.

Or I could expect. But I didn't stop.

The cranky downstairs door at the CP building was unlocked because the museum was open. I let myself in and up. Nora, looking tired, smiled when I poked my head through her office door.

"Come on in," she said, dropping her pen onto a neat pile of papers. "Save me."

"You're sure it's an okay time?"

"I'm drowning in paperwork. Didn't you take an EMS training course?"

"Paperwork rescue isn't covered until the advanced session."

Nora's office wasn't as warm and cozy as Roger Caldwell's had been. The furniture was older, the decoration more sparse. The view out her window was of the building across the street, not the broad sky over Central Park. Seating myself in the chair across the desk from her, watching her fold her files and paperclip her papers, I realized with a quick gulp of guilt that, in spite of what I'd said to Roger Caldwell, of course I had met a museum director before.

"Did you find out anything?" she asked. Then, "Wait, I'm sorry. Do you want some tea?"

"Yes, thanks." I unbuttoned my coat but kept it on. "And I don't think I found out anything, but I might have some leads. Can I ask you some questions?"

"Sure." Nora handed me a steaming cup. I cradled it against me, then lifted it to drink. It was chrysanthemum this time, sweet and light like morning sunshine in summer.

Lowering the cup, I asked, "You pay your lucky money to the Main Street Boys?"

Everyone in Chinatown knows what "lucky money" is. Nora picked at something on her spotless desk, shook her head. "We don't pay."

I stared at her in disbelief. "You don't pay?" I felt hot blood surge into my face. "You're sending me out there asking questions like an idiot, sniffing around gangsters, and you don't pay?"

Nora blinked involuntarily, as though my anger was something I'd thrown at her. "Wait, Lydia, I don't get it. What's one thing got to do with the other?"

"Oh, come *on*, Nora! You don't pay, they steal your porcelains. You start to pay, you get them back. Probably tomorrow some gangster will come up here with a bagful of broken pieces. 'Got some nice porcelain for sale. Like this, but not broken—yet.' Nora, I don't believe this."

"Oh, no, Lydia!" Her voice was shocked. "That's not what I meant."

"What's not?"

"Lydia, I wouldn't do that to you! The Main Street Boys didn't do this. Or, I mean, I don't know, maybe they did, but not to keep us in line or anything like that. We don't pay because they don't come around."

"What do you mean, they don't come around? Trouble from the Golden Dragons said this is their corner now."

"You talked to Trouble? How could you do that? Lydia, if I thought this had anything to do with gangs I would never have hired you. I don't want you going near those guys—"

"You want your porcelains back? What did you expect me to do?"

She stopped short. "I don't know. But not that." She picked up her pen, watched it turn in her fingers. Then she put it down, poured herself a cup of golden tea. "You really think the gangs are involved?"

"I don't know. But I think it would be crazy not to check it out."

Nora sipped her tea. Without looking at me, she said, "I heard rumors these Main Street Boys had taken over this corner from the Golden Dragons. I waited for them to come selling orange trees,"—which means the same as "lucky money"—"but they never did. We don't pay because no one asks us."

Now it was me who was confused. "How can that be? They're paying the Golden Dragons good money for this corner. Like rent. Why would they do that if they're not making anything on it?"

"Rent? That's how it works?"

I gave her a brief rundown of Trouble's entrepreneurialism.

"Unbelievable." She shook her head slowly. "They're not stupid, you know, those kids. God, it's such a loss. We lose twice, the community: by what they do, and by never having what they could have contributed."

"Trouble's not a kid. And he's not from the community."

"He was a kid once. And we're all immigrants here, Lydia."

"Is that why you wouldn't talk about this yesterday in front of the *low faan?*"

Her look was blank; then she said, "Oh, Dr. Browning? No, not entirely. It's not just that he's *low faan.* He's also . . ." She tapped the pen on the desk, searching for words. "Well, he's sort of . . . innocent. He's in his own world. Porcelains are what he cares about; otherwise he doesn't exactly know what's going on. You should see him down there opening boxes with this little smile." She smiled gently herself.

"You were protecting him?"

"Is that a bad thing?" she asked defensively.

"No, but Nora, it's not your job to protect the whole world from reality. Anyway, I'm going to have to talk to Dr. Browning."

She nodded. "I expected that, and I told him. And maybe I was being silly yesterday. Anyway, I wish I'd answered you about the gangs, because then you wouldn't have gone and gotten involved with the Golden Dragons."

"I might have anyway. It's also not your job to protect me."

"It's not *your* job to be tougher than everyone else, Lydia."

"My job is to get your porcelains back." And be tougher than everyone else. "Nora, I have to ask you this. Is there any way Dr. Browning could be involved?"

"Oh, Lydia! Oh, I don't think so. He's so . . ."

"I know. Innocent. But just sort of logistically, Nora. Could he have actually done it? Did he have a key, for example?"

"No. He loses keys. I let him in in the morning and lock up after him at night. We leave together, in fact." She smiled. "And he wasn't carrying any crates the evening this happened."

"Very funny. And the alarm code? Does he have that?"

"No. There'd be no point in giving him that. He can't remember his own phone number."

"Okay. But I had to check. You understand?"

"Of course. I'm glad you're being thorough. I just wish you didn't have to go near gangsters."

I reached forward and poured myself more of the sweet tea. "And I wish I knew why the Main Street Boys took over this corner and aren't hitting you up."

Nora leaned back in her chair, frowned in thought. "Well, we're not the only people here," she reasoned. "And it's obvious we don't have much. Maybe they're only bothering with people who can pay worthwhile amounts."

"If that's true, it would be news. But the Main Street Boys are new in town, and their *dai lo* is from the West Coast, I hear. Maybe they do things differently out there."

"Maybe." Nora looked uneasy. "Lydia, maybe this wasn't such a good idea. Hiring you, I mean. If these gangs are involved—either one of them—then maybe we should go to the police."

Tim would love that, I thought. You're fired, baby sister. This case was too big for you. It was too hard.

"Your reputation," I said. "Face. Your other donors."

"Well, maybe that's not so important."

"Your porcelains. You said yesterday that I had a better chance of getting them back than the police have. Dr. Browning said so."

"Yes," she said reluctantly. "That's true. But Lydia . . ."

"Give me a few days." I cut her off before she could talk herself into the idea that she was being irresponsible by letting me go on putting myself in danger for her. "If I don't get anywhere, you can go to the police. But maybe I'll be lucky, and you won't have to do that."

"Well . . ."

"Thanks," I said, standing quickly. "Good seeing you. Great working for you. Gotta go."

And before she could change her mind, or even speak it, I went.

E IGHT

I went home.

It was late, it was dark, it was dinnertime. The streets of Chinatown weren't any less crowded, but the crowd was different: fewer families and older Chinese, because everyone was home eating. More young people in groups now, and more couples, some Chinese, some white or black—*low faan* of different kinds—and a few mixed. In front of me, a young Chinese man squired his long-haired blond girlfriend through the streets of the old neighborhood. Two white men in camel-hair topcoats, their wives in furs behind them, headed down the stairs to a famous restaurant where I'd never eaten. I maneuvered around a mixed group of young teenage boys pawing through a sidewalk vendor's tray of watches.

The salty smell of soy sauce and herbs washed out the

door of a restaurant I passed. I hurried along, hungry for my mother's cooking. The air was bitterly cold now that the sun had gone down. Everyone, *low faan* and Chinese and me, wore our hats pulled down to our ears and hunched our shoulders as deeply as we could into our coats.

Except for the hatless white guy in the open jacket in the doorway across the street.

I scurried down the block, turned right at the corner, toward home. At the first building, which wasn't mine, I slipped into the shadow of an alley, and waited.

A figure sauntered around the corner, didn't even look in the direction of the shadow I was hiding in. He crossed the street, ambled down the block to the old brick building I live in, stood in front of it for a moment. He looked at his watch, scratched his hatless head, and wandered on.

I stayed behind him for a block and a half, and I was pretty good at it, too. He shouldn't have spotted me. But a young woman in high heels tripped off the curb, and the hatless guy—a true gentleman—turned to catch her.

As he did that he caught sight of me watching him.

Leaving the high-heeled woman in mid-rescue, he whirled and dashed away. I broke into a run, too, and made Canal Street in time to see him jump into a cab and disappear in the direction of the Manhattan Bridge. I looked around wildly, but on a freezing night at dinnertime in New York a cab is a hard thing to find. By the time the light had changed and a fresh batch of traffic, including two empty cabs, was headed my way, he was halfway to Brooklyn.

I comforted myself, as I seethed on the way home, with the hope that he hadn't wanted to go there.


I was still seething as I stomped up the three flights of stairs to the apartment where I've always lived. Seeing the hatless guy in Chinatown, where white people, to Chinese, are visible and not part of the background, had brought him suddenly into focus for me. It made me remember his red-tipped ears this afternoon crossing the street in the same direction Bill and I did on the Upper East Side, and, yesterday, dashing in front of a Jeep outside a cafe in the Village.

This guy had been following me. It had taken me two days to make him, and now I'd alerted him and lost him.

You're an idiot, Lydia, I pointed out to myself. A total idiot, a complete loss.

I took a few deep breaths when I got to the door, to try to approach normal before approaching my mother. I stood with my key in my hand, listening to old Mr. Tam's television across the hall. Old Mr. Tam has lived here since before I was born. He doesn't speak English, but he watches endless hours of American television. You can hear him cackling to himself over the antics of the white-skinned ghosts any time you walk by.

When I was calm, I twisted my key in each of the four identical locks on our door in turn. "It takes a thief as long to pick the same lock four times as to pick four locks once," my mother had declared, standing over the locksmith to insure his competence, as well as his diligence. "And this way my foolish children will have fewer keys to lose."

None of us, in my memory, has ever lost a house key, but I'm the youngest so maybe there are things I don't remember.

"Hi, Ma," I called, taking off my shoes in the tiny vestibule, hopping around as I put on my embroidered slippers. "Mmmm, smells great."

"Oh, are you here?" my mother grumbled from the kitchen. "Well, I'm so lucky. Hurry now, dinner is almost ready."

My mother has been saying this all my life, making it sound as though if I'd been five minutes later I'd have kept everybody waiting or caused everything to burn. The fact is Chinese food is always almost ready. It's the original fast food, everything cut small and served crisp, sauces made in advance to be added at the last minute to vegetables quickly fried, noodles rapidly boiled, fish steamed whole.

The fish—a big perch—was sitting next to a pot of simmering water when I walked into the kitchen. My mother was at the kitchen table chopping greens. Beside the cutting board was a bowl of mung bean sprouts and bamboo. "Hi," I said. "Have a good day?"

"You're in my way." She stood, wiped her hands on her apron, bustled past me. Then, theatrically, she turned. "Oh, I'm sorry, Miss. I was expecting my daughter, Ling Wan-ju. You'd know her if you saw her, she wears a leather jacket and trousers and thick clumsy shoes. I think she has a good coat like that, and even a silk suit that I made her, but she never wears them. It's because of her job, of course—"

"Oh, Ma, give me a break." "Give me a break" wasn't exactly the expression I used, but I came as close as I could in Chinese. "Anyway, the suit was a hit uptown. I'm going to change now so I don't get it dirty. You need help here?"

"I don't think snooping helps cooking. You can set the table. But first go and change. I don't want you to get that suit dirty."

"Hey, good idea." I headed for my bedroom.

"But hurry. Your brother is coming for dinner."

This is something else my mother's been saying all my life: "your brother," as if in any given context it should be obvious to me which of my four brothers she's talking about. Even if it's Ted, his wife and three kids, or Elliot, his wife, and their two, it's "your brother is coming to dinner."

"Which brother, Ma?" I called as I pulled my sweater over my head. "Andrew?" I hoped it was. He's one brother up from Tim, and he's my favorite. He was also the most likely, since he's single, a great eater, and, like me, not much of a cook.

My mother stuck her head around the corner of my door, turned up her nose at the chaos in my room. She smiled triumphantly. "Tien Hua," she said.

Which, of course, meant Tim.

*  *  *

60

After I was in jeans and sweatshirt, before I set the table, I called Bill.

He wasn't there.

I left a message with his service telling him to call me, and telling him to be careful. I didn't know who my tail had been, or what his purpose was, but maybe Bill had one too.

Then I set the table. Rice bowls, soup bowls, teacups, chopsticks. All the Chins have a pair of chopsticks engraved with our names in red Chinese characters. My parents' were a wedding gift from my father's brother. Then he gave each of us a pair when we were born. My father's and my brothers' are ebony, black and shining; my mother's and mine are ash, glistening white.

I straightened up the living room, which was also the dining room, not because it needed it but because I didn't want to straighten it up for Tim because who did he think he was anyway?

"Whose idea was this, Ma?" I called, organizing the photographs next to the bowl of oranges on the shelf. Every room in our apartment already had its New Year bowl of oranges and tangerines, every door had its gold-lettered red banner proclaiming this as a place of health, good fortune, prosperity, and joy in the coming year.

"Whose idea was what?" Somehow my mother can mutter from the next room.

"Tim coming for dinner."

"What do you mean, idea? Your brother called and said he would be in Chinatown this afternoon and he'd like to come for dinner. It wasn't an idea, it was the right thing to do."

Meaning that a good son, when in the neighborhood, can be expected to pay his respects to his mother. As opposed to a lousy daughter who, though she lives with her mother, can be expected half the time not to show up for dinner because she's running around with the type of characters it humiliates her mother even to know she knows.

Except that, according to Nora, Tim had been at his of-

61

fice this afternoon, in midtown with all the other stuffy lawyers.

The sharp rat-tat-tat of knuckles came from the front door. I pulled it open, and of course it was Tim.

"Don't you have your key?" I asked. Maybe one of the foolish children had lost a key after all.

"Of course I have it." He pushed past me, handed me his hat while he took off his shoes. "But how do I know which of the locks you locked?"

The first half of dinner, for all that, wasn't too bad. Tim talked about his work, which is trusts and estates and bores me but fascinates my mother. She plays the stock market and is always interested to know what Tim is recommending to his clients and why. Her record is actually better than his, but no one but me knows that because it would embarrass her deeply to outshine her son.

After the soup, however, when my mother disappeared into the kitchen to steam the fish and stir-fry the scallions, the action started. And I must admit I started it.

"You were not in the neighborhood this afternoon, Fourth Brother," I said, spearing some bitter greens from the platter, dropping them in my rice bowl. "What's the deal?" I said this in English, just in case the scallions weren't sizzling very loud.

Tim flushed. "How do you know where I was?"

"I'm a detective. Is that what this is about?"

He glared. He doesn't like to be one-upped, especially by someone who isn't a lawyer. "All right, Lydia, yes, it is. I didn't want to embarrass you in front of Nora and Dr. Browning, but I want you to resign from this case."

"Lawyers resign. P.i.s quit. And I won't."

"Lydia, don't be pig-headed. You're going to embarrass Ma, and worry her, too. Think how upset she'll be if you get hurt." He was trying a rational tone of voice and emotional blackmail.

"I won't get hurt. And nothing I'm doing could embarrass her, even if it got back to her, which there isn't any reason why it should do." I hate it when he gets me so riled up my English grammar goes. His never does.

"What if she hears you've been meeting with Golden Dragons? She'd be ashamed to show her face on the street. And," he added, looking at me seriously, as though he was about to tell me something I'd probably never considered, "Lydia, they're *dangerous.*"

I didn't deny that. I also didn't tell him that somewhere, in some place deep inside me that I don't look into very often, I enjoy that part.

"She won't find out, unless some low-down rat tells her," I said pointedly. "And how do you know, anyway?"

"Oh, for Pete's sake, Lyd, it's all over Chinatown."

"Then Chinatown hasn't got anything worthwhile to talk about. Anyway, Tim, be honest. You're not worried about Ma and you're not worried about me. What you're really afraid of is that I can't solve this case. You're worried I'm going to screw up and then everyone, not just you, will know what a jerk Tim Chin's little sister is. Your face. That's what this is about. Your face, not my ass."

The aforementioned face was splotchy purple. I thought lawyers had better control than that, but maybe not.

"Damn it, Lydia, I have a reputation to protect!" he sputtered. "I'm up for partner this year. I have to be careful where I go, who I'm seen with—CP is already a little far to the left for some of the partners, and then to have my own sister running around stirring up trouble—"

"Stirring up trouble! *You* guys came to *me* because you already had trouble, because you couldn't hold onto the best gift you'd ever gotten!"

Tim's mouth formed a shape that was going to lead to a word, and I had a feeling that that was going to lead to disaster, but at that point two things happened: My mother came back with a beautiful perch on a beautiful platter, and my phone rang, the line in my room that rings through from my office.

I smiled sweetly and excused myself. I dashed to my room and grabbed the phone, thinking it might be Bill.

It wasn't.

"Lydia? It's Mary."

"Serving and protecting, as always. You just saved Tim's life."

"What?"

"I was about to kill him. What's up? Did you find something for me on this Bic person?"

She ignored that question and asked another one. "Can you meet me at Reggio's?"

"What, now?"

"Can you?"

"Sure. Fifteen minutes. Give me a hint?"

"See you there." She hung up. No hint.

I clipped my gun to my belt, untucked my sweatshirt so it would ride over it. I picked up my leather jacket, braced myself, went back to the dining table.

"I'm sorry," I said. "I have to go out."

"Lydia—"

"Ling Wan-ju—"

They spoke simultaneously, in the same disapproving tone.

"Think of it this way," I said brightly, putting on my shoes by the door. "You can visit with each other, just mother and son. That's why Tim came, after all. Don't wait up, Ma. I'll do the dishes when I get back."

At the idea of having Tim to herself, my mother visibly cheered up.

Tim did not.

I smiled and left.

# NINE

**M**y cab dropped me at the corner, just because I like to look over the street before I get where I'm going. Most of the cab ride I'd spent looking back over my shoulder. I was pretty sure I hadn't been followed.

Reggio's is a old dark-wood-and-marble cafe in Greenwich Village. The walls are crowded with ornate picture frames around mediocre pictures and the music leans toward violins. Mary and I spent innumerable hours in Reggio's in high school, before we were old enough to hang around in bars and drink, and many more while I was in college and she was in the Academy, after we had discovered that, like a lot of Asians, neither of us can drink anyway. It was in Reggio's that she talked me through my breakup with Matt Yin, and here, years later, that I talked her through the times when being a small Asian woman in a big white man's department was almost not worth it to her.

Mary was waiting when I got there, in the corner at a round table with a carved pedestal and a cracked marble top. She was watching the crowd, the window, and the street, with those eyes cops develop, the ones that never stop noticing.

The waiter, a slight, unsmiling young man with a haircut more asymmetrical than mine, got to Mary's table at the same time I did, bringing her cappuccino. I ordered a pot of Earl Grey tea, shrugged out of my jacket, sat down.

"Well?" I said. "Hi, by the way."

"Hi." She stirred sugar into the froth, waited for me to get settled. When I did she got straight to the point. "Why were you asking about the Main Street Boys this afternoon?"

"I told you, I can't tell you."

"I need to know."

"I'd need to know why."

"I can't tell you."

I smiled cheerfully. "Can we skip this part?"

"It's not funny, Lydia. There's a problem."

"What's the problem?"

"The problem is . . ." She paused as the waiter came back carrying a tray with my tea. He set down the pot, the cup, the lemon slices, the little plate for the teabag, the napkin, the spoon. Then, because he had nothing left to do and he still hadn't found out what the problem was, he turned on his heel and stalked away.

I let my tea steep. Mary went on. "A detective I know named Ferguson caught a homicide this afternoon. A fresh stiff. Young male Asian."

Mary talks about death the way all cops do, words like stiff, whacked, burned. It always throws me, but I try not to show it.

I asked, "Who is it? Do they know?"

She nodded as she sipped her cappuccino. "One Hsing Chung Wah. FOB, 19." An FOB, in Chinatown, is a new immigrant: someone Fresh Off the Boat. Some people lose the title right away, as they get into step with the dance of the community; some wear it for years. "The street says he was a wild man. Not well-liked." She put down her cup. "He had a dragon tattooed on his right arm."

"A Golden Dragon?"

"A Golden Dragon," she agreed.

Holding the top of the pot down so it wouldn't slide into my cup, I poured my sweetly fragrant tea. "But there's more to it than just this," I said, "because he wasn't a Main Street Boy, and you got me here to ask about the Main Street Boys."

"To ask why you were asking."

"Hmmm." I regarded Mary curiously. "Why does the death of a Golden Dragon get you interested in the Main Street Boys?"

"Are you mixed up with them, Lydia?"

"I told you, I don't even know them. I'm looking for their *dai lo.*"

"Well, don't."

"Why not?"

Mary drank her cappuccino some more. "Hsing Chung Wah was found in Flushing," she told me. "In an alley off Main Street. And: He was killed by a bullet through the eye."

I said, "Executed."

Everything has fashions; the current rage in street execution was this, a bullet through the eye.

With a spoon Mary chased the froth around the sides of her cup. "Now tell me why you wanted to know."

I sighed. "I can't. You know I can't. My client came to me specifically to avoid going public."

"Once there's a homicide everything's different, Lydia."

"This could have nothing to do with what I'm working on," I protested. "Gang members get in trouble all the time for being in each other's territories."

"When Ghost Shadows go around the wrong corner in Chinatown and the Fuk Ching blow them away I'll buy it," Mary said. "When Golden Dragons go all the way to Queens to turn up dead I don't think it's just guarding your territory. The Golden Dragons don't share borders with the Main Street Boys."

Mary had told me some things, just now, that she didn't have to. Partly, I knew, it was to scare me away from the Main Street Boys and Bic; but partly, I also knew, it was in case, for whatever I was working on, it was useful. Now I was obligated; now it was my turn.

I said reluctantly, "Yes, they do."

She looked up sharply. "They do what?"

"Share borders." I told her about the Main Street Boys' sublease on the corner of Mulberry Street.

She listened. When I was through she was quiet, her face thoughtful. The violins played a romantic, Russian-sounding melody.

"How do you know that?" Mary said.

"Don't ask me, okay?"

She didn't answer that, but said, "I'm going to have to pass it on. We didn't know what the connection was."

"You would have found out sooner or later." Mary nodded in absent agreement. I wondered if Trouble would see it that way. "But that arrangement may have nothing to do with this murder," I added.

"Maybe," she said, "but it gives us someplace to start from. We need that, Lydia. We need to find out who killed this Hsing kid and take them up before the Golden Dragons get to them. We can't let that get started."

She didn't say what she meant by "that" but we both knew. "That" was gang war, when icy, crowded streets and steamy restaurants become as dangerous as minefields, when any minute a car could whip around the corner or a door could burst open and rattling gunfire could turn a wedding banquet or a child's birthday party into a horror of screams and blood.

"I hope it helps," was all I said.

The sulking waiter reappeared to see whether there was anything else we wanted.

"No," Mary said. "I've got to be getting back."

We left together, zipping and buckling and wrapping up against the cold. "How'd you come?" Mary asked me as we walked down the street together, her breath forming a question mark of steam to punctuate her words.

"Cab."

"I'll drive you as far as Canal."

"Okay."

Her car was parked illegally one block over. We got in and she started it, gave it about twenty seconds, then turned the heater on full blast.

"It won't ever heat up if you don't give it a chance."

"It's a department vehicle, it doesn't heat up anyway. Listen, Lydia." I listened, but until she'd pulled out into the traffic she didn't say anything else. "Whatever you're working on, if these guys are any part of it you've got to tell me, okay?"

"If I find anything I think has anything to do with this I promise I'll tell you."

"No." Exasperation shortened the syllable. "Not if what you're working on has to do with this killing. If the gangs have anything at all to do with your thing. That's what I meant, and you know it."

"All right," I said meekly. "If I find out they were involved. I promise."

She dropped me on the north side of Canal, near my office. It's not quite Chinatown here—though in a couple of years it might be—and not quite Tribeca or Soho either. My neighbors are mostly electronics discounters and bare bones job lot places, and my office is in the back room of a storefront travel agency. It's an easy, anonymous spot for both Chinese and *low faan* to come to, and anyone who doesn't want the world to know they need a detective can pretend they need a trip to Hawaii.

I headed across Canal, hat pulled down and collar pulled up, cheeks burning with the cold. I thought about my talk yesterday with Trouble, and the one today with Nora. I thought about what Mary had told me and what I'd promised her.

And I couldn't help thinking that, more intriguing than the idea that the Main Street Boys had been involved in the robbery I was working on, was the idea that, in their territory, they had not.

## T E N

Tim was gone when I got home. My mother had already done the dishes and was in the living room knitting a sweater for Elliot's new baby and listening to Tom Jones on some lite radio station.

"That's very sappy music, Ma," I told her as I took off my gloves and blew on my fingers to warm them. "If you understood the words you'd hate it."

"Then it's a lucky thing I don't, so my pleasure isn't spoiled." She changed the color of her yarn as I came and flopped down on the couch beside her. She went on: "I think your brother is working too hard, Ling Wan-ju. He seemed worried and preoccupied. What were you fighting about?"

"We weren't fighting, Ma."

"You always fight in English when I'm out of the room. I hope you weren't provoking him again. He has enough on his mind, all his important responsibilities to his clients and partners. You really have to try to be nicer to him and not add to his burdens. It would be easier on all your brothers if you had a safe, secure job, you know."

"Oh, Ma!" She'd sneaked that one up on me. I got up, headed toward my room. "Did I get any calls?"

"Yes. One. I think it was from the white baboon."

That would be Bill. I punched the button on the machine, listened to the chipmunk sound of a message rewinding. Then I listened to the familiar sound of Bill telling me to call him at home or, if he wasn't there, to try Shorty's.

He wasn't at home, but he was at Shorty's.

"What's up?" he wanted to know.

"Are you being careful?"

"I always do everything you tell me. Someday you'll appreciate that in a man."

"Uh-huh. Someone was tailing me."

"Shit. When?"

I told him about the hatless guy.

"Damn," he breathed. "I should have spotted him. Damn."

"He's Mr. Anonymous," I said. "I never would have noticed him myself except in Chinatown. Here he stood out."

"Well, I'll watch my back, but there's no one in here I don't know. If there's someone on me he must be out in the cold freezing his butt off."

"Good." I liked that idea.

"You have any idea who they are and what they want?"

"No. You?"

"Santa Claus, seeing whether we're naughty or nice?"

"Christmas is over."

"Maybe he's checking for Chinese New Year, to see if you deserve your presents."

"We don't give presents on Chinese New Year."

"Then you can be as naughty as you want. In which case . . ."

"I'm already as naughty as I want. Good Chinese daughters don't get any naughtier than this. Speaking of which, my brother Tim came over for dinner to give me a hard time about this case. He wants me to drop it."

"Tell him he should have thought of that before his organization called you."

"I'm sure he did. Luckily we didn't get a chance to really get going, because something else came up." I told him about my meeting with Mary at Reggio's. "Of course," I finished up, "it might be completely unconnected to our case."

"It might."

"You don't think so?"

"It seems strangely coincidental, a Golden Dragon killed on Main Street Boys' turf the day after you talk to the *dai lo* of one and go looking for the *dai lo* of the other."

"But it could happen."

"Happens all the time," he agreed.

"I don't think so either." I sighed. "But I hope so. Mary says all the cops are on alert now, in both precincts."

"Waiting for the payback?"

"Well, it doesn't seem likely the Golden Dragons will just let this go."

"No, it doesn't."

"What about the rest of your day?" I asked him. "Did you get anything accomplished?"

"My laundry," he said. "And twenty new measures of the Bartok. But I'll bet that's not what you mean."

71

"Astonishing, Holmes. How do you do it?"

"Modesty forbids my mentioning my prodigious—"

"Don't."

"I was going to say intellectual capacity. Anyway, yes, I saw all of Roger Caldwell's porcelain dealers."

"Do you really know two of them?"

"I really know all three of them, but one might not want to admit that he knows me."

"Why not?"

"Remember I told you about my friend, who knows a guy who might know a guy who might know what to do with hot porcelain?"

"You're kidding. That guy is one of these guys?"

"Franco Ciardi, at the Morpheus Gallery."

"Ah. Did you tell him Caldwell sent you?"

"Uh-huh. And he said the same thing he said yesterday, the same thing the other two said: It's too soon to expect these things to start turning up. In a way, that's good. Now they know we're looking. If they're offered anything from the Blair collection they won't get taken in. They'll know to call us."

"Do you trust these guys?"

"The other two, sure."

"And Ciardi?"

"Ciardi owes me, but he'd rather I owed him. If he can put us on to our stolen porcelain he'll see it as a way of making points with me. It'll show me what a good, cooperative guy he is."

"And he thinks you'll believe that?"

"If he helps us out it'll be true," Bill pointed out.

"Doesn't motive count?"

"Not to me. Pure action, that's all I'm interested in."

"Hah. All right, here's some action: You want to come uptown tomorrow?"

"I love to go uptown with you. Why?"

"I want to talk to Dr. Browning."

"I think that's a good idea. When?"

"Nine? I'll have to call him."

"See you then."

"Bill?"

"What?"

"Don't forget to be careful."

"I won't." I could hear his voice smile. "Thanks."

I took a hot bath with a couple of spoonfuls of Mr. Gao's relaxing herbs in it. When I settled into bed I was pleasantly tired and finally warm. I don't remember the dreams I had that night, except that there was sunshine, and peach trees, and a duck and a drake.


## E L E V E N

I called Dr. Browning early, at home, because that's what Nora had recommended the day before. First she'd asked, "Why don't you talk to him here? He comes in in the afternoons, after his seminar, to work on the rest of the collection."

That had surprised me. "He does? Still?"

"Well, it still has to be done. We put in a new alarm system and bars on the insides of the basement windows."

"Oh. I guess I just never thought about the rest of the collection."

"Let's hope the thieves haven't thought about it either," Nora said drily. "Do you want to meet Dr. Browning here tomorrow?"

I considered. "No. I prefer to talk to people in their natural habitats when I can. It gives me a better sense of them."

"Then get him before he goes in to school. If he gets buried in his research he won't even answer the phone."

So I called at eight. At first the soft, hesitant voice on the other end of the phone seemed unsure of who I was. Then he placed me. "Oh, I'm so sorry! Nora's detective. Yes, of course, come whenever you like. I'm anxious to help. When should I expect you?"

I suggested nine and he agreed. At eight-thirty I met Bill and we took the IRT to the Upper West Side. We did some doubling back and we did some looking over our shoulders and we both decided we weren't being followed.

Which was too bad; because if someone isn't following you, you can't find out who he is.

The day uptown, like the day downtown, was bright and blue and sunny. We could see the bare trees on the Jersey side of the river through the bare trees in Riverside Park as we walked down the block. Dr. Browning's address turned out to be one of those old brown brick apartment buildings on a side street off West End. There was fancy tan trim around some of the windows and in a line up by the roof. It looked like stone to me, but Bill said it was terra cotta.

I told the doorman who we were, and he told the handset of an ancient intercom system, and then he hung it up and told us to go up to eight.

The elevator wheezed and creaked and finally got us there. At the end of a hallway whose beige carpet was thinning down the middle we found Dr. Browning's apartment door and knocked.

Immediately, the door opened a wedge. The thin, spectacled face of Dr. Mead Browning peered out. His eyes fell on Bill first, and he looked him over with a puzzled frown.

"Good morning, Dr. Browning." I smiled. "This is Bill Smith. He's working on this case with me. We'd like to ask you some questions, if that's all right?"

Dr. Browning's glance shifted to me and his face cleared. I had the funny feeling that he not only hadn't seen me, he hadn't remembered I was on my way up. He smiled shyly. "Miss Chin. Yes, please, come in. I was just trying to remember whether I'd met this gentleman. I lose track, you know."

The shy smile remained on his face and he remained

standing in the doorway. Bill and I stood dopily in the hall for a few more awkward moments. Then Dr. Browning flushed. "Oh, I'm so sorry. Come in, come in."

This time he moved aside, and I stepped quickly into the vestibule, Bill right behind me. We didn't want to lose our chance.

As Dr. Browning closed and locked the door behind us I took a look around. The living room was straight ahead, the kitchen to the right. The bedroom and bath, I assumed, were off to the left, through a small archway. I was intimidated at the thought of going that way, because it seemed to me just getting to a living room chair was going to be challenge enough.

Or finding one. Dusty piles of newspapers, magazines, and books rose lumpily in Dr. Browning's dim living room like snowbanks from a paper blizzard. Dark curtains, possibly blue once, hung half-opened around two grimy windows that might have a view of the river, if you could see through them. My nose wrinkled with the smell of must and mold; I unzipped my jacket, uncomfortable in the close, warm air. Bookcases, books stacked haphazardly, surrounded what was probably a writing desk; across the room, an upright piano held papers and more books. A squat brass vase dropped petals from a bunch of ancient dried flowers onto a graying cloth on a shelf. A hard wooden chair was pulled up to the desk; the other chairs, three of them, were snowed under.

Only one thing in the room seemed to gleam: A small china cabinet hung on the wall, all dark polished wood and sparkling glass. Inside it, three shelves displayed a dozen pieces of shiny porcelain.

Gingerly, I stepped closer to examine the cabinet and contents. Dr. Browning hovered just behind me. I let my eyes wander from piece to piece, knowing I had very little idea what I was looking at, knowing also that last week I probably wouldn't even have stopped to look.

The pieces were all small, teacups and saucers, mustard pots and salt cellars, a sugar bowl, a cream pitcher. A gravy boat stood on tiny clawed feet; a white cup as translucent as a shell had a red tiger painted on its side and another curling around the knob on its cover. Six salt cellars held miniature silver spoons and were each painted with a different stylized blossom. The pieces' shapes varied, in ways that I knew told something about their origins, but didn't tell it to me.

The designs painted on them, also, had meaning: more than one meaning. Each swirling line and lotus leaf, each glowing cobalt phoenix and fierce orange tiger meant something to the artist who'd put them there: a symbol, a talisman, a joke. They meant something else to a scholar like Dr. Browning: a clue to the origin of the piece, and to its destination, its intended fate.

And something else to me, something I was surprised to find myself feeling: a connection to people I'd never known in a place I'd never been to, people who dug this clay out of the ancient earth, formed it and colored it and sent it halfway around the world.

"How do you like my little ones?" Dr. Browning's wistful voice, close behind me, brought me back with a little jolt to this dishevelled room in this city where I was born.

I turned and smiled. "They're lovely. I didn't realize you were also a collector."

His eyes didn't meet mine; they rested instead on the china cabinet as he said, half-apologetically, "Oh, I'm not, not at all. On a professor's salary, I couldn't possibly collect. But the occasional piece, here and there . . . something too special to leave behind . . ." He trailed off, looking lovingly at the porcelains, which stood at attention on their shelves as if on their best behavior to make a good impression on the strangers.

I suddenly recalled the large platter, also standing proudly, in the sun-touched case by the stairway at the Kurtz. "But you're a donor," I said. "We saw a plate at the Kurtz Museum that you gave."

"Oh, hardly a donor. Occasionally I acquire a splendid piece which really must be seen. I do try to find a home for those. It's quite marvelous, isn't it, the platter at the Kurtz?

And they're displaying it so handsomely. So many people are given the chance to admire it. Did Roger Caldwell point it out to you?"

"No, his assistant showed us around. Do you know Dr. Caldwell?"

"Yes, of course. He's very well known in the field. We were all very proud when he was given the post at the Kurtz."

" 'We'?"

"Those of us involved in the study of export porcelains. Exports are widely considered the field's stepchildren, you see. Because of the purely commercial intent behind their production. As if the early imperial ware—or Limoges, for that matter—were created for any other reason." He said this with a sense of resigned bitterness, as though the injustice he was pointing out was so entrenched he had given up all hope of redress. "In any case," he went on, "that a member of our small fraternity has been given the opportunity to direct a museum is quite gratifying. Even a museum such as the Kurtz."

" 'Such as the Kurtz'?" I repeated, not sure what he meant.

"Well, for all its virtues, the Kurtz is not widely accepted as an institution of the first rank, is it? My understanding, in fact, is that that is a source of frustration for Dr. Caldwell: that he cannot quite get the museum taken seriously in the professional world."

"Because it's directed by an export porcelain person?"

"Sad, isn't it? And a man like Roger Caldwell, with so much to offer. I'm given to understand that he feels his professional career to be rather stymied."

I thought about Roger Caldwell, stymied and growing bitter in his beautiful office in his Upper East Side townhouse; and about Nora, dreaming and planning and working late into the night in her vinyl-floored room with the peeling paint.

"Oh." Dr. Browning suddenly turned away from the cabinet. "Oh, but you haven't come here to talk about my little ones, or the intricacies of the museum world. I'm so sorry. You have questions for me. Why don't we . . ." He looked around helplessly, taking in the book mounds, the magazine hillocks, the paper snowbanks.

I was at a loss, unsure what proper etiquette required of a guest when the host can't produce a chair; but Bill walked smoothly into the room, moving around precarious-looking piles as comfortably as though he'd put them there himself. He lifted books and magazines off one side of a tiny sofa, didn't react at all to the clouds of dust that puffed from them as he placed them neatly on the floor. He repeated the performance with a leather armchair and settled in that.

Dr. Browning beamed a grateful look at Bill and gestured me to the sofa.

"May I use your bathroom first?" I asked.

"Oh, my, yes, of course. It's right through there."

I thanked him and made my way through there, leaving Dr. Browning to turn to Bill with a flustered smile.

The bathroom was fairly tidy, though obviously the domain of someone unused to guests: a threadbare bathrobe hanging behind the door, towels damp from a morning shower. I spent the bare minimum of time in it that modesty demanded. Then I left it silently and I slipped into the small, dark bedroom, poked quickly into the closet and under the bed.

When I returned to the living room, Bill had Dr. Browning absorbed in a serious conversation about the changes in university education in the city since Bill's college days.

They both looked up when I came back, and ended that discussion, apparently on a note of agreement. I sat on the sofa I'd been offered before. Dr. Browning, sitting straight in the desk chair, knees and ankles pressed together, looked at me expectantly.

"Dr. Browning," I began, removing my jacket carefully, laying it across my lap, "what can you tell us about the pieces from the Blair collection that were stolen from CP's basement?"

"Tell you about them? Well," he looked at his shoes for

inspiration, "well, they're really quite wonderful. The entire collection is quite wonderful, quite special."

"Can you be more specific? Is there anything about them, for example, that would make anyone want to steal them particularly, rather than anything else in the collection?"

"Do you mean, are they perhaps worth more? Can one sell them for a higher price?" A strange overtone echoed in Dr. Browning's thin voice, something that, in a context where it made sense, I might have called resentment.

"Yes, I suppose that's what I mean."

"It isn't likely. I haven't gone through the entire collection yet, of course, but all of Mr. Blair's pieces seem to be of very high quality. The stolen pieces were marvelous, but most of the collection is equal to them."

"Were they all somehow the same?" My newly acquired knowledge of porcelain was leaving me flat; I couldn't think of very many ways in which porcelain could be the same. "From the same kiln, or made for the same patron, or something?"

"Oh, I doubt it. They appeared to represent quite a wide range of periods and styles, as far as I'd examined them."

"What about," Bill asked, "from the same source? The same seller, I mean? These were all the new acquisitions, weren't they?"

Dr. Browning pursed his lips. "Yes, they were, but from the same source? I wouldn't think so. So many diverse pieces . . . of course, it's hard to say." He trailed off, shaking his head at the difficulty of saying.

"Is information about the source of each piece on Mr. Blair's list?" I asked. "Can we check that?"

Dr. Browning brightened and smiled. "Oh, of course." His eyes wandered the room. His smile began to fade, but when he spied an old battered briefcase at his feet it rekindled, as though he'd unexpectedly run into an old friend. He extracted a file folder from the briefcase, laid it on his perfectly horizontal lap, ran his finger down a typewritten page. His smile held for a short time, then faded again.

"Oh," he said. "Oh, dear. That's a shame."

"What is?" I asked.

"Well, as it happens, those were the crates where Mrs. Blair had placed the new acquisitions. A lovely lady, Mrs. Blair," he added, as an aside. "Quite classically patrician." Eyebrows raised, he asked Bill, "Have you met her?" Bill shook his head. Dr. Browning dropped his eyes to the list again. "And she seems quite methodical. Her late husband, sadly, does not." He pursed his lips in gentle disapproval.

"They're not there?" I asked.

Dr. Browning blinked great big owl-eyes at me. I suddenly wondered if he needed the night vision of an owl to live in the permanent dimness of his own living room. "No. They hadn't been catalogued. The inventory process," he added quickly, "is, I must admit, rather tedious if it's done painstakingly, as it should be. One can quite understand Mr. Blair's reluctance to give time to such an enterprise. I've been working on the Blair collection at Chinatown Pride for some days now, and I haven't yet finished."

"If you haven't finished," Bill asked, "how do you know for sure what was in the boxes that were stolen and what's in the others?"

Dr. Browning turned his eyes to Bill, then quickly back to the paper in his lap. "Well. Well. I haven't a list or anything of that sort, but I did look through all the crates before I began the actual cataloguing process. I couldn't help myself." He said that anxiously, as though Bill and I might think less of him for such unprofessional behavior. "It was all so lovely. And I had heard of the Blair collection for so many years." The small smile I'd first seen in Nora's office played on his lips again. Then he seemed to give himself a mental shake. He looked to me. "And I photographed some of them. In those pictures you have."

"And you remember the others, enough to know they aren't on this list?" Bill wanted to know.

"Oh, yes. Oh, I remember them all."

"Dr. Browning," I asked, "who knew the Blair collection was at the CP building?"

He pursed his lips, folded the file shut. "I told no one. Nora asked me specifically to tell no one."

"So no one knew but you, Nora, and Tim?"

His owl-eyes blinked at me again. "And Mrs. Blair, of course. And anyone she might have told."


The icy New York morning, when Bill and I stepped back out into it, shone so brightly I had to pull my sunglasses from my jacket pocket. I looked up at Bill; he was squinting, too.

We walked back toward the subway, breathing in air that suddenly seemed fresh and clean to me. Cars drove by that hadn't been in the same place for thirty years, and when the wind blew, pushing papers and the smell of frying eggs, I didn't mind it.

"What do you think of Dr. Browning?" I asked Bill as we walked.

Cupping a cigarette against the wind to light it, he said, "Do you mean do I think he stole the Blair porcelains?"

"Well, I could just mean do you think he's sort of batty."

"You could, and he is, but you don't."

"Well, then?"

"He could have. He would have had to have hired someone, at least to help, probably to do it for him."

"Someone who knew how to disable an electronic alarm."

"Lots of people know how to do that."

"Yes, and most of them are friends of yours. But how would someone like Dr. Browning find one?"

"You'd be surprised." We stopped at a light. Both of us, as we talked, scanned the street, looking for anyone who seemed to be looking for us, finding no one. "Or maybe he knows someone who could do that and that's what gave him the idea. You're the one who went strolling through his apartment. Did you find anything interesting?"

"No boxes or crates, no recently disturbed dust. Do you think he plays that piano, by the way?"

"I don't think he knows he has a piano."

"If he stole them," I asked, "what's he going to do with them?"

"Sell them?"

"And do what? Buy a red Miata? Look at his apartment, Bill. I don't think he cares too much about *things*."

"Except his porcelains. His little ones."

"That was weird, that he called them that," I admitted. "But they were all small. And he's given bigger things away, like that platter. He could have kept that."

"That's true. Are you a p.i. or a defense attorney?"

The light changed. As we crossed, I said, "I guess I don't want him to have done it. I guess I like him."

"I guess you do. And maybe he didn't, and so far nothing says he did. But he's someone who knew where they were, and knew what they were worth. He's a possibility."

"So's everyone who knew those things. Maybe Nora did it. Maybe Mrs. Blair did it herself. Oh, hey, maybe Tim did it. Oh, I like that. Can you arrange for that to be true?"

"No, but for a price I can probably prove it."

We'd reached the subway. I searched my pocket for a token. "We really have to look into all those people, don't we?" I said. "Nora and Tim and everybody. Just to be thorough and eliminate them."

"Yes."

"Because any of them might have done it."

"It's always possible."

"It always is, isn't it?" I sighed. "You always have no real idea what anyone is up to. I hate that."

"That's why you love this job."

I looked up, surprised. "What do you mean?"

"Because in the course of finding out what happened in whatever case you're investigating, you get to find out what everyone is up to."

I considered that. "You're right. Why do you suppose I want to know that?"

"I have no idea. I've always found knowing that kind of depressing, myself."

We stepped from the shadow of a building into a patch of bright sunlight, and I thought of the musty dimness of Dr. Browning's living room. "But not as depressing," I told Bill, "as being in the dark."

## TWELVE

**B**ill went crosstown, I went downtown. He went to cruise the galleries, just sort of to listen, in case there was anything to hear. I went to see if anyone in Chinatown could tell me anything that might help about the robbery, or about the Main Street Boys, or about anything else.

A bright sunny day in Chinatown brings everybody out, even in the cold. People wove through the packed streets like dancers, finding openings, halting, starting, spinning suddenly to head the other way. Their music came from the words they spoke: the Cantonese and English I understand, the Mandarin and Fukienese and Spanish and Korean that I don't. The percussion was their footsteps slapping and tapping the pavement in syncopated rhythm. Their costumes were marvelous: bright ski parkas, patterned scarves and mittens, plaid coats, black leather and brown leather and puffy white fur sweeping by one another in intricate, fast-moving choreography. The set was good, too. Crimson New Year's banners with glittering gold letters snapped in the wind across Mulberry and Mott. In crowded store windows chains of red-wrapped firecrackers hung waiting for the lion dancers who would come to scare away the evil spirits on New Year's Day.

I stepped into the pattern, took my place. Not a soloist, just another member of the corps, I worked my way down Mulberry close to the corner where CP's building stood. Then I stepped off stage, into the wings.

I started with the bakery, six doors up. "Couple buildings each direction" was the amount of real estate Trouble had said he was renting out to the Main Street Boys. I didn't know if the bakery was included, but there was a fifty-fifty chance they would tell me, if I asked.

Warm, scented air enveloped me as I stepped out of the sharp cold and inside the bakery door. It was welcoming, comforting, and a strong reminder that breakfast had been a few hours ago and lunch wasn't close. I ordered a cup of tea and a lotus-seed cake from the tiny woman behind the counter. I didn't know her and our transaction was in English, since the people who own that bakery are from Fujian province and it would have taken us hours to puzzle out each other's dialects.

I had found a table and taken my hat and jacket off by the time the tiny woman brought my tea and cake on a tiny tray. The cake was small too, but the tea was in a big white cup—porcelain, I mentioned off-handedly to myself. Undoubtedly new, with garish colors and sloppy lines. Not the fine workmanship you got in the old days.

"Excuse me," I said to the woman as I paid her, "may I see the manager?"

She gave me a look full of suspicion and empty of comprehension. "Manager?" She repeated the syllables as though she'd never heard them before.

"The owner," I said. "The boss."

"Oh, boss." Understanding came into her eyes but the suspicion didn't leave. She nodded quickly and slipped away toward the back of the shop.

The tea was strong and fresh, astringent but not bitter, with a woody taste I didn't know. I sipped it slowly, enjoying the warm glow. As I took the first bite of my lotus-seed cake a short man with thinning hair and a very round face appeared by my elbow.

"You want see me?" he asked.

My mouth full of sweet lotus-seed paste and light flaky pastry, I nodded and gestured to the chair opposite. He sat. I swallowed and smiled.

"You make wonderful cakes," I said.

He shook his head, looking glum. "Not so good, like grandfather in China. Not possible here get right things for use."

He denied the compliment in the good old-fashioned Chinese way. Praise from a stranger is almost rude; to accept it would have obligated him to me. It warmed my heart to see him sticking to the old ways in the new land.

The proprietor said nothing as I took another bite. His eyes were small and the look in them said that he didn't quite believe I had asked him to my table to compliment his pastry.

And, of course, I hadn't.

I reached into my pocket, gave him a business card, Chinese side up. He read it, turned it and read the English side too. He flipped back to the Chinese side, then looked at me.

"Investigator?" he said. "Got nothing to investigate, my shop."

"No," I said, sipping my tea. "And I'm not INS, FBI, NYPD or the Health Department." Though it never hurts to remind people you know those names. "And what I'm investigating has nothing to do with you."

"Okay, then why you here?"

"I'd like to ask you some questions that might help me."

"How I can help, got nothing to do with me?"

"The building at the end of the block," I said. "Chinatown Pride. Do you know them?"

He nodded, almost reluctantly. "Sons play basketball there, go to English. Wife also, English class."

"Those classes are free, aren't they? And the basketball league too."

"Free sure, don't pay. Got no money to pay. Bakery business not so good." His voice took on the tone of a complaint, as if to prepare me for being turned down when I hit him up for a donation.

"They have a museum there that's also free," I said. "Did you know that?"

"Don't know it." He shook his head.

"Well, it is. They don't charge money for any of their services. They're gifts for families like yours, because they want you to have what they can give you. They give gifts, but now they need help."

His eyes narrowed. "What kind help?"

"Just the answers to some questions."

"Don't know anythings."

"You may know more than you think. Will you just listen to my questions? For the people at Chinatown Pride? I'm working for them."

Now I had him. Now he was stuck. Accepting a gift puts you under an obligation to the giver; his reaction to my trial-balloon compliment had let me know he would take that obligation seriously. He clearly didn't want to talk to me, but, just as clearly, he felt he had to.

Now just don't step over the line, Lydia, I told myself. Just don't get cocky because you're so smart.

"There was a robbery there three nights ago. Have you heard about it?" I hadn't waited for him to agree to answer, but I knew he would.

"No. Not heard."

"Well, some things were stolen from their basement. Porcelains," I said, watching my teacup turn in my hand. "Very beautiful ones. They would like to have them back."

"Anyone lose something, want it back," the proprietor said cautiously.

"That's true," I agreed. "And interesting to discuss. If I knew who had these porcelains, I could have an interesting discussion with them."

"Well," he said, sounding relieved, "hope you find out, then."

The relief was because he'd been able to answer me without either lying or giving anything away. Okay; I'd made the offer. Maybe something would come of it, maybe not. In a quiet voice that didn't carry beyond our table at all, I asked, "Who collects your lucky money? The Golden Dragons?"

Looking alarmed, he glanced around, behind, at the door. Then, without looking at me, he shook his head.

"The Main Street Boys," I said, still just above a whisper. "When did they take over?"

He shrugged. "Few months. Don't remember."

"What happened? They just came in one day and said, 'We're in charge now'? It was that easy?"

"Easy?" His eyes suddenly flared; I was surprised. "Not easy! Golden Dragons come, I pay. Main Street Boys come, I pay. Then some Golden Dragons comes back, say, Main Street Boys go to hell, you pay us. Too much money! Bakery business not so good!"

I'd hit a nerve. I guess the bakery business was not so good. "What did you do? Do you pay them both now?"

His round head shook slowly back and forth. "Complained."

"Complained? To the police?"

"No no no. Police." He winked to show he understood my ridiculous joke. "Find someone told me how find Golden Dragons' *dai lo.*"

"You went to him yourself?" That showed a streak of courage I might not have expected. But people always surprise me.

"Sure I went. Say, 'Who I pay? Not both!' "

"And?"

"He tells, 'Main Street Boys. My boys don't coming back.' "

"And do they?"

"No. No more Golden Dragons. Main Street Boys only, every months."

"How much do you pay them?"

"Hundred dollar! Too much money!"

It sounded like a lot to me, too.

But it wasn't so much that Chinatown Pride couldn't have handled it.

## THIRTEEN

That was how it went all morning. Six businesses in each direction from the corner on both sides of the street seemed to be about the limit of the Main Street Boys' sublet. I hit the second-floor operations, too, the doctors and travel agents and CPAs. The story was the same, and I averaged maybe one in four people willing to tell it. I didn't push anybody. I wanted the word out that I was interested and could be reached. I didn't want to appear to be in the muscle business myself. CP wanted their porcelains back, and if I had to make a deal to get them I'd do it.

Though if someone had handed me the name of the thief and some hard evidence, like fingerprints, that could have locked him up, I wouldn't have turned it down.

After a couple of hours of sitting in waiting rooms or leaning over counters I was down to three more places. The first of them was a restaurant. I took that as a sign. The smell of garlic and black beans almost knocked me over as I pushed through the door, so I ordered shrimp in black bean sauce and gave myself half an hour off.

I called Bill from the pay phone by the door, to see how his day was coming, but he wasn't there. By the time I got back to my table my tea was waiting for me, and by the time I was halfway through the first cup my food arrived, plunked down by a harried and surly waiter. By the time I opened my mouth to say thank you he'd charged back into the kitchen again.

This place—Lucky Seafood—was small, unatmospheric,

and sort of a dive, but still at least half the customers were white. Lawyers from the courts and city workers from the area around City Hall, which both border Chinatown, wielded chopsticks with practiced ease, talking, eating, and thrusting the sticks at each other to emphasize important points. They passed the platters of breaded pork and jade scallops so everyone could scoop some onto their plates. The tables of Chinese ate the way I did, reaching across each other onto the stationary platters for the morsels they wanted, dropping pieces into their rice bowls so the rice could soak up the sauce. The lawyers and city workers didn't eat out of the rice bowls, but scooped rice, also, out onto their plates.

The restaurant, with its plastic-laminate tabletops and tin ceiling, was noisy, here at the heart of lunch hour. The sound of the white voices was lower and slower, the Chinese higher, quicker, more insistent. I eavesdropped idly on as many conversations in both languages as I could manage, but I didn't hear anything so compelling that it distracted me from my shrimp.

When I was finished I sat back, sipped my tea, and thought about where to go from here. I'd need to converse with the remaining shopkeepers, including the one who ran this place, just so I could say I'd been thorough. And then, depending on whether Bill had turned anything up, I really really wanted to meet this Bic.

The waiter brought my check and my fortune cookie. I was a little insulted about the cookie; usually they save them for the *low faan*. I opened it anyway.

Patience, it told me, is the key to joy.

Good, I thought, I'll have to remember to tell that to Bill next time he comes on to me.

I took out some cash and waited for the waiter. As he took the money and the check I asked to see the boss.

The waiter gave me a curious look, as though I were something interesting to see. I discounted it; maybe at Lucky Seafood no one ever had anything to say to the boss.

"Sure," he said. "You go this way." He pointed to the swinging doors into the kitchen.

I did think it was strange that he didn't go back and check with the boss first. For one thing, the boss might not want to see me. For another, I might be with the Health Department, in which case the boss might not want to see me wandering through the kitchen all by myself. But maybe the kitchen at Lucky Seafood was so faultless that a surprise visit from an inspector was no problem at all.

I thought all that, but no warning bell went off in my head, no little voice suggested that, in the absence of anyone else to do it, I should be watching my own back.

I just gathered up my things, pocketed the fortune from the cookie, and marched through the kitchen doors.

And into Trouble.

He and three of his boys—gelled hair, black leather jackets, no socks—were lounging against the stainless steel counter in the cramped kitchen, picking boiled baby shrimp out of a bowl, spitting shell fragments on the floor.

The rich aromas of simmering sauces were overpowered by the stinging smells of ammonia and soap in the small, bright, crowded room. Trouble and I stared at each other, wordless. I felt my face rearrange itself in astonishment. His didn't. He smiled a sneering smile as the eyes of the others swept over me in a way I could almost feel, a way that made me want to sock them.

"So." Trouble smirked. "Little private eye must lost. Door to leave Lucky Seafood back that way."

"You're right," I said. "I went the wrong way. Nice seeing you." I turned calmly, right into one of the boys, who held a nine-millimeter automatic a foot from my chest.

I turned back to Trouble. I hadn't really thought that was going to work.

"Okay," I said. "Now what?"

"Since you here, maybe we talk."

"About what?"

"Private talk."

One of the others clamped his hand, greasy with shrimp, on my jacket sleeve. I swung my arm sharply up and over, broke the grip. For a second I considered a front kick to the gun and a dash for the door, but I didn't have room for much of a kick, and it probably wasn't the only gun. The kitchen help in this tiny room were standing, silent and riveted, pressed against walls as far away as they could get. They knew better than to leave—that might look as though they were going for help—and they knew better than to help.

"Tell them to keep their stinking hands off me," I ordered Trouble, in the voice of someone used to being obeyed and totally unafraid. I wondered whose voice it was. "What the hell do you want?"

"Just private talk, little private eye. Outside, where pots don't got ears."

Well, there'd be more room outside for me to maneuver, too. And maybe someone who saw us from a window, where they could be anonymous, would call a cop.

So I went outside with the Golden Dragons, to the courtyard behind the kitchen of the Lucky Seafood restaurant. Other restaurants opened into this courtyard too, and different kinds of stores, and the back hallways of apartment buildings, but nothing opened into it right now.

The sun, angling overhead, cut sharp shadows from the garbage cans and back stoops and meaningless piles of junk strewn around here. Trouble cast a shadow too, and his boys, and they all pointed toward me. Mine, hiding behind me, pulled away from them, as far as it could.

"Well?" I said, trying to sound impatient.

"Little private eye spending a lot of time this block, this morning," Trouble began unhurriedly.

"I had shopping to do. What do you care?"

"Shopping," he scoffed. "Shopping for porcelains."

"I'm in the market." I was cautious. "You knew that."
Don't look interested, Lydia, I told myself. Don't look anxious. He'll let you know if he wants to make a deal.

"Get out."

"What?"

"Get out that market. Little private eye don't want porcelains more."

"Why wouldn't I?"

"Porcelains," Trouble said. "Robbery. Golden Dragons, Main Street Boys. All this don't matter to little private eye now."

"Yes, they do."

"No." He stepped closer to me. "No, they don't. No more questions, no more bother people."

I was curious. "Why do you care?"

In a flash he'd backhanded me across the mouth hard enough to send me staggering. I tasted salty blood, but an adrenaline rush drowned the pain I knew I'd feel later.

"See," I heard Trouble say, as I grabbed a garbage can to keep from falling, "too many questions."

Hot fury filled me. Some black belt, Lydia! You didn't even see it coming.

"Hurts?" Trouble's voice sounded concerned.

"No." I let go of the garbage can, straightened to face him again.

"Why you crying?"

"I'm not," I snarled. It's true my eyes were tearing from the blow, but that didn't count.

"Little private eye like to be tough," Trouble grinned, talking to his boys. "How tough you think?"

"Oh, I think she's real tough," the one with the greasy hands snickered. He had no trace of a Chinese accent: ABC, like me. "Too tough to be tasty. I think we'd better soften her up." His slimy hands curled into tight fists at his sides as he started forward.

"Hold on, Jimmy," Trouble said easily. "I do this, I think so."

Jimmy looked disappointed, but he shrugged and stepped back. "Now," said Trouble to me, "maybe we don't hurt you too much, little private eye. Just enough show you how stupid, asking questions Trouble don't want you ask."

"Which questions?" Oh, shut up, Lydia! I told myself, but I couldn't do it. "Yesterday you didn't care—"

His fist whipped out again but this time I was ready. I blocked it overhead, came in low, slammed my fist into his stomach and the heel of my palm up into his nose. He tottered back with a muffled sound and I swung to the side to be ready for the guys who were sure to be coming at me.

They were. I stopped the first with a flying side kick. As I delivered it, and the roundhouse that brought down the next, I howled my loudest, bloodiest yells. I wanted to concentrate my *chi* and focus my power; I also wanted anyone with windows on this courtyard to know I was in trouble out here.

Those two went down but I misjudged the next guy. He dove low, under the kick I had for him. I caught him on the shoulder but it didn't matter. He clamped onto my standing leg as I brought the kick down. The buildings spun crazily as I flew backwards, crashed to the pavement on my back with him clinging to my ankle like a lead weight tail on a kite. I doubled up to reach him, pounded my elbow against his temple twice, three times. My angle was bad but my power was good: His grip loosened. I yanked my foot free and started to stand.

A tremendous crashing noise, like the firecrackers and bass drums of New Year's Day, exploded all around me. A pounding weight of pain crushed my back, my head. The asphalt came swirling up and met me with a dull thud. I lay, willing my legs and arms to move, but they wouldn't.

A far-off voice, Trouble's, rasped through the black-edged fog I was fighting. "Little bitch private eye! Stupid, stupid bitch! Teach you more than lesson now—teach you keep away from Trouble, keep away from Golden Dragons, little bitch!"

I saw his foot coming. I moved feebly no distance at all. The slamming pain in my side forced a sound from me, a sad-sounding moan. The foot moved again and crashed into my jaw. A web of fire sizzled around my head, into my eye and my shoulder. I almost didn't feel the next kick, in my stomach, but I knew it had happened because I couldn't breathe. I was choking, gasping for air out in a courtyard behind some old brick buildings in Chinatown.

A few more blows, and then they stopped. In a bitter sneer Trouble said something I couldn't make out. I tried to focus on him but my vision was blurry and dark. Moaning, I moved weakly; then I felt something else. Greasy hands rolled me onto my back, unzipped my pants, yanked them down. Cold air washed over my thighs. I reached out blindly for those hands, to stop them, but one of them smacked me twice across the face.

Then: "No." It was Trouble's voice. "Jimmy, I say no!"

I felt movement, watched a blurry Jimmy tumble over backwards as Trouble pulled him off me.

"Hey, come on," Jimmy whined.

"No," Trouble said again. "Old Gao doesn't likes that."

"Who gives a shit what that old asshole likes?"

"You got to learn respect elders," Trouble lectured. "Not good idea, piss off Old Gao."

"Jesus, man." Jimmy straightened his jacket, smoothed his moussed hair. "Oh, all right. Who wants an ugly bitch like her anyhow?"

"You right." Trouble leaned over me. It hurt my eyes to try to focus on his sneering face. "You hear that, little private eye? No one want ugly bitch like you around here. This your warning. Get it?"

I couldn't form any words. Trouble grabbed and shook me. Pain throbbed through my skull. "Get it?"

Still no words, but I managed a sound. He took it for whatever he wanted and let go.

Unable to move, I watched as the four of them stood over me for another few sniggering moments. Then, as a group, they turned, walked back through the door of the Lucky Seafood restaurant, and closed it decisively behind them.

## FOURTEEN

**A**ll right, a voice said in my head as my unfocused eyes lingered absently on Lucky Seafood's back door. You're lying with your pants down in a pile of garbage, Lydia. Get up.

Oh, shut up! I snarled at the voice. Where were you when I was waltzing merrily into that ambush? I don't have to listen to you anymore.

I let my eyes start to close.

Get up, the voice insisted. You'll freeze to death out here.

So what? I demanded. What's one brainless p.i. more or less? My head hurts. Leave me alone.

If you're found like this, the voice said in a smug, superior tone, your mother will never be able to show her face in Chinatown again. And your brother Tim will say "I told you so."

Unfair, you creep! But I opened my eyes. The sun seemed very close over the looming tops of the tenement buildings, close and too bright, but not at all warm. I was freezing, and something smelled terrible. I lowered my eyes to where I lay, turned my head painfully. It was true about the garbage, and not far away was the can it had come from. That's what the crashing noise had been, that's where the pounding in my head was from: Trouble, that motherless stinker, had clobbered me with a garbage can.

That was too much. Galvanizing anger thawed me enough that I managed to roll achingly onto my side, then work my way onto hands and knees.

Even better, Lydia, the voice said. On all fours with your pants down. We like this a lot.

95

I'm trying! I snapped, and I tried. I clung to the corner of a building and pulled myself up very slowly. When I was standing I held the building awhile to keep it from reeling around the way all the other buildings were doing. Then I reached all the way back down to my ankles for my pants.

In a dizzy stupor I hauled them up as far as they were willing to go, zipped and buttoned them. Something was wrong, something was weird. Well, of course, the voice said. You're a mess. The Golden Dragons just beat you up, remember?

I ignored the voice and ran my hands around the waistband of my pants. My holster, that was what was weird.

It was there, but it was empty.

Damn, I thought. Damn, damn, damn! I liked that gun. I cleaned it a lot.

I started to cry.

Oh, no, the voice said. Lydia, you jerk! If you lose it now you'll end up back in the garbage and freeze to death. Stop snivelling and try this: Walk through some restaurant's back door—maybe not Lucky Seafood's—and go home.

I wiped my eyes and tried that. A step. Another. Another. Maybe this wasn't so hard.

More steps.

An earthquake.

It must be that: I couldn't get my footing, the buildings spun and shimmered, the ground was moving. It headed up in my direction; helpless, I watched it come.

Then I was caught, then I was floating. No, being carried. A tall figure, good black overcoat, black hair combed straight back over his balding head, was holding me.

"Put me down," I slurred. "I can walk."

"No doubt." Mr. Gao, however, did not put me down.

"Leave me alone!"

I squirmed, but the movement hurt, and his strong arms just accommodated to me, still holding me up.

I stopped squirming. A doorway passed us. We went down a flight of stairs; I thought my head would break at each jarring step. The pipes of a long, dank, convoluted hallway went by overhead; then stairs up. Then a door, then another. The second opened into the dim, tranquil interior of Mr. Gao's apothecary shop.

Mr. Gao deposited me gently on the cushions of the carved teak couch. As soon as he did I started to stand. He had to catch me when I fell.

Mr. Gao pulled the shade on the apothecary door, spread a soft wool blanket over me, and told me not to move.

I didn't move, just shivered under the blanket while he opened drawers and jars and lit a fire on the small stove in the back. He brought me an ice pack for my jaw and one for the back of my head. I lay in a completely blank twilight, no thoughts at all, until Mr. Gao brought over a steaming cup of black liquid. He sat on the couch next to me, took away my ice packs, and lifted my head more gently than I would have thought possible.

"Ow," I protested anyway.

"Ling Wan-ju, drink this."

"I don't want your tea! You let them do this to me!" I turned my face away from the cup he held to my lips.

"I didn't know. Come, drink it."

The tea smelled inviting, a spicy smell over something deep and rich and earthy. And it was warm. I sipped.

"It tastes terrible!" Betrayal was everywhere. I felt the tears returning.

Mr. Gao chuckled. "Yes, of course. Now finish it."

He held it and I did. It warmed me, I grudgingly admitted, and though it still tasted terrible, it somehow also tasted right.

"I will give you some to take home. Brew it twice a day. And I will give you herbs for your bath." He let my head rest back on the pillow.

"My bath? My *bath?*" I stared in disbelief. "Why did you let them do this to me?"

"I told you: I didn't know."

"One of them wanted to—" Flustered and angry, I realized I didn't know the Chinese word for "rape." "To assault me." I hoped he would get it. "But Trouble wouldn't let him. He said you wouldn't like it."

"And I would not have."

"Then—"

"Ling Wan-ju, I don't control the Golden Dragons. They have no loyalty to me or to anyone."

"Then why does he care about what you wouldn't like?"

Mr. Gao looked at me for a moment, wordless in the peaceful dusk of his ancient shop.

"I cannot control their actions," he said. "Or instruct them, or advise them. They are a mountain cataract, racing over rocks. A river is contained by its banks, perhaps more than it knows, but it does not consult them."

I wasn't in the mood for philosophical Chinese nature metaphors. "Three Brothers is a powerful tong," I said. "And Trouble is afraid of you."

He nodded. "I cannot control them," he repeated. "But I can bring justice."

"Justice? What are you talking about?"

"If you want, they can be punished for this attack."

"They can?" Visions of Trouble stuffed head first into a garbage can filled my mind. "You can do that?"

"Yes. But," he fixed his black eyes on me steadily, "you must consider carefully, Ling Wan-ju."

"Consider? Why? I want them stomped and kicked and punched and walking barefoot on broken glass!"

"I know you want that. In your place I would want that and more." He paused, looking into the dimness. I realized my head was hurting less, and I was warm. "I have known you all your life," Mr. Gao mused. "I knew your father's family in China. I think your father would be pleased at the woman you are becoming."

"My mother says I'm causing him indescribable agonies in the afterlife."

"Your mother is concerned for your well-being and your

98

future. As are your brothers. The path you have chosen is unusual, and therefore, some think, unsafe."

I shifted a little, felt my ribs ache. "Maybe they're right," I said gloomily.

Mr. Gao smiled, a small soft smile. "Danger can mean many things. For you, not to do this work might be even more dangerous."

"Grandfather, don't. I can't think well enough to follow you right now." Something occurred to me. "Why did you come get me? How did you know what happened?"

"A shopkeeper called me. The baker, from further up the block."

I thought. "The bakery doesn't open on to the court-yard."

"He didn't know what was happening, but he told me you were going along the block asking questions about the Golden Dragons. He had seen some Golden Dragons go into Lucky Seafood, and you had gone in also. They had come out, and you had not."

A smart man, that baker. An astute observer. A hero. I promised to buy all my New Year's sweets from him forever.

"Can you drink more tea?" Mr. Gao arose.

"Not if it tastes like that. Grandfather, can you really punish them for this?"

He clinked and stirred in the rear of the shop, returning with a cup of clear, golden liquid. "Yes," he said. "But are you sure you want that?"

"Why wouldn't I?"

He handed me the tea, sat again. "Did the meeting you had requested with the Golden Dragons' *dai lo* come about?"

"Yesterday? Yes." I noticed he had delicately refrained from asking me if it was I who had been at that meeting.

"And whatever business it is that has gotten you involved with the Golden Dragons, is it concluded yet?"

"No." Suspiciously, I lifted the tea to my lips. This one had a thin, delicate scent and a mild, sweet taste.

"Perhaps, then, the river should be allowed to flow to the sea."

He didn't elaborate. I drank my tea. When I'm king, I decided, nature metaphors will be outlawed. "You mean, as long as it's cost me this much already, I shouldn't mess up my chances of solving this case by taking Trouble out of circulation?"

He smiled. "I'm glad you're feeling better." Then he said, "There is another reason also. When I greet you on New Year's Day, we will exchange oranges for luck."

I got that one. That's how it works, on New Year's: You give someone an orange, and he gives one to you. That's how it works any time. If Mr. Gao and the Three Brothers tong punished the Golden Dragons for attacking me, I would owe them. Mr. Gao was suggesting I think twice before incurring that kind of debt.

"Grandfather," I said, "you're a quiet man. Quiet men keep secrets, and therefore many people speak to a quiet man."

He nodded without an answer.

"Has anyone spoken about a robbery? Three days ago, porcelains taken from the Chinatown Pride building?" Nora would kill me for telling Mr. Gao, but I'd already spilled it to Trouble—assuming he hadn't known already—and quiet men keep secrets.

"Porcelains," Mr. Gao repeated. "No, I haven't heard about this. This is your case, Ling Wan-ju?"

"Yes, Grandfather. For many reasons they—Chinatown Pride, I mean—don't want anyone to know. I thought the Golden Dragons must have been involved somehow, because it was their territory, but now I find out it's not anymore."

"No. It isn't."

"Do you know the gang who've taken it over? Bic, and the Main Street Boys?"

"Do you intend to continue to pursue this?" he asked.

"Yes, I do. I was hired to do a job and I haven't done it yet."

"Then be prepared."

"For what?"

"For danger."

"Are you telling me not to let the Main Street Boys bushwhack me the way the Golden Dragons did?"

His unblinking black eyes fixed on me in a way they never had before, a way that made me almost unable to continue to meet them. "I am telling you, as I told you before, that danger comes in many forms. Anyone with eyes and ears would be frightened of the Golden Dragons. Anyone's ribs can be bruised by a kick."

Meaning what? I asked myself wearily. Lydia Chin doesn't have the brains she was born with?

Or meaning that some dangers are less obvious than others, and not, perhaps, dangerous to everyone in the same degree?

## FIFTEEN

I ran a hot bath, according to Mr. Gao's directions, and opened one of the square, paper-wrapped packages of herbs into it. While it was filling I called Bill.

"Hi," he said. "How're you doing?"

"Terrible," I said. "Rotten lousy horrible bad terrible."

I told him what had happened.

"I'm coming over," he said.

"No. You can't."

"Watch me."

"No, Bill, please. If you're here when my mother gets home she'll know something's really wrong."

"If your face looks like a pillowcase full of eggs she'll know anyway."

"I can handle it. But just seeing you upsets her."

"That's not my fault."

"No, it's not. But it's my problem. Listen," I said, and I swallowed. "I'd like to have you here. I would. I . . . but please don't come, okay?"

There was silence on his end of the line. "Tell me you're really all right," he said.

"I'm really all right. Mr. Gao gave me herbs for my bath. He says I don't have any broken bones or concussion or anything. Actually, I've been hurt worse than this in bouts in the days when I used to fight Tae Kwon Do tournaments."

"Actually, you have not."

I listened to the rush of bath water. The empty apartment felt lonely and sad. "You're right. I've never been beat up like this and I hate it. I want to be all right and I want you to come over and I want to solve this stupid case so we don't have to work on it anymore. But my head is killing me and I'm all sore and you can't come over anyway, so unless there's something I need to know right now I'm going to take a hot bath and go to bed. I'll call you later, when maybe I'll be able to think like a detective and we can work on the case. Okay?"

He agreed about as reluctantly as I'd ever heard him agree to anything.

"You'd better call," he said. "Because I'll call you if you don't. And you know your mother hates that."

"I'll call."

The bathroom was full of rolling steam and of scents that made me think of silent stands of pine on high mountains, of mist and moss and tiny creamy white flowers and no gangsters anywhere at all. I lowered my aching self into the water tinted green with Mr. Gao's herbs. The enveloping heat was so comforting I almost started to cry. A dried chrysanthemum blossom floated by. I brushed the surface of the water, watched the leaves and twigs bobble away.

Maybe I should give up this detective nonsense. Think of all the people I'd make happy. I could become an apothecary, studying with Mr. Gao until I knew all the Chinese medicines, all the plants and roots and ground bones and their uses and properties. Maybe knowing that would satisfy my need to know, to get to the bottom of things, to dig and dig until nothing was hidden from me anymore.

Maybe that was a good idea.

Maybe I'd think about it.

After I found the Blair porcelains, and found a way to let Trouble know he couldn't do this to Lydia Chin.


The bath was beginning to cool, and I was aching a lot less, when I realized with a guilty start that there was one phone call I was going to have to make, now.

I dried off, pulled on a long-sleeved T-shirt and some leggings, and dialed the Fifth Precinct. I was hoping Mary wouldn't be there, but she was.

"Hey," she said cautiously. "What's up?" I rarely call Mary at work. If she'd come up with anything about Bic that she thought I'd want to know—or that she could tell me—she would have called me, and she knew I knew that.

"Don't yell at me," I started.

"That means you did something bad."

There wasn't any better way to tell her than to just jump in and tell her. "I got roughed up a little by some Golden Dragons this afternoon."

" 'Roughed up a little'? What does that mean?" I could almost see her propelled out of her seat in the noisy squad room. "Where are you? Are you all right?"

"I'm all right. I'm home. It's okay, Mary. I'm only calling you because they took my gun."

"Your gun? The Golden Dragons? What happened?" she demanded.

I gave her as short a version as I could come up with.

"God, Lydia," she said, blowing out air with an exasperated sound. "You're nuts. They have a dead boy, a dead

Dragon in another gang's territory, and you yell both gangs' names all up and down the block and then you wonder why you get hurt!"

"I don't wonder," I said huffily. "I didn't call you to ask why I got hurt. And I didn't get all that hurt. And I wasn't yelling!"

"How hurt are you?" Her voice was cold.

"I saw Mr. Gao. He sent me home with herbs." I didn't tell her he'd rescued me. I didn't want her to know I'd needed rescuing.

"He says you're okay?"

"Uh-huh."

"All right," she said. For Mary, as for me, Mr. Gao's word was enough on things like this. She seemed to warm up just a little. "Now tell me why you needed to know who's protecting which businesses on that corner."

"I can't."

"Lydia! When the Golden Dragons go to all that trouble to keep you out of their business it must be important business. We have a dead Dragon in Queens and any minute now we're expecting the streets to be littered with Main Street Boys. I want to know why."

"They're not yet?"

"Who's not yet?"

"The streets. Littered with Main Street Boys."

"The retaliation hasn't come. But hey, it's only been a day. These guys can nurse grudges over less for years."

"Over less. But don't they usually take care of important stuff pretty fast?"

"Yeah, but not necessarily this fast. Or maybe there's something else going on here, other factors they're considering. Like what you're doing. So tell me about it."

"Mary, I can't. Too many people's face is involved."

"Including yours?"

"Of course including mine. If I get known as a p.i. who tells all, I'm finished, and not just in Chinatown."

"You could be finished faster if you don't take Trouble seriously."

"I am taking him seriously." Which might mean something different to me from what it meant to Mary. "But I can't believe the dead guy is related to what I'm working on."

"Excuse me? Which one of us has a bloody nose?"

"What I think happened," I said, feeling my nose, "what I think is that the Golden Dragons are planning to deal with the Main Street Boys soon and they don't want anybody pointing out the connection too loudly. That's all."

"Just a coincidence."

"Right."

"Ridiculous."

"It is not! Oh, come on, Mary. I'm sore and I have a headache. I want to report a stolen gun and then I want to take a nap."

"In a minute. I'll pass you to a uniform for paperwork on the gun. You don't want to press charges?"

"No. Why? There won't be any witnesses, and Trouble and his boys will have a dozen respectable citizens to alibi them."

She didn't argue with me about that; she knew it was true. But she said, "I don't like this, Lydia. I don't like having to deal with you like cop and p.i."

"I don't either, Mary. And the minute I feel like it's okay to tell you what my case is I will. Or the minute I feel like it's more important that you know than that I keep my promise to my client."

"I don't think you can make that decision on your own."

"I'm going to have to."

In her silence I could hear cop conversations around her. "All right," she finally said. "All right, Lydia. I just don't want you to get hurt."

"Too late. But I'm okay, Mary. I really am."

"Really?"

"Really."

She sighed, then said, "Look, I'm sorry about your gun. I know it meant something to you. Maybe we can get it back."

That's what I love about Mary. She knows what's important in life.

"Thanks."

"Lydia? What are you going to tell your mom?"

"I fell off a roof?"

"I think you used that last time."

"I think you're right. What haven't I used lately?"

"Runaway horse? Tripped on the sidewalk?"

"Slipped on a banana peel? What do you tell your mom when you get hurt?"

"I never get hurt. I'm a cop. This is the safest job in the world."

She transferred me to a uniform who took the information about my gun and the permit for it. When I hung up, I peeled a tangerine and wandered around the apartment eating it. The juice was sweet but it stung my lip where it was cut. Coincidence, I'd told Mary. My case and the dead boy and Trouble's warning to me had nothing to do with each other.

Mary hadn't believed it.

Neither did I.

But if there was a connection, I sure didn't know what it was. I washed sticky tangerine juice off my hands and climbed into bed. I snuggled under the covers and tried to cut my mind loose from the demand for logic, to see if just free associating would help me figure anything out.

Within minutes, I was asleep.

## Sixteen

The only real piece of luck I had that day was that my mother wasn't home when I got there.

But she did come home. The clinking of keys—or, a single key—in four locks woke me up. I pushed the covers aside and sat up stiffly as my mother poked her nose into my room.

"Ling Wan-ju! Why are you in bed in the middle of the day? Are you sick? Let me see you."

"I'm fine, Ma." That wasn't going to work, but it was a good position to retreat from. I got carefully out of bed.

"Fine? Look at you! Your cheek is swollen. You're moving as though you're made of porcelain and you're afraid you'll break! What happened to you?"

Made of porcelain, I thought. Very funny, Ma. "Nothing. I made a mistake. I'm fine."

"A mistake? What does that mean?"

"It means I'm as foolish as you're always saying I am." I moved gingerly to my dresser, trying to keep my face from showing the clamps of pain that grabbed my ribs and back in syncopated rhythm.

"What are you doing? Get back into bed. I'm going to see Grandfather Gao."

"I already saw him, Ma. He gave me those." I pointed to the two kinds of square packages piled on my desk.

My mother sniffed at them. "For tea or for the bath?"

"Both." I pulled a thick snuggly sweatshirt over the long-sleeve T, replaced the leggings with quilted trousers. I sat on the bed and stuffed my feet into heavy wool socks, stood again feeling about as warm and enveloped as I could outside of my blankets.

"What are you doing?" she demanded again.

"I drank the tea. I had the bath. I'm going out."

"To get in more trouble? Ling Wan-ju . . ."

"Ma, I'm working. I'll try to be home for dinner but don't wait." At the door I put my shoes on; bending down was hard, so I sat on the floor. My mother's lips flattened into a thin line. As I worked my way into my jacket and left she was lighting three sticks of incense at the little altar in the living room. I didn't know who she was talking to, or about what, but I could guess.


At the first pay phone I came to I called Bill's number. I got his service, told them I was at my office, and headed there.

It was late afternoon. Neon glowed red, yellow, and blue against the purple-gray sky. The fish and five-spice smells were strong as the restaurants prepared for the dinner crowd. People hurried home with bags of groceries as I walked slowly the other way, out to my office beyond the outskirts of Chinatown.

I needed to think and, if I could find him, to talk to Bill: two things I couldn't do at home.

The three women—two Chinese, one white—who ran the travel agency were doing end-of-the-business-day things when I got there. We all smiled and greeted each other, and no one asked about my swollen jaw. Maybe it didn't look so bad. Or maybe their mothers had just raised them well.

I unlocked the door with my name on it at the end of the narrow hall that led off the street doorway we shared. Inside, I flipped on the light and put the kettle on the hot plate to boil. The radiator was spitting merrily under the window and everything was warm and cozy, though maybe not as tidy as it could have been. Well, my job was to find things, not put them away.

I brewed tea, a mixture of oolong and chrysanthemum, and settled in my desk chair to drink it. I resettled twice until I found an almost-comfortable position. The tea, a good mixture, woke my brain gently. My eyes drifted from the print of misty brush-painted Guilin mountains on one wall to the poster opposite, of the first rays of sun reddening the northern Rockies. I'd never been to either place, but both pictures were beautiful.

Why had Trouble cared enough today about the questions I was asking to give me a very unpleasant warning about it, when he'd answered pretty much the same questions himself yesterday?

Why didn't the Main Street Boys extort money from Chinatown Pride?

Why hadn't there been any retaliation yet about the murdered Golden Dragon?

Who had been following me, and why, and where was he now?

And who had stolen two crates of the Blair porcelains, and where were *they* now?

The phone rang, startling me into splashing my tea and pulling my shoulder painfully as I reached for it.

"Chin Investigative Services, Lydia Chin speaking." I said this first in English, then in Chinese, because you never know.

"What are you doing out of bed?" said Bill.

"You sound like my mother."

"Never. How do you feel?"

"Lousy. You want specifics?"

"If it'll make you feel better."

I considered briefly. "It won't. The only thing that would make me feel better is for you to tell me right now that you solved this case."

"No, it wouldn't."

"Why not?"

"Because *you* want to solve this case. Especially now. Now you have a chip on your shoulder the size of the Chrysler Building, right?"

I bristled. Who asked him to read my mind? "*You* might, under the circumstances. I'm not just like you, you know."

109

"You're not like me at all. You're gorgeous and young and Chinese. And a woman. And you have a chip on your shoulder the size of the Chrysler Building. Don't you want to know what I did today?"

"Why would I?"

"You're paying me."

"Oh." I ran my hand through my hair. "I'm sorry," I said. "Am I being obnoxious?"

"It's just the chip—"

"Oh, shut up. Tell me what you did today."

"I went back to the Upper East Side. I talked to some art dealers. And I had lunch."

"Which was most interesting?"

"Lunch."

"Why?"

"Because I ate in a pizza place on Lexington and Eighty-second. You would have liked it, by the way. Huge calzone with olives in them."

That did sound good, I admitted. I have a weakness for Italian food. "And?"

"I was hungry. And cold. I was there awhile, sitting by the window. Nice view up Eighty-second."

"Eighty-second?" Wake up, Lydia! "Lexington and Eighty-second is where the Blairs live. Lived. She lives. You were doing a surveillance?"

"Me? I was having lunch. I had to walk two blocks over and nine blocks down from where I was to find the right greasy pizza place, that's all."

"Bill, come on! You were up to something. What was it?"

"Just curiosity. The Blairs were beginning to intrigue me. I just wanted a look at the house, and I figured maybe I'd get lucky and get a look at Mrs. Blair. I wanted to know what gorgeous Chinese women look like when they're sixty."

"Did you see her?"

"No."

I was disappointed. "That's not a very interesting lunch."

"Yes, it was. The reason I didn't see her was that it was

the maid who came to the door when Roger Caldwell rang the bell."

"Caldwell? Wait, what? Caldwell went to see Mrs. Blair?"

"Uh-huh." I could hear the pleased grin in his voice.

I hesitated, mystified. "What do you suppose that means?"

"I don't know what it means. I'm just the employee, reporting in. The boss is supposed to figure out what things mean."

"Where are you?"

"Home."

"Can you come over?"

"Do you have coffee?"

"No."

"I'll bring my own."

Sometimes it's best not to think too much. If you ignore something maybe you can sneak up on it later when it isn't trying to hide from you. I balanced my checkbook and shuffled some papers while I waited for Bill. The radiator hissed and the Rockies glowed. The yellow mug made my tea cheerful, and the tea made me relaxed. The mug had a chip, I noticed. So did the blue one, and the one from the Hong Kong and Shanghai Bank. Maybe I should get some decent teacups. Porcelain, something nice. I didn't want to lose face in front of people when they saw my stuff.

When the street buzzer buzzed I jumped. I tore myself from the Guilin mists I'd been lost in and answered it.

"Let me in," Bill said. "I brought you a present."

"Goody." I buzzed, waited for him at the end of the hall.

When he reached me he stopped, examined my face critically. Then he touched his fingertips to my chin and softly kissed my forehead. His arms wrapped around me, the cold of the evening he'd walked through emanating from his jacket and his skin. He held me so gently that it didn't hurt even where it should have. I hugged him, letting myself feel, just for a moment, sad and small and safe.

111

Then I moved away.

He let me go without protest, looked me over as we stood apart in the corridor. "You don't look so bad," he told me.

"I love compliments. Where's my present?"

He lifted a white cardboard box tied with string.

"Cookies?" I brightened, led the way into my office.

"White-trash medicine," he said, settling on the guest chair. "Eat sugar, you'll feel better."

In the box were miniature Italian pastries: tiny cannoli in three flavors, silver-dollar-sized cheesecakes, thumbprint cookies with red and green cherries on them. My mouth started to water; lunch had been years ago.

"Okay," Bill said, opening the large container of black coffee he'd come with. Its rising steam joined the steam from the radiator and from my fresh cup of tea. "Do you have any idea what's going on?"

"None whatsoever." I took a cannoli with microscopic chocolate chips in its rum-flavored cream, passed Bill the box. "I want to hear about Caldwell and Mrs. Blair."

"You've pretty much heard it all. I was uptown gallery hopping. I saw some interesting stuff, by the way. Some rusted steel sculpture you might like."

"Sounds lovely."

"Lovely's the wrong word, but it's graceful and tough. It made me think of you."

I was flattered and surprisingly touched. I hid it with a bite of cannoli.

"Anyway," Bill continued, when it was obvious all I was going to do was eat, "afterwards I figured I was so close, I'd take a look at Mrs. Blair's place."

"Thinking what?"

"Thinking it's possible someone had had his eye on those pieces for a long time, but the Blairs' security was so good that there was no opportunity to grab them until they were moved."

"I knew you were thinking something. I knew you didn't just want a look at Mrs. Blair."

"Why would I want to look at her when I can look at you?"

I crossed my eyes for him and bit into a cheesecake with a quartered slice of kiwi on it.

"Anyway, I was halfway through my calzone when Caldwell trotted up the street, climbed the steps of the Blair house, and rang the bell."

"Did he seem to be known there?"

"I couldn't tell, I couldn't see the maid's face well enough. But he wasn't searching the buildings for their numbers."

"How long did he stay?"

"Through the rest of the calzone, two cups of coffee, and a browse through the bookstore down the street."

"How did he look when he left?"

"In a hurry. He went back to the museum," he added before I could ask.

"You followed him?"

"Why not?"

I pulled the chewy green cherry off a cookie. "Of course, there may not be anything sinister about this at all. Nobody ever said they didn't know each other."

"Nobody ever said they did."

"But why would anybody? She had no reason to mention him to me that first day, and we didn't tell him yesterday whose porcelains had been stolen, so he had no reason to mention her."

"Unless he recognized the pieces."

"Supposedly no one's seen the collection in years. And those were the new acquisitions. Which makes your theory that someone's had an eye on them for a long time sort of unlikely," I added.

"But maybe someone was interested in whatever he could get from that collection, and those two boxes just happened to be what he got."

"Only supposedly no one's seen it."

"Supposedly."

"Mrs. Blair might be lying about that?"

"People do."

"Why?"

"Because," he said, "people are evil and malicious and wicked—"

"I mean why would Mrs. Blair in particular lie about this?" I said with something approaching patience.

"To protect the person who'd seen the collection."

"Because she thinks he's the thief."

"Or knows he is."

"Wait," I said. "If this is someone she knows and likes well enough to protect, why not give the stuff to him in the first place and not to CP? Or sell it to him, or whatever?"

"I don't know." Bill munched a chocolate cannoli.

"And why agree to hire me?"

"Well, it was you or the police. She couldn't exactly have said to Nora, 'Oh, let's just forget about it.' This gives her a couple of days float, for the trail to get cold."

I felt the muscles in my shoulders tighten, and it hurt. "That only works," I said, "if I'm no good."

"Or," Bill said reasonably, "if, as you told them yourself, you have fewer resources than the police, and art isn't your specialty."

"You mean you think I—we, let me point out, white man—were hired because they figured we couldn't solve this case?" The radiator hissed. I felt like hissing with it.

"I don't think that necessarily. But haven't you ever been hired by a client just going through the motions, who'd just as soon you didn't do what he hired you to do?"

"No. I always assume they want what they're paying for."

He didn't answer me. We were quiet for a few minutes, he drinking his coffee, I my tea. Then I picked another cannoli out of the box and asked, "You think this could be some sort of complicated insurance fraud?"

"I thought of that. But if that were it, they'd report it to the police right away."

"They." I looked at him. "That could mean Nora and CP were involved, couldn't it?"

"Well, this didn't happen until they had the porcelains on their premises."

"But these are the pieces that weren't recorded, so they weren't even insured." I thought about that and said reluctantly what I was thinking: "Of course, all *that* means is that it's not likely to be insurance fraud, or, if it is, someone screwed up. It doesn't necessarily mean that whatever it is, CP's not involved."

"Or someone at CP."

"Or someone."

Through the pebbled wire-glass windows in my office faceted light shone from the building behind, like lights in a pool when you open your eyes underwater.

"Tim really doesn't want me on this case," I said to Bill.

"Tim? Tim's afraid of losing face. He doesn't want you to embarrass him. That's what you said."

"Think how embarrassing it would be if I found out he'd stolen the porcelains."

Bill lowered his coffee. "You're not kidding, are you?"

"When he came to dinner last night he tried to get me to quit again."

"You told me."

"He said my mom would be humiliated if she heard I'd met with Trouble. He said all of Chinatown was talking about it."

"She would, wouldn't she?"

I poked my fingernail at the chip in my mug. "Nora didn't know about it. She was mad when I told her. And this afternoon, Mr. Gao didn't know either."

Bill lit a cigarette, dropped the match in his empty coffee container. "Oh. All of Chinatown isn't talking about it."

"Mr. Gao didn't know, and he set it up! How did Tim know?"

He breathed out a stream of smoke, leaned back in his

chair. "Jesus." Then he said, "Lydia, there are other explanations."

"I'm sure there are loads of them. But how *did* he know? And how come Roger Caldwell went to see Mrs. Blair? And how come Trouble beat me up?"

I looked at him, and he looked at me, and neither of us said anything. Then he put out his cigarette and stood.

"And how come you're not home in bed?" he asked. "Come on. There's no point in trying to do anything else tonight. I don't think Tim had anything to do with this, but if he did we'll find out and then we'll worry about it. You need to get some rest now or you won't be any good tomorrow."

"I probably won't be any good tomorrow anyway," I said glumly.

"Come on, with that Ho Chi Minh medicine? It'll fix you right up."

"Ho Chi Minh medicine?"

"Oh, never mind. Generation gap. Let's go."

Bill rinsed out my mug while I, who was moving more slowly, pulled on my jacket and scarf and gloves and hat. He got wrapped up too, minus the hat, and we left, switching off the light and shutting the door behind us. I took out my key to lock up; then I pushed the door back open, grabbed the half-empty pastry box and, with it under my arm, locked my office and walked with Bill into the night.

SEVENTEEN

I had another cup of Mr. Gao's foul-tasting tea that night, and another bath, and more tea in the morning. After a late morning bath I did some gentle stretching exercises and except for my jaw, ribs, back, shoulder, stomach, and head, I felt almost okay. Wrapped in a thick flannel bathrobe, I ate oil sticks and rice porridge my mother had made for me while she hovered and fussed.

I hadn't told her what had happened, and by now it was clear that I wasn't going to, but that didn't stop her.

"I called your brother," she said, standing over the table while I ate. "He said I should lock the door and not let you out anymore until your brothers find a husband for you."

"I'll bet he'd like that," I muttered darkly. I didn't give her the satisfaction of asking which brother. Andrew wouldn't have said that. If Elliot had said it he'd have been half-kidding. The other two didn't bear thinking about. "Did he have anybody in mind?"

She began seriously, "He said it would be difficult, such a headstrong girl, but that—"

"Oh, Ma!" I stood, tightening my jaw so she wouldn't see the pain. I took my dishes to the sink. She followed me and grabbed them away to wash them; she doesn't think I get dishes very clean.

Back in my room I dressed, slowly and carefully. Tournament Tae Kwon Do bouts in my teens and through college had taught me a lot about isolating pain, but this was a lot of pain to isolate. I reached for my sweater the way I always reach and my shoulder shrieked. Anger flamed in me, knotted my stomach and flushed my skin: anger at Trouble, at Mr. Gao, at Tim and whatever other brother wanted me married and no longer embarrassing him, at Lucky Seafood's kitchen help and all the people with windows on the courtyard who didn't call the police. I was angry at Nora for not paying the Main Street Boys and at my mother for not getting off my case, at Mrs. Blair for owning the porcelains in the first place and at whatever rat had stolen them.

Calm down, Lydia, I demanded. I sat on my bed, tried to slow my pulse and focus my breathing. I thought about Bill, and the baker from up the street, and Mary who knew how important my gun was to me, and the incandescent Steve at the

Kurtz Museum. Not everybody connected with this case, or my life, was bottom-feeding slime whose only goal was to give me a headache. Not everybody.

The phone rang as I was finishing dressing, not my office line but the phone in the kitchen. My mother spoke in rapid Chinese, too softly—deliberately, I thought—for me to catch. Then she came across the living room to call through my closed door, "It's Grandfather Gao. Come, hurry, don't keep him waiting."

In the kitchen I picked up the phone, which my mother had left dangling within an inch of the floor.

"How are you feeling?" Mr. Gao's soft, even voice asked me.

"Better than I expected, thank you, Grandfather." Even in the nasal cadences of Chinese I could hear the wariness in my own voice, and I knew he could, too. Mr. Gao has been treating illnesses in the Chin family for thirty years. Calling to check up on you is not one of the things he does.

"You must reassure your mother when you hang up the telephone." Mr. Gao's voice smiled. "She thinks I've called to inquire after your progress, and she is very worried about what that might mean."

My mother, who knew Mr. Gao's habits as well as I did, was fluttering anxiously nearby. She probably figured this meant I was going to die.

"Yes, I'll do that, Grandfather," I said. And what does it mean, I wondered; but I didn't ask. I could be as discreet as he was.

"I am concerned with your progress, of course, and delighted to hear you're improving," Mr. Gao went on, "but that is not why I'm calling."

"No, Grandfather." And the little voice in my head screamed, Well, then, why, for Pete's sake? but I waited patiently so my mother wouldn't get more upset.

"The choice not to ask for retribution for what has happened to you is a wise one, Ling Wan-ju."

He seemed to be waiting for something from me, so, with my mother practically breathing down my neck, I said, "Yes, Grandfather." Let her try to read something from that.

"However," he went on, "I feel that, because of my role in this situation, as well as my long association with your family, I am nevertheless in your debt. I have gotten a call this morning that I think might interest you."

"Yes?" I was practically out of non-committal responses, and my mother was practically climbing the walls.

"Are you well enough to go out?"

"Definitely."

"Then come to my shop, and we will go out."

"I'll be there as soon as I can."

"Ling Wan-ju?"

"Yes, Grandfather?"

"Tell your mother you sound so much better to me I've decided to give you a different prescription." I could hear the smile again.

"She won't believe me."

"No, but after you leave she'll call me to ask whether it's true."

As I put on my shoes and jacket I told my mother what Mr. Gao had said to tell her. She didn't believe me, but at least she had the grace to wait until I'd shut the door behind me before she grabbed up the phone to call him.

Outdoors, the day was still and cold, the cloud-covered sky luminescently pearly and the air bright with reflected light. I made my slow way to Mr. Gao's shop, different muscles aching with different steps. I wore my big round sunglasses even though there was no sun. On the street corner people who sold other things at other times of year were selling gladiolas now. The long stalks' blooms huddled defensively against the cold, ready, once they were warmer, to burst into flares of scarlet and salmon and peach to celebrate the New Year.

Mr. Gao was alone in the shop when I got there. The two-note chime tinkled behind me; the shop was as dim and soothing as ever. The brass scales were set up and on them Mr. Gao was weighing golden flowers that I recognized as useful in cases of cough. Valuable now, in flu season.

He smiled, finished his work, and then stepped around the counter to look at me. I'd taken off the sunglasses; they made the dimness of the shop into impenetrable night.

"Well." He smiled. "A remarkable recovery."

"I feel terrible." He wasn't getting off the hook that easily.

"I'm quite sure that's true. But your spirit is like your father's. He was always able to turn fear into anger and anger into work. A very productive ability."

At least it wasn't a nature metaphor.

"Grandfather, why did you call me? Where are we going?"

"Come." He put on his coat, the good wool coat I had rested against yesterday as I was carried up and down stairs. He pulled down the blind on the shop's glass door and we went out.

We crossed Canal on Mulberry, and then we crossed Hester. The building we stopped at, half a block up, used to be in the heart of Little Italy. Now the Italians, all third and fourth generation, are moving to the suburbs, and Chinese—from Hong Kong, from Taiwan, from the People's Republic and Singapore and Viet Nam—are buying this property, living in these tenements, cooking food from home, and depending on their children to learn English and guide the family through its new life, as immigrants have always done.

Mr. Gao led the way into the building, whose outer door lock was broken, and up to the second floor. There, in a dank hallway with grime at the places where the vinyl tile met the baseboard, he knocked on a door, like my mother's, with four locks.

A quavering voice called in Chinese, "Who is there?"

Mr. Gao answered calmly, "It's all right. It's Grandfather Gao, with a friend. Please let us come in."

I heard bolts thrown and the clinking of a chain; then the door moved, widened until someone's eye appeared, blinked, stared. It was a runny brown eye, located about the height of my shoulder. Then the door finished opening, and we stepped inside.

The woman who'd let us in was shorter than I am, although she probably hadn't always been. Stooped and arthritic, with unkempt thinning gray hair framing a dry, lined face: There's your future, Lydia, I thought. If you live that long.

Probably an apartment like this was my future too, mismatched furniture, a threadbare carpet, a non-working fireplace whose mantel was crowded with photographs of family members who didn't live here. One, a picture of a young man, had, I noticed, a black mourning band across it.

The woman took Mr. Gao's hand in both of hers and thanked him for coming. She didn't look at me at all.

"I'm grateful for this opportunity to be of use to you in this sad time, Mrs. Hsing," Mr. Gao said. "Please, sit down."

She led him to a seat and made sure he sat; then, because I was with him, she offered one to me, without eye contact and without much interest in whether I took it or not. Then she seated herself on the edge of a straight-backed chair, her hands resting on the shapeless housedress that covered her knees.

"Please," Mr. Gao said, as silence filled the shabby room. "My friend knows all about your suffering, Mrs. Hsing. She is only here to listen and to help."

Actually, I knew nothing at all about anything, since Mr. Gao hadn't spoken a word to me on our way over, but I got it: You're here to keep your mouth shut and learn something, Lydia. Let's not hear from you.

Well, for Pete's sake, I thought. It wasn't my bright idea to come here in the first place. Now I'm supposed to sit here like a potted plant? An actual potted plant, a rubber tree, drooped in the corner. I tried to think of it as my spiritual brother.

Mrs. Hsing, after a glance at me, rose slowly and made her way into the bedroom. She returned holding in both hands a glossy red box. She looked at it with a slight hesitation, then handed it to Mr. Gao, and sat again.

"If you tell me I must return it to him, Grandfather, I will," she said, and something about the way she said it was touchingly brave. Feeling like an intruder in something I didn't understand, I looked away, let my eyes wander the room again. They were drawn to the mantel, found the black-banded picture of the young man.

Suddenly, things fell into place in my potted plant brain.

The Golden Dragon who'd been killed on Main Street Boys' turf had been named Hsing.

I threw a quick glance at Mr. Gao, to let him know I'd figured it out, but his attention was fixed on the box he was opening. I watched as he removed the top and moved red tissue paper aside. Then he lifted out the contents, a paper-thin white porcelain cup. An orange-red tiger coiled around it and another one wrapped itself around the knob on the cup's lid.

Mr. Gao held it to the window's cloudy light. "It's quite beautiful."

"It was the last time I saw him," Mrs. Hsing said, in a steady voice. " 'A gift for my mother,' my son said. He was a good son." Her voice caught. She swallowed and continued. "I would like to keep it."

"And please tell me," Mr. Gao said, "who is demanding its return."

"Lee Kuan Yue," she said simply. I searched my memory, but the name meant nothing to me.

"And on what grounds?"

"Lee says my son worked for him. Lee has an import-export business, and my son made deliveries. This cup was part of a shipment, Lee claims, and was missing when the shipment arrived."

Mr. Gao nodded, regarding the cup thoughtfully. "Did

you know, Mrs. Hsing, that your son was employed by Lee Kuan Yue?"

Mrs. Hsing shook her head emphatically. "My son was a cook at Lucky Seafood."

Oh, swell, I thought.

"Part-time," she went on. "He was a student at City College, in electrical engineering." She said this proudly, and her eyes moved to the black-banded picture. Then they misted, and she looked down into her lap.

"Still, many people in Chinatown work at two jobs," Mr. Gao mused. "Even students. How does Lee know you have the cup?"

"He doesn't know. He called to say items were missing from the last—" her voice quavered, but she recovered, "the last shipment my son handled. He said that to avoid bringing great disgrace upon my family and my son's memory, he would urge me to see that the missing pieces found their way back to him."

"Pieces? What other items were missing?"

"Another cup like this. There were two, Lee said."

"Did your son give you both?"

"No, Grandfather. My son gave me this. It was the first, he said, of many beautiful gifts for his mother."


Mr. Gao and I walked back down Mulberry toward Chinatown in silence. He had carefully restored the white porcelain cup to its box and promised to weigh the matter and attempt to guide Mrs. Hsing to a proper course of action.

When we stopped for the light at Canal, I spoke. "Stolen porcelains," I said. "And Golden Dragons. That's why you called me."

"I thought Mrs. Hsing's situation might interest you. I also hoped it would prove useful." Mr. Gao surveyed the bustling Chinatown scene with the air of a patriarch whose children's flaws were only too well known to him but who found them, on the whole, satisfactory.

"Her son was Hsing Chung Wah, wasn't he?"

"Yes."

The light changed and we started forward. "Do you know Lee Kuan Yue?" I asked.

"An importer with a business on Mulberry Street."

"Do you," I tried to be at least a little subtle, "know him to be involved with the Golden Dragons?"

"All the merchants on Mulberry Street have an acquaintance with the Golden Dragons," he said. Which meant: You've gotten everything you're going to get for free, Lydia.

But it also meant Mr. Lee wasn't a well-known major bad guy, because Mr. Gao would have warned me about that.

What else it meant, I had no idea.

Taking a deep breath, I tried something else. "Grandfather, do you remember that I asked you about the *dai lo* of the Main Street Boys? A boy named Bic?"

Mr. Gao glanced at me, then returned his eyes to the street. "Ling Wan-ju, I would have thought you had had your fill of that sort of young man."

"It would make me happy never to speak to another of that sort of young man again," I admitted. "But there is a connection here, Grandfather. Hsing Chung Wah was killed in Main Street Boys' territory. It's more important than ever to me to know why."

Staring straight ahead, he said nothing at first. Then he asked, "And if you were to find out why from someone else?"

"I would still like to speak to the Main Street Boys' *dai lo*, Grandfather."

With a look I couldn't read, but one that gave me a very uncomfortable feeling, Mr. Gao said, "Very well. You will hear from me." He unlocked the door to his shop and, without inviting me in, stepped inside and closed it behind him.

# Eighteen

I turned down Canal to my office, where I'd left my file of Dr. Browning's descriptions and photographs of the stolen items. That beautiful cup had seemed familiar, though why, if it had been part of the Blair collection, an importer named Lee Kuan Yue would be demanding its return—and the return of its mate, which she didn't have—from the mother of a Golden Dragon found dead in Main Street Boys' territory, was beyond the mental powers of a potted plant.

However, my instincts were in fine Chinese harmony with Mr. Gao's: Any reference to stolen porcelain or, in this case, porcelain of contested ownership, was worth, at least, close attention.

In my office I put the kettle on and flipped through the file. The cup didn't appear either on the list or in the photographs. I reached for the phone to call Bill; maybe it was obvious what all this meant, to someone with a brain in the animal kingdom. My hand was on the receiver before I noticed the message machine blinking. No kidding, I thought, someone called me? Probably the thief giving himself up.

The first message was from Bill. "Something interesting," he said. "Call me."

Well, I was just about to, I grumbled to myself. But there was another message also, so I played it first.

"Hi," a voice said eagerly, and, I thought, a little furtively. "This is Steve Bailey. You know, from the Kurtz Museum? That's so cool, that your machine answers in Chinese! Anyway, could you call me? Something strange happened. Well, maybe. I mean, it's definitely strange. But maybe it has nothing to do with why you were here, because, I mean, I don't know why you were here. But it's about the porcelains. I mean, I don't want to get anyone in trouble. But I thought maybe you'd want to know. But you're not there. Shoot. And I'm going out. Oh, wait, I know—I'll call your partner. But anyway, call me back, okay?"

My kettle whistled as he clicked off. I set some jasmine tea to brewing and called the Kurtz, but Steve Bailey was, as he had represented, out. So I called Bill.

"You have a lot of interesting things for me, right?" I asked when he answered.

"More than you know."

"Do me a favor, stick to the ones that have to do with the case. Did Steve from the Kurtz call you?"

"You're no fun," he complained. "Yes. He said he'd left you a message."

"I just got it, but all it says is he found something strange and he's going out. I called the museum, and he's out."

"Predictability. Among my people, it's a virtue."

"Among your people mayonnaise sandwiches are food," I reminded him. "What did he find?"

"I'm going to put that crack down to the strains of your weakened physical state. How do you feel, by the way?"

"I'm fine. Come on, Bill, you're driving me crazy."

"Just doing my job, ma'am. Apparently," he said, just before I could sputter something, "he was snooping in his co-executive-assistant's files. Trish Atherton, remember her?"

"Beautiful blond hair."

"Really? I didn't notice."

I slurped my tea noisily.

"Anyway," he said, "she's in charge of the porcelains at the Kurtz. Processing them in and out, recording, what they call in the museum biz 'acquisitioning.' "

"Now that I *know* isn't English. So? What did he find?"

"Irregularities."

My heart shifted into a higher gear. "What sort?"

"He said it was complicated and he didn't have time to

126

talk. I also had the feeling he didn't want to be overheard. Anyway, he wants us to meet him at the Kurtz tonight, six o'clock. The museum will be closed, we will be alone, and he will reveal all."

"Six o'clock! I can't wait that long. God, Bill, what do you think it means?"

"It could just mean sloppy recordkeeping at the Kurtz. Just because it's porcelains doesn't mean it has anything to do with us."

"That's true." I poured more jasmine tea and warmed my fingers around it. "Okay, let's think about something else."

"Can I suggest a topic?"

"Not a chance. Now: You called before Steve did, and you said you had something interesting, which obviously wasn't him because he hadn't called you yet."

"Your deductive powers amaze me."

"I practice. What was the other thing?"

"I got a call from Franco Ciardi."

"Your shady art dealer friend?"

"You'd break his heart if he heard you call him that. Yes, him."

"What did he want?"

"To see me."

"Why?"

"He said he'd rather not say over the phone."

"What is this, everyone in New York thinks their phones are tapped? Did you go see him?"

"He said late this afternoon. Want to come?"

"Are you kidding? I wouldn't miss it."

"Great. He's about ten blocks from the Kurtz, so we can make an evening of it on the Upper East Side."

"Good," I said. "Now, do you want to hear how I spent my morning?"

"You weren't home in bed?"

"Hey, I've been working on this case too, you know. I mean, I'm not just a potted plant."

I told Bill about my visit with Mr. Gao to the home of Mrs. Hsing.

"Stolen porcelains and Golden Dragons," he said when I was through. "I get the idea we have a theme going here."

"Does that cup sound familiar to you?" I asked. "I had the feeling I'd seen it, or a picture of it, but it's not in the file."

"I don't remember it, but I'll think. But I do think you're right: This has got to be related. Even if the cup isn't a Blair collection piece, the fact that the dead Golden Dragon was messing with it can't mean nothing."

The radiator whistled weakly under my window as I thought about a nineteen-year-old kid whose whole life had been reduced to that: He was "the dead Golden Dragon."

"Bill? She loved him. His mother. It was so sad to see her. She just wanted to keep the last gift he'd given her. She was so torn between that and doing what she had to to keep his memory and her family's name from being disgraced."

"That's understandable," he said quietly.

"I'm not even sure she knew he was a Golden Dragon. She told us he was a college student." A thought struck me like a blast of icy air in a stuffy room. "Bill?"

"What is it?"

"Would studying electrical engineering teach you how to disarm an electronic security system?"

"Is that what he was studying?"

"Yes. It would, wouldn't it?"

"It could. You're thinking he could be the thief?"

"Well, I was sort of thinking that anyway, assuming that's one of our cups. Weren't you?"

"Uh-huh. But then who's Lee Kuan Yue? The guy Hsing fenced the stuff to?"

"And then Hsing double-crossed him? Possible. Maybe we should look into Mr. Lee."

"Here's something else: Would this mean this was a Golden Dragon job and Trouble lied to you?"

I thought about that. "I don't see why he would. What was I going to do about it? No, if the Golden Dragons had

128

done it Trouble would have been bragging. Maybe Hsing was operating on his own."

"Do they do that, the gang kids?"

"They're not supposed to. It's very bad; the *dai lo* loses face. But Mary told me Hsing was a loner, not well liked even in the gang."

"If he had been operating on his own, would that explain why the Golden Dragons haven't retaliated for his murder?"

"You mean, Trouble just sort of wrote him off?" I considered, sipping the cooled remains of my tea. "No, I don't think so. It's like family. You may not like someone, but you're obligated to take care of them. If you didn't manage that, you're supposed to avenge them. But it would explain why the Main Street Boys killed him."

"Because he was poaching."

"In their rented territory."

"Okay," Bill said. "Let's work on the theory this Hsing kid stole the porcelains. Where are they? Is there a way we can get a look around his apartment?"

"Actually, his mother did that. She said that she searched everywhere for the other cup after Lee said there was one. In case her son had been saving it for a gift for another occasion, or something. She didn't find anything."

"Do you think we can believe her?"

"Why would she lie?"

"To protect her son's reputation?"

"She was the one who called Mr. Gao. If she'd actually found anything that says her son was a thief she'd never have called him. She's torn because she doesn't believe it but she's afraid it might be true."

"All right. Assuming he stole them and did something with them we don't know about yet, here's another question: why?"

"Why? Because they trade in the five-figure range, according to Dr. Caldwell."

"Would he know that? An electrical engineering student, a gangster? If he could disable an alarm like that, why not knock over a jewelry store on Canal Street? He could fill his jacket pockets and be doing a lot better than he could with two heavy crates of porcelains."

"Maybe he was a porcelain kleptomaniac and he stole the stuff from everybody who had some, CP and Lee and who knows who else," I offered brightly.

"How did he know CP had some?"

"Oh." I deflated a little. "Someone told him?"

"Uh-huh. Who?"

"Oh, I don't know. That's too hard." I rubbed my forehead, suddenly tired. "Bill?"

"What is it?"

"I'm going to have to tell Mary, aren't I?"

"Tell her what?"

"They don't know why Hsing was killed. This could be why."

"It could be."

"I promised her if I actually made a connection, I'd tell her. God, Nora's going to hate that. And Tim. He'll say he knew from the beginning I wouldn't be able to keep it quiet."

Bill didn't say anything.

"Do you think it would be terrible," I asked, "if I didn't tell her until tomorrow?"

"Giving us a chance to wrap up the case?"

"Well, we could, if we get a lucky break and find out where he hid them."

"If he's actually the guy," Bill said.

"You mean, if that actually is one of our cups."

"Right."

"You know what I think?" I asked.

"What?"

"I think we need to go see Mrs. Blair."

130

**M**rs. Blair, of course, was the most likely person to be able to tell us if the cup Mrs. Hsing so desperately did not want to give up was from the Blair collection. I could ask Dr. Browning, but he might not remember, or might not have gotten to it. He'd claimed, when Bill and I had talked to him, to have looked at everything in all the boxes, but this cup hadn't been in the photographs, and, judging from the state of his apartment, methodical precision wasn't his style.

It was, however, Mrs. Blair's.

I very much wanted to see her. Before that, though, I wanted to do some other things.

One was eat. I was starving. Healing always gives me a big appetite; I'd discovered that when I was eight and I broke my wrist in the schoolyard running away from Tim, who was following me around everywhere just to annoy me. "You should have paid no attention to him," my mother had scolded me, as she bustled around the kitchen and I examined my brand-new cast at the kitchen table. My brothers, including Tim, were still at school; they'd had to stay and finish the day. I was home in the early afternoon being plied with tea and sizzling rice crust.

It was after that incident that my father decided all his children needed the discipline that the study of martial arts provides. The Kung Fu academy in Chinatown where he sent my brothers didn't take girls, so, outside the community, he found a Tae Kwon Do school for me. By the time he died five years later I was the only one of his children still practicing.

Right now, I was stiff and sore and too hungry to focus my thoughts. In my desk's top drawer I keep various boxes with various things in them. From the business card box, which was divided up into sections, I took a couple of the cards with the Taiwan address. The kind of gag I was planning to use I'd used before.

I locked my office, but before I did I climbed up to the closet shelf for the .22 Smith & Wesson I keep there and rarely use. I checked it, loaded it, and stuck it in my pocket. A .22 is almost not a real gun and I liked my .38 a lot better, but the Smith & Wesson had two advantages. One, it was small, light, and could be carried around in a roomy pocket so a person with bruises all over her didn't have to wear a holster.

And two, I, not the Golden Dragons, had it.

I left, headed to the Peacock Rice Shop. There I ate Seafood Chow Fun Soup and pondered Bill's question: If Hsing Chung Wah was our thief, where were the Blair porcelains now? If he was, of course, and we could find the answer to that one, then maybe the case would be over and the rest of this wouldn't matter. The Golden Dragons' delay in avenging Hsing's murder; the Main Street Boys' lack of interest in squeezing CP; the mysterious Lee Kuan Yue; Roger Caldwell's visit to Mrs. Blair; and whatever Steve Bailey and Franco Ciardi had to offer, would all be irrelevant, useless, not of interest.

And the guy who'd been following me.

And my brother Tim's knowing I'd been to see Trouble.

All coincidental, innocent of any involvement in the Case of the Purloined Porcelains.

It could turn out that way.

Except that every ounce of p.i. instinct I had was yelling that it wouldn't.


The Peacock Rice Shop isn't on Mulberry Street, but nothing in Chinatown is far from anything else, so after I'd eaten my soup and drunk some restorative tea I strolled over to Mulberry to see what the importers were importing this year.

I knew where I was going, because from my office, before

I'd gone to eat, I'd looked up import-export businesses in the Yellow Pages, called the three on Mulberry Street, and asked for Lee Kuan Yue. At the third they told me he was on the other line and would I like to hold? No, I said, I'll speak to him later.

Now it was later. I paused before entering Spring Moon Imports, admiring the silk shirts and large porcelain vases in the front window. The day wasn't quite as cold as the past few had been, the sun peering through small breaks in the clouds every now and then as though it were trying to decide whether this day was something it wanted to get involved in. It was already past two, though, and, being winter, it wasn't long until evening; if I were the sun I'd figure it wasn't worth it.

Inside the shop a few customers were browsing up and down the stainless steel shelves, looking through neat piles of silk and cotton clothing and tablecloths, displays of porcelain teacups and painted bells. Cases down the center of the airy, mirrored store held jade and enamel jewelry and hair ornaments.

I browsed with the other customers for a short time, then approached a saleswoman at the jewelry counter and asked to see Mr. Lee. The saleswoman looked younger than I was, with long straight hair pinned back by a silver and topaz clip. She cheerfully called over the manager and conveyed my request.

"Of course." The manager, a smiling, short man, folded his hands in front of his gray suit. "I'll see if he's free. You are . . . ?"

"Chin Ling Wan-ju," I said, speaking, as he had, in English, using my Chinese name and my Chinese accent. I handed him one of the business cards I'd taken from the box in my desk. "I'd like to see him about the possibility of a business venture."

The manager went to check on Mr. Lee. I spent the few minutes he was gone examining jade bracelets with the help of the cheerful saleswoman. I had just chosen a particularly pretty piece of cloudy jade with a small gold lotus flower inset as a birthday present for Elliot's daughter when the manager came back and said Mr. Lee would be very pleased to meet me and was on his way down. As the bracelet was being gift wrapped, a tall man in his mid-fifties approached us through the doors from the back of the shop.

"Miss Chin." He greeted me in the traditional way, one hand folded over the other and a small bow. I extended my hand and we shook. "Please let me offer you some tea."

"I won't trouble you," I said, but he insisted it was no trouble, and soon we found ourselves in his office in the back, sipping a lovely pale oolong out of small white cups. Mr. Lee's office, like the store, was airy and modern. Papers and pens were neatly arranged on his glass-topped desk; a computer hummed on one corner of it.

After a few minutes of general chat, so that neither of us would seem rude and only interested in business, we got down to business.

"My family has a small firm in Taipei," I told Mr. Lee, keeping the Chinese accent going, "dealing in antiquities and *objets d'art* from Asia. We haven't until now done business outside of Taiwan, but my eldest brother has decided this is a propitious time to explore the possibility of expanding. He's sent me here on what you might call an exploratory expedition. I'm searching for business partners—firms who might be interested in bringing our goods to the American market."

Lee Kuan Yue smiled in an interested way. "And what, may I ask, led you to us?"

"Spring Moon Imports is an established, respected firm, the sort of concern we would be honored to be associated with." I smiled also. I had no idea if that was true, but it's the kind of thing people's vanity always lets them believe you believe if you tell them you do.

"Well," Lee Kuan Yue said, "we're always interested in new sources of merchandise for our customers. Can you tell me more about the kinds of items your family deals in, Miss Chin?"

"As I said, our specialty is Asian art and antiquities. We've recently acquired some small Indian bronzes, and we have some lovely Thai shadow puppets, for example. But your inventory here is all Chinese, isn't it?" I looked around innocently, though there was nothing to see in the office except a few framed pictures and calligraphy scrolls.

"Yes, we deal exclusively in Chinese goods."

"And may I compliment you on your jade, by the way. We don't deal much in jewelry, but we have somewhat of a reputation for high-quality Chinese porcelains of varying antiquity, from imperial ware from the Tang period to some exceptional export porcelains made for the British and American markets."

I smiled as I said this and held out my cup for more tea.

Pouring my tea, Mr. Lee said, "I'm afraid antiques aren't something we handle, Miss Chin, although we are very interested in modern porcelains. Does your family have any association with any of the new kilns in Guangdong province?"

His tone and his look were friendly, interested. I sampled my new cup of tea, thinking fast. "No, we don't deal in modern goods at all. Each of my brothers is a specialist in a different area of antiques, and we've concentrated there." I sampled some more, thought some more. "We're not a large firm and we're not necessarily interested in large orders. Perhaps you have a particular customer or two for whom you might want to examine our porcelains, as a special service, even though they're not the sort of goods you generally deal in?"

Mr. Lee gave a short, good-natured laugh. "No, I'm sorry, antiques are something I know nothing about, and my customers know that. If any of them are looking for older pieces, they won't come to me."

"Even if," I said cautiously, "these are goods they might not find anywhere else?"

He said apologetically, "I'm not sure what you mean."

"We're an old firm," I told him, "and we have many long-established relationships with dealers and with certain . . . individuals. Occasionally we are offered items which for one or another reason are not to be sold on the open market. The porcelains we have now fall into that category."

"Oh?" He held his teacup lightly between the fingertips of both hands. "Intriguing." He sipped at his tea and went on, "However, as I say, I have no expertise in the antiques field and therefore no clientele. I'm not sure I'm young enough to start into a new line of work, Miss Chin. I appreciate your offer, and I'd like to do business with your family, but I'm afraid this may not be the right opportunity."

I gave him my most mysterious smile, as a last-ditch effort. "I'm sorry to hear that, Mr. Lee. I was hoping we would be able to work together."

"I'm disappointed also, Miss Chin. But if you and your brothers decide to deal in modern goods, please get back in touch with me. I'm always, as I say, interested in new sources of merchandise."


I made my achy way along the sidewalk, trying to avoid being bumped by my fellow pedestrians, and hailed a cab on Canal to take me to Bill's. It was a ridiculously short walk, but I was cold and sore and tired and had a long afternoon and evening ahead. Traffic on Canal was snarled and couldn't seem to figure out how to get itself moving; sitting in the cab I heard a lot of horn blowing but saw very little action.

I felt just like the traffic myself.

Why had Lee Kuan Yue denied dealing in antiques, at the same time as he accused Hsing Chung Wah of stealing them from him?

One possibility was that my clever ruse hadn't fooled him in the least, that he knew who I was and what I was working on. But in that case, why sit there and talk to me at all? Maybe so he could find out what I knew. But then why not lead me on, ask me about the porcelains, get me to describe them?

And what would I have done if he had?

And what would I have done if he'd thrown me out of his office?

And what would I do if every question I asked in this case

just kept on leading to more and more confusing questions and I never, never found any answers?

## TWENTY

I was sitting in another car, Bill's, as we made our way uptown. Driving had been his idea, and I hadn't tried to talk him out of it.

"Otherwise your mother might think that I'm not looking after you well enough," he said. "In your condition."

"You're not supposed to be looking after me!" I snapped at him. "And it doesn't matter what my mother thinks. And I'm not in any condition."

"Nope."

"And it's freezing in here."

Bill rolled the window on his side most of the way up. He'd been driving, as usual, with it down; he'll do that in any weather, unless the rain is actually falling sideways.

"Rough day?" he asked me, glancing over.

"Oh, stop being so understanding; you're making me feel guilty. Yes, it was a rough day. First poor Mrs. Hsing, who doesn't want to give Lee Kuan Yue back a cup that's probably ours anyway, and then Lee Kuan Yue, who denies knowing or caring about antique porcelains in the first place."

I'd told Bill about my visit to Lee's shop as we'd walked to the lot where he keeps his car. Now he asked, "Even the suggestion that what you were offering him might be hot didn't light his fire at all?"

"Not a flicker."

Bill pushed the car's lighter in, waited for the little pop, put it to his cigarette. "Maybe he just likes to know who his fences are."

"You mean, he wouldn't want to buy stolen goods from my family because he didn't know us?" I thought about it. "If that were true he'd have strung me along while he checked me out. Every Chinese-American has someone he can call on Taiwan who can call someone else who knows everybody. Especially an importer."

"What would you have done if he had?"

"Well, I could have gotten lucky. There may be a Chin family on Taiwan who deals in Asian antiquities."

"There may be." Bill's tone of voice implied it was entirely possible pigs could fly, too.

"Or I might have had to drop the whole gag and tell him who I really was and what I really wanted. I don't know. But anyway, it didn't happen. Lee Kuan Yue just wasn't interested in my goods."

"Hard to believe," Bill said with a slightly lewd grin.

"You know, it's a good thing you're obnoxious." I made my seat recline, closed my eyes. "Otherwise I might fall for you. Tell me when we get there."

As the gentle motion of the car lulled me, my mind went back to Lee Kuan Yue's spare, modern office. I pictured myself sitting up squarely, telling him straight that I'd been to Mrs. Hsing's and whose cup was that, anyway? I wasn't sure, now that I thought about it, why I hadn't. My first instinct has always been toward subterfuge, fakery, and disguise; but maybe that's not necessarily a good way to go. I could have gone in straight.

It just didn't occur to me.


When we got to the Upper East Side we had to park two blocks away and walk through an afternoon that was colder than the morning, though the sun, more ambitious than I would have been, had come out after all. I had a flash, maneuvering around a newsstand on Lexington, of how good a hot bath would feel right now, with the warmth and the mountain scent of Mr. Gao's herbs surrounding me, but I pushed the whole idea out of my mind.

Mrs. Blair lived in a four-story brick rowhouse—the kind of building that's called a brownstone in New York, no matter what it's made of—two houses in from Lexington on Eighty-second. The maid, a fair-skinned Irish woman in a black uniform, told us Mrs. Blair was expecting us and would be right down.

The maid showed us into a bay-windowed room filled with satin-striped furniture with carved legs, a Turkish carpet, and diluted sunlight flowing gently through sheer curtains. In my room at home the sun charges in as though it's trying to burn a square hole in the floor.

The maid took our coats and invited us to sit, but we both stood, admiring the portrait of Mrs. Blair in a formal gown over the fireplace and the small objects of porcelain, silver, and crystal placed in elegantly eye-catching spots. A silver-framed photograph of a smiling man in waders holding a large flopping fish dominated the mantelpiece.

"Do you suppose that's him?" I whispered to Bill, pointing at the fisherman. "Mr. Blair?"

"Betcha," he answered.

The click of heels on the marble foyer floor made us both turn as Mrs. Blair entered the room. Wearing a silk blouse and a wool skirt—and, I noticed, stockings and high heels in her own house—she smiled at us graciously.

"Ms. Chin. It's a pleasure to see you again."

"Hello, Mrs. Blair." I introduced her to Bill, although I wondered as I did that whether I was supposed to introduce Bill to her first. There's a rule of etiquette that covers these occasions, but I don't know what it is.

"Please, sit down." She gestured to the pristine-looking furniture, chose a chair with graceful wooden arms for herself. Bill remained standing until both Mrs. Blair and I were seated. Well, at least someone in this partnership had manners.

"Mrs. Blair," I began, after everyone had crossed their

legs and tugged at their trouser creases—or, in Mrs. Blair's case, her skirt hem—"something a little odd has happened and I wondered if you could help us."

"If it will help Chinatown Pride recover my husband's porcelains I'll certainly try."

"I'm not sure. But can you tell me about the porcelains that were stolen: Was there a white cup with a red tiger on it?" That seemed to me a shabby description of the delicate, translucent vessel painted with the fiery beast that Mr. Gao had held to the window's light, but if she'd owned it she'd recognize it. "It had a top, with a tiger on that, too."

Mrs. Blair paused, gave me a small smile. "This may seem strange to you, Ms. Chin, but I'm not sure. As I told you, the collection was my husband's; I wasn't really involved with it." Her eyes went to the photograph of the fisherman, lingered a moment. "No, I don't think so. I don't think that sounds familiar. Why?"

"There were two of them," Bill interjected. "Two covered cups like that, identical."

Mrs. Blair turned her gaze to him. "Well, as I say, I'm not sure, but I don't believe they were my husband's. Why do you ask?"

"One of them has turned up," I said. "It was a long shot, but porcelain . . . we just thought we'd check it out. Mrs. Blair, may I ask you something else: Are you acquainted with Dr. Roger Caldwell, from the Kurtz Museum?"

I thought, for a fraction of a second, something hard passed over her face, but it might have been a cloud momentarily darkening the sunlight in the room.

"Yes, of course," she said. "Dr. Caldwell's particular field is porcelains. I believe he and my husband consulted on occasion."

"Had Dr. Caldwell seen your husband's collection?" I asked. "Would he recognize the pieces?"

Mrs. Blair looked down at her perfect, French-tipped nails. "I don't believe so, no. Apparently they occasionally bid against each other at auction, and I suppose whichever pieces my husband was successful in acquiring Dr. Caldwell might remember and recognize. But he was not a guest in this house."

I thought I heard, in that, an echo of the icy Hong Kong lady I'd heard in Nora's office. I glanced at Bill; if he'd heard it too, he wasn't showing it.

Interested in the source of the chill, I asked, "But you didn't consult Dr. Caldwell about the disposition of Mr. Blair's collection?"

"As a matter of fact, I tried, but Dr. Caldwell was in Europe, on an extended purchasing trip, as I understand. He wasn't aware my husband had passed away until his return. But all in all I'm very satisfied with—in fact, grateful for—Dr. Browning's advice and assistance."

"Yes, I'm sure," I said. "Well, Mrs. Blair, we appreciate your seeing us, and we won't take much more of your time. Let me just ask you one more question: Do you know a Chinatown importer named Lee Kuan Yue?"

Her clear brown eyes blinked. "Of course," she told me. "He's my brother."

"We need a cup of coffee," Bill said. "To help us think."

We were walking south on Lexington, toward the art gallery that was our next stop. The sun had packed it in and the city was cloudy and gray, approaching the early twilight of a January afternoon.

"I never need coffee," I pointed out. "But I could use help thinking."

We chose the first place we came to, a white-and-green tiled cafe that was mostly takeout but had a line of tables opposite the pasta-salad-filled glass cases. Bill got black coffee and a blueberry scone; I got Irish Breakfast tea. We carried them to a table, drank, and tried to think.

"I'm such an idiot," I told Bill, squeezing my teabag around my spoon. "Did I cover well enough?"

"You were perfect. I'm sure she has no idea that you're an idiot."

"Gee, thanks."

After Mrs. Blair's revelation about her relation to Lee Kuan Yue, I'd told her I'd only asked because his firm was known for dealing in porcelains and we were checking on all such firms. If I'd known he was her brother, of course, I wouldn't have bothered. It sounded lame to me, but she appeared to buy it.

"You knew I had a brother doing business in Chinatown, of course? I believe I mentioned him to you when we first met." She seemed slightly amused at my confusion.

"Yes, of course. I just never connected the two."

"I should have thought to arrange for the two of you to meet. Have you talked to Kuan Yue? Was he able to help you?"

"Well, as I say, it was only a background check. Actually, he told me he's not interested in antiques."

"No, I don't believe he ever was. We were raised to look to the future, my brother and I."

Now, picking blueberries out of Bill's scone, I said to him, "Maybe he's the guy you were theorizing about at the beginning. Lee Kuan Yue. The one who had his eye on the collection for a long time but couldn't get at it until it went to CP."

Bill leaned back in his chair, sipped his coffee. "Keep going."

"Well, he could have seen the collection. I mean, her *brother*. No matter how much of a recluse Mr. Blair was, his wife's brother could easily have been in and out of the house all the time."

"Ummm. It's possible. But he'd also have known Blair was dead. Why not try to make a deal with her then?"

"Maybe they're not on good terms?"

"She didn't make it sound like that. Maybe we should ask him."

"Maybe we should," I agreed.

"That would fit with your other theory," Bill said.

"I had another theory?"

"That Mrs. Blair has an idea who did it, and is lying about no one seeing the collection to protect whoever that is."

"Ah, that theory." I leaned back in my chair, too. "You know, there's a way to test that theory."

"I thought of that."

"Did you?"

"Uh-huh. There's an Irish bar on Second Avenue where all the Irish maids I know go for a pint in the evening, after the mistress retires."

"You know a lot of Irish maids?"

"Doesn't everybody? What's Mrs. Blair's number?"

I gave it to him. He pushed back his chair and went to the pay phone.

"Okay," he said, sitting down again. "I have a date with Rosie O'Malley at nine."

"What did you tell her?"

"That she was beautiful as a summer's evenin', that her eyes were like the sparklin' waters of home."

"You didn't."

"Well, it's true."

"She didn't strike me as the kind of woman who'd fall for that kind of stuff."

"She didn't. So I said I was a p.i., I'd like to ask her some questions, and I'd buy her a beer."

"That worked better?"

"It usually does."

He went back to his coffee. "Leaving her brother out of this," he said between sips, "the guy Mrs. Blair doesn't seem to be on such good terms with is Roger Caldwell."

"You picked that up too?" I asked. "I wonder why."

"And I wonder why, if it's true, he was over at her place yesterday."

"Maybe we should ask him."

"Maybe we should."

"But if they're not on good terms," I broke off a crumbly

piece of scone, "why did she try to consult him about the collection when Mr. Blair died?"

"Who says she did? Maybe that was just to throw us off."

"Could be. You think she's that sneaky?"

"I don't know her. The only Chinese women I know well are you and your mother."

I narrowed my eyes at him. "What's your point?"

"I wouldn't dare make one."

He grinned. I dabbed crème fraîche on my pebble of scone. "What do you suppose it's about, her and Dr. Caldwell?" I mused. "The pieces her husband beat him out for at auctions?"

"That sounds to me like a reason for Caldwell to carry a grudge, not Mrs. Blair."

"Well, maybe it worked the other way too. Maybe he snarfed up some soup bowl Mr. Blair's heart was set on."

"For a woman not involved in the collection, it seems pretty heartless to dislike him over a soup bowl."

"Not involved in the collection. But very involved with her husband. Suppose he'd wanted something very badly, and Dr. Caldwell had stolen it."

"Literally?"

"Well, no. But used some seriously dishonorable means to get his hands on it. I'll bet that would have upset her, if it upset him."

"Possible. But you know, it didn't sound to me as though *Mr.* Blair had a lot of trouble with Caldwell. She said they consulted sometimes."

"True." I finished my tea, noticing that I ached, wishing I didn't, or, if I had to, that I could do it home in bed. "I don't know, maybe she just doesn't like his cologne. But I can't get over the feeling that there's something real there."

"I think so, too," Bill said. "I think there is. We just haven't figured out what, yet."

\* \* \*

Our visit to the Morpheus Gallery was short, because Franco Ciardi's little tidbit of information was short, though very interesting.

The gallery was a hushed, white-walled space on Madison, three square rooms at the top of a flight of carpeted stairs. The glow of the bare wood floor, the tranquil oil-painted landscapes, and the refined sounds of a string quartet gave you the sense that this was a warm, calm refuge from the scurrying and the chill outside.

Of course, all the paintings had price tags, and the string quartet was on CD, available at Tower for $14.95.

"Smith, my boy!" Ciardi, a sharp-nosed man in his fifties, beamed as we walked through his glossy door. "I would have closed, but I waited for you."

He said this modestly, as though waiting for us was some impressively generous act he didn't want any fuss made over.

"Uh-huh," Bill said. "Franco, this is Lydia Chin."

"Enchanted." Ciardi turned the beam on me. It was like being caught in someone's headlights; I wondered if he could turn it down. "Absolutely enchanted."

I murmured something I hoped was enchanting. Ciardi squeezed my hand meaningfully, though I had no idea what it meant. Bill wandered into the room, stood in front of one of the landscapes. Ciardi looked his way.

"Oh, don't waste your eyes, dear boy. Marvels of mediocrity, very popular with the matrons." He winked at me. I had no idea what the wink meant, either. "Still, one must make a living."

"In all sorts of ways," Bill said, turning back to him. "You called me?"

"Certainly. I certainly did. About your porcelains. Come sit down."

He showed us to the corner where his desk angled, to two highly finished wooden chairs with needlepoint seats. He perched himself against the graceful, curved-legged desk, folded his arms, beamed some more.

"So what's the story, Franco?" Bill asked. "Someone try to sell some hot porcelain to a friend of a friend of yours?"

"No. No no no. Your pieces aren't on the market, as far as I know. Not, of course, that I would have any real way of knowing that sort of thing. Only what I inadvertently hear, that's all."

"Of course that's all," Bill said in total agreement. "So why are we here?"

"Well," Ciardi hugged himself a little closer, with the look of a man about to share a delicious piece of gossip, "the point, the point about your porcelains is, someone else is looking for them."

Bill and I glanced at each other; then I said, "Who?"

"Ah," Ciardi said. "Unfortunately, I don't actually know."

"If you don't know who, how do you know he's looking?" Bill asked.

"He was here," Ciardi said triumphantly. "But he gave me a false name. Never con a con man, dear boy. I looked him up as soon as he left."

"When was this? What was he like?" That was me.

"It was early this morning. Early in the art world, that is: before ten. He was, if I may say so, like the pair of you: He claimed to be a private investigator. That may be true. But he also claimed his name was Jim Johnson, which sounded phony enough to be true—sort of like 'Bill Smith,' dear boy—but it wasn't."

"You checked?" Bill asked.

"Thoroughly. Although he showed me a license that looked very like yours, no one bearing that name is licensed to ply your trade in this great state. Or the surrounding colonies."

"What did he look like?"

"A very average gentleman. Brown hair, brown eyes, five foot nine or ten."

"Did he wear a hat?" I broke in.

"A hat?" Ciardi seemed delighted at the randomness of the question. "He didn't. No hat."

"The guy following me," I said to Bill. "It could be him." To Ciardi I said, "What did he want?"

"He wanted porcelains. Chinese export porcelains, though," turning his eyes to Bill, "I have even less faith that he had any idea what that meant than that you do, dear boy. But he described some pieces, rather vaguely. His descriptions were too similar to the photographs you showed me for coincidence."

"He said they were stolen?"

"He did. From his client, who, he implied, would be willing to pay for their return."

"How did he get to you?" Bill wanted to know.

"My dear Smith, do you think I'm your personal trade secret? One has a reputation, you know."

"I'm sure one has. Did he leave you any way to get in touch with him?"

"No." Ciardi gave himself a moment, to add to the drama. Then he said, "He told me, however, that he would be calling me."

"Franco," Bill said, "this is fascinating. Did you send him to the Kurtz also?"

"That," Ciardi seemed affronted, "I would not have done."

"Not for free, anyway," Bill said.

"Most certainly not for free. You and I, after all, have a history. This is a gentleman I don't know. However, as it happens, he'd already been there."

"To the Kurtz?" I asked.

"He asked me about the Kurtz. Whether I'd heard of them acquiring porcelains lately. I had to say I hadn't, and he said that's what they had told him, too, but he'd wanted to make sure it was true. Unfortunately I couldn't enlighten him further." Ciardi beamed at us. "Have I been useful?"

"Franco, you're invaluable," Bill said. "Tell me one more thing. In your line of work, have you come across an importer named Lee Kuan Yue? Lee's his last name."

Ciardi rolled his eyes. "My dear boy, I'm well acquainted

147

with the Chinese custom of placing the family name first. A quite sensible way to proceed, actually." He smiled and bowed to me. "No, I don't believe I've heard the name."

"You wouldn't expect him to be interested in our stolen porcelains?"

"I have no reason to, no."

"How about Hsing Chung Wah?" I asked.

"I've not heard of this gentleman, either. Is this case of yours turning out to be a far-flung international conspiracy? It's beginning to sound quite fun."

"Not fun, Franco," said Bill, standing. "This sort of case is never fun."

"My dear boy, I'm sorry to hear that," Ciardi answered as I stood also. "One's joy and one's reputation are quite everything in life."


### TWENTY-ONE

"Okay," I said to Bill as we stood on the windy corner below the Morpheus Gallery. "I think it's time to go to the Kurtz Museum and find out what's going on around here."

"Misguided optimism is one of your most adorable characteristics."

"Get lost. But before you do, do you have any aspirin?"

"You have a headache?"

"I have an ache everyplace. Don't sympathize," I cut him off. "You'll make me feel sorry for myself."

"You have a right."

"But I don't want to. You don't think Steve Bailey's big news will make all this crystal clear?"

From his look I got the idea there was something he

wanted to say, but he didn't say it. He shrugged. "So far everything we've learned today has just made it murkier. Here's a drugstore; I'll treat you to some aspirin."

We bought aspirin and a seltzer to down them with. Bill looked at me critically while I drank.

"You do look beat," he said. "Let's take a cab to the museum."

I was going to protest that it wasn't that far, which it wasn't; normally it would have been a nice brisk walk through the winter evening. Right now, though, the thought of slogging all the way to the Kurtz made me feel like a sled dog on the last day of the Iditarrod race.

"We'll be early," I said. "Do you care?"

"What's a little bad manners compared to protecting the health of your partner, the vigor of your companion, the bloom in the cheeks of your—"

"Taxi!" I hollered, stepping into the street.

The cab dropped us a block down from the Kurtz; Bill and I think alike about that. Probably because I learned it from him.

As we approached the limestone building it seemed cozy and inviting, a soft light glowing from the third-floor window and another over the broad front door. Catching our breath in the wind charging out of the park, we climbed the stoop, and this time I rang the bell, seeing myself just for a moment as a daughter of New York's glittering turn-of-the-century society paying a social call.

Then I saw something else.

The door was ajar.

"Bill?" From watching the street, Bill turned, looked where I was pointing, at the thin dark shadow line between door and frame. We exchanged glances.

"Ring it again," he said. I rang the bell again. No one came.

"It's not normal, is it?" I asked. "For a closed museum to be open?"

"No."

"Well," I said, "it's not breaking and entering if the door is open. And it's not trespassing if we were invited."

"Sounds right to me."

We could, of course, have called the police then. The museum is closed and the door is open, we'd have said; something's wrong. But I was still hoping, then, to keep the police and this case apart.

And maybe nothing was wrong. Maybe Steve was just waiting upstairs, and the door hadn't quite caught when he'd closed it, and he hadn't heard the bell.

So we pushed the door open, silent on its heavy brass hinges, and we went in.

The downstairs lights were off, but enough light filtered in from the streetlights outside the high windows for us to see our way. I shut the door behind us, and I locked it.

"Wouldn't you expect a museum to have an alarm system?" I whispered to Bill.

"I'm sure they do."

"Wouldn't you expect it to be on?"

"Not if there's someone here and they haven't actually closed up yet."

We looked at each other. "There's a light on upstairs," Bill said.

"What are you suggesting?"

He shrugged. So did I. We went upstairs.

The light we had seen from outside was in the third-floor windows of the director's office. The dim outlines of glass cases shimmered in the pale glow from the streetlights. The pad of our footsteps on the marble stairs disappeared into the carpeted silence of the second floor.

The stairs from the second floor up were dark polished wood; they creaked under us. Beside me, Bill reached into his jacket, softly withdrew his gun. My hand was already on the .22 in my pocket.

On the third floor, light spilled onto the carpet from the

half-opened door of the director's suite. Soundlessly, we moved toward it, took up positions on either side of the door.

Bill looked at me; I nodded.

He kicked the door wide. We both went in, crouching, guns up, each covering half the room and each other's backs.

We didn't need to.

The room was a disaster. Drawers were dumped, computers smashed, papers everywhere. Shards of a broken computer screen sparkled in the light of the lamp. And next to the lamp, as wrong and unmoving as everything else, lay Trish Atherton, lamplight glinting off her golden hair and off the blood, still fresh, that soaked her beautiful silk blouse.

My bones went cold.

Bill stood, looked at me. He nodded toward the door into Caldwell's inner office. On autopilot, .22 ready, I stepped back to where I could see both that door and the hall one. Bill toed the inner door open, waited. He stepped inside, made a quick trip through the room and out again.

"No one here," he said. He crouched by Trish, put two fingers to the side of her throat. The carotid artery, I thought uselessly, one eye on him, one on the hall doorway. That's what's in the throat. That's what throbs, moves, pulses more than once a second, every second of your life. She'd need an ambulance. Call an ambulance, Lydia.

I reached for the phone, stopped. Fingerprints. Don't mess. I pulled on a glove I'd taken off downstairs and dialed 911. When the operator asked me the nature of my emergency, I said, "A woman's hurt. She's bleeding badly."

Bill looked up. He said, "She's dead."

## TWENTY-TWO

I was sitting on the sofa in Roger Caldwell's office. My head was throbbing. Back and forth in front of me, an overweight detective named Bernstein paced the room, seeming unwilling to trust any of the delicate furniture with his bulk, swearing at the furniture for it. The streetlight stabbed through the window and joined the desk lamp in poking me in the eyes whenever I tried to do more than squint. In the other room, beyond the closed door, the crime scene technicians were finishing up their photos, sketches, and measurements. They'd already found a letter opener covered with blood discarded near the door. Soon the medics would be able to zip Trish Atherton's body into a thick rubber bag and heft it down the twisting stairs.

"Tell me again," Bernstein growled.

I told him again, giving him the most compressed version yet, because this was the third. "We're investigating the theft of some porcelains. We came here yesterday because we thought the thief might try to sell them to the Kurtz. Steve Bailey, who works here, called Bill today and said to meet him here at six. When we got here the door was open. We came up and found her. Then we called you."

"Why did Bailey want you to meet him?"

"I don't know."

"You always go places you don't know why?"

I felt stretched with patience. "I hoped he had some information that would help us solve our case."

"Which is?"

"I told you, a theft. Porcelains."

Never lie to cops, if you can help it, and never tell them more than they absolutely have to know. Especially if you don't know them.

Bernstein scowled at me. "What else?"

"There's nothing else, except the name of my client. I won't tell you that without my client's permission."

"Withholding information's a crime, Miss Chin. Even for a p.i. Now I think of it, *especially* for a p.i."

"Only if it's relevant."

"Oh, sure. And you're in a great position to say what's relevant. Who socked you in the jaw?"

That threw me. I straightened my shoulders. "A Chinese boy I know."

"Why?"

"He doesn't like the way I behave."

Bernstein gave a cold chuckle. "How's that?"

"I'm not afraid of him." That wasn't quite true, but it would serve Bernstein right to believe it.

"He involved in this case?"

"I don't see how he could be." Assuming, of course, that the case Bernstein was referring to was his, not mine.

"What's his name?"

I shook my head.

"Tell me his goddamn name!"

I took a breath. "Detective," I said, trying not to grit my teeth, "there's a lot I haven't told you. My birthday. My brother's favorite foods. If you want to know everything I ever knew I'll tell you, but as far as anything that will help you find whoever killed this woman, there's nothing else."

Bernstein stopped pacing. "Lydia," he said quietly, "—it's Lydia, right?—Lydia, there's only one thing gets under my skin worse than a killer, and that's a wiseass p.i. Don't get smart with me, okay?"

"I wasn't trying to." Control yourself, Lydia, I suggested, or you and your headache will spend the night in a holding cell at the 19th. I tried to sound reasonable. "But I've told you everything I know. This," I fingered my tender jaw, "this was a private quarrel."

He stared down at me for what must have been a full minute before he spoke. "Look, Lydia. I have here two p.i.s and a dead woman in a closed museum. The p.i.s won't tell me what they're doing here except they came to meet someone who's not here. They won't say how they got in except the door was open. They won't say what the dead woman was doing here except she worked here. I don't give a shit about your private quarrels, 'scuse my French, but in my experience, which I think is maybe a little bit broader than yours, the things people hold back are the things I want to know. Where's Steve Bailey?"

"I don't know."

"Who else knew you'd be here?"

"I don't know."

"Trish Atherton?"

"I don't know."

"Who'd want to kill her?"

"I don't know."

"How did—"

Bernstein didn't get to finish that one; a uniformed black cop stuck her head in the door from the outer office. She shifted her wad of chewing gum and spoke around it. "Caldwell's here, Bernstein."

"Yeah?" Bernstein gave her a narrow-eyed stare. "All right. Bring him in here." The cop shut the door again. Bernstein hissed out a breath. "You can go," he said to me. "Just hope your partner's story was the same as yours. And don't leave town."

I didn't believe real cops actually said that, I almost told him, but my better self knew better, so I shut up.

As I gathered myself to leave, the uniformed cop returned, ushering Roger Caldwell through the office door. Caldwell's face was ashen above the silk scarf in the neck of his fine tweed overcoat. He was subdued, but with a tightness about his mouth and shoulders that suggested costly control, not calm. At first he didn't notice me. When he did he almost jumped, as though he'd heard a sudden noise.

"Ms. Chin. What are you doing here?" Caldwell looked from me to Bernstein, back to me.

I opened my mouth, not sure what was going to come out, but Bernstein beat me to it.

"Miss Chin and her partner found Trish Atherton's body."

"I don't understand," Caldwell said to me. "Were you here to see Trish?"

I'd caught on to what Bernstein wanted, and it was the same thing I wanted. "We were hoping to talk to someone," I said. "The door was open when we got here, so we came up."

"Open? It wasn't supposed to be open." Caldwell sounded a little vague, as though he wasn't sure any of these words made sense.

"Not wide open. Ajar."

"It wasn't supposed to be open," he repeated. "Did Trish call you?"

"Why would she have done that, Mr. Caldwell?" Bernstein jumped in. Caldwell must have been seriously distracted; he didn't flinch at the "Mr."

"I don't know," he mumbled. "Why would she want to talk to a detective?"

"Why does anyone?" Bernstein said. "What was her relationship to Steve Bailey?"

"Steve? Trish and Steve? They worked together. I—they seemed to get along quite well."

"Anything more than 'get along'?"

Caldwell stared at Bernstein. "Are you asking if they had a romantic relationship? Implying that . . . that this could be the result of some sort of lovers' quarrel?"

"Did they?"

Caldwell bristled. "Steve Bailey is a fine young man. It's ludicrous to think him capable of such a thing."

155

"I'm sure he'll appreciate the testimonial when we find him. Now answer the question, please. Was there a romantic relationship between Bailey and Miss Atherton?"

Caldwell's face seemed to pale even more. He shook his head, and, without looking at Bernstein, said, "I don't know."

Bernstein shrugged. Then seeming to become aware of me suddenly, he said, "Oh, Miss Chin." He sounded almost apologetic. "You can leave. I'm sorry for keeping you. I'll be talking to you again, I'm sure." Hand on my back, Bernstein propelled me to the door and closed it behind me.

I stood uncertainly in the outer office as the zipper was zipped on Trish Atherton's relationship to this world. It occurred to me that someone was going to have to break the news to her family. I hoped it was someone with more gentleness about him than Bernstein.

I eyed the mess in the room. Now that the body was gone, a detective was sifting through the computer innards and scattered papers, looking for something in what was there—or what was not—that would speak through Trish's silence.

The gum-chewing cop who'd brought Dr. Caldwell in said to me, "Bernstein said you could go." Her tone of voice hinted that it would be a good idea. She smirked. "Unless you thought of something else you want to tell us?"

"No," I said evenly. "But I'd like to wait for my partner."

"Smith? Connors, you still got Smith here?"

The detective, papers in both hands, shook his head. "Nope. Gone."

The cop turned to me. "He left," she said.

I descended the curving stairs, wondering how cops can think you're smart enough to be keeping things from them and dumb enough to need an English word translated at the same time.

On the street outside, three patrol cars and the detective's unmarked one were distributed randomly, along with the crime scene van and the medical examiner's wagon. A uniformed cop, the earflaps down on his uniform hat, guarded the front door. The crowd that materializes from nowhere had materialized. I guessed they'd gotten their money's worth a few minutes ago when Trish's body was lifted into the wagon for its trip to the morgue.

A small colony of reporters was swarming. Just like the mosquitoes in my brother Ted's backyard, they spotted me coming out the door and surrounded me.

"What's your name?"

"Do you work at the museum?"

"Who's the dead woman?"

"What was your relationship to her?"

I gave them all a sullen "No comment" and pushed through. It took me until I got to the corner of the next block to lose the last of them.

On the corner of the block after that, I found Bill leaning against a lamppost and smoking a cigarette.

"Do you have any idea what a cliché that is?" I glared at him.

"Took you long enough."

"What made you think I'd come?"

"North," he said. "It hasn't failed yet."

That was true. We had a standing plan, if we got separated at a place where one or both of us was no longer welcome, to meet a few hundred yards north of the last place we'd seen each other. This was the fourth time it had worked.

Bill's lamppost was on the park side of Fifth, near a park bench. The bench suddenly looked wonderfully welcoming. I sat.

Bill sat next to me, the orange tip of his cigarette glowing. "Bernstein give you a hard time?"

"Bernstein," I said, "is an unpleasant, condescending, sneaky creep. He probably didn't give me as hard a time as he thought I deserved, for being a woman, a p.i., and there. But it was hard enough to give me a splitting headache."

"You had a headache already. He ain't so tough."

"No," I declared. "He ain't."

He threw the cigarette away, turned to look at me. He

wrapped his arm around my shoulders. I moved closer, to get warmer. I realized my insides were shivering.

"Bill?" I whispered.

"Hmm?"

"Nothing."

"Hmm," he said.

We sat like that for awhile, bare trees throwing long dancing shadows on the sidewalk and on us. A pack of cars whished past. Some of them got trapped behind a stoplight, halted, stood panting and growling to move again.

"Did Steve do that?" I asked Bill, when the silence had been long enough.

"I don't know."

"I don't think he did."

"Why?"

"He knew we were coming. That would be the worst time to kill someone, when you were meeting two p.i.s in a place you were supposed to be alone in."

"Unless you had to."

"Why would you have to?"

He didn't answer.

"They brought Dr. Caldwell in as I was leaving. Bernstein asked whether there was anything between Trish and Steve. He said he didn't know."

"It's a motive."

"I don't think it was him," I said again.

"Why?"

"Because—oh, because he was so *enthusiastic* on the phone. Because he called us. Because when he was showing us around he got excited about the porcelains and it's not even his field."

"Because you like him."

"Well? That's my p.i. instinct."

"No, it's not. But it's one of the best things about you." He said that seriously. Then he leaned over and kissed me.

Usually, Bill's kisses are light, half-kidding; usually, mine are like that too. Not this time.

This time, his kiss was long and warm and made me forget that we were sitting on a park bench in a New York January evening. It made me forget Trish Atherton's golden hair and her ruined silk blouse. And it made me forget that I didn't let him kiss me like this.

Then I remembered something.

Pulling away so that I could look him in the eye I said, "What do you mean it's not my p.i. instinct?"

He stared for a moment; then he laughed. "Boy, remind me to never play on the other team from you."

"Yeah, yeah, yeah. What do you mean?"

"I mean," he said, "that a p.i.'s instinct is what says not to trust people who seem trustworthy. I'm not sure it works the other way around."

"Mine does." I pulled my jacket to straighten it. "You have lipstick on your cheek."

"You don't wear lipstick."

"Just checking to see if you're awake." Then I thought of something else. "Bill, we have to find Steve."

"The cops will find him."

"What if he saw something? He may be in danger. Maybe what he wanted to tell us had something to do with . . . with this." I flashed on bloody silk; I blocked the picture out.

"I'm sure he's on top of the NYPD Hit Parade right now," Bill said. "Which, by the way, we're not. And we don't even know where he lives. They'll look for him, and this is a good time to keep out of their way."

"Yeah," I said. "Okay. You're right. I hate that."

"Me being right?"

"That too. No, sitting around waiting for something to happen."

"Well," he said, stretching and standing, "that's your problem. I've got a date."

"What are you talking about?"

"A brew with Rosie O'Malley, the queen of Killarney."

"Oh." I looked at my watch. "I forgot about that. Can you really do that? After—after this?"

"It's better to keep moving. It's always better."

That made sense to me. I stood.

"What are you going to do?" he asked as we walked along the park.

"I don't know," I said gloomily. "Maybe go home and go to bed."

"That's not a bad idea."

"At eight-thirty? You're crazy."

"Hey, I didn't suggest it."

"Good."

He went on, "The last time I was in a fight I was sore for two weeks. I slept a lot. Of course, maybe that's just me."

"You sleep. I eat. And I feel fine." That, of course, was a major lie. "Call me later? Especially if Rosie O'Malley has anything to say."

"I'll call you no matter what."

We kissed again, lightly, the old way; then I hailed a cab and headed downtown. I turned back to see Bill still standing on the corner, watching my cab as he got smaller, finally disappearing in the darkness.

## TWENTY-THREE

I didn't go home. The cab left me off at the noodle shop across from my office, where, being as famished as I was, the need to choose among the various smells and sizzles and steaming noodle vats practically immobilized me. In the end I bought pork dumplings and vegetable chow fun and promised myself I could come back for soy sauce chicken over rice if it was necessary.

The travel agency had long since closed when I unlocked

the street door and deposited my dinner on my desk and myself behind it. I threw my hat and coat on the guest chair. Mouth watering from the gamey pork odor of my dumplings, I grabbed my chopsticks from my pencil cup. I'd eaten two dumplings dipped in hot oil before I noticed the blinking red light on my phone.

I bit off another half dumpling and hit the rewind button. The machine raced backwards through three messages.

The first two were almost the same.

"Ms. Chin? Oh, god. It's Steve Bailey." The words were breathless; traffic noise filled the background. "We have to meet somewhere else. I have to see you. Can we . . . oh god, I don't know. I'll call your partner. I'll call you again."

Damn, I thought. Steve, where are you? I pressed the button again.

"Ms. Chin? Oh, why aren't you there? I have to talk to you. Please be there. Please pick up the phone. Oh, god. I'll call you back."

That was it.

I pressed the button a third time. The tape was silent for a few seconds; I thought it was a hang-up. Then, just as I reached for the rewind button, came a soft male voice.

"Lydia Chin? This is Bic. Grandfather Gao wants me to tell you I didn't steal any porcelains. So: I didn't steal any porcelains. Now stay out of my way and stay out of my life."

The click of the phone being hung up was the only sound in the room. I realized I'd stopped chewing with my mouth half full. I started up again while I rewound and replayed that message. "Stay out of my way, and stay out of my life."

Damn! I slammed my fist on the desk, slopping hot oil out onto the mail. Steve and Bic, while I was smooching with Bill on a park bench! What kind of detective was I? I glared at the silent answering machine. The timer that automatically marked each call told me Bic's had come in barely ten minutes ago. Ten minutes! I should get a cellular phone. Then I could get my Call Forwarding to call it, and then I could smooch with anybody I wanted without . . .

161

Oh, I thought. Oh, Lydia. Oh, Lydia, you are an idiot. I grabbed up the receiver, before the phone had a chance to ring again.

I didn't have a cellular phone. But I had Call Forwarding. And Call Waiting. And Three-party Calling.

And, brand-new from Nynex, Call Return.

I punched the buttons that automatically let my phone call back the last number that called me. Bouncing my foot up and down rapidly as I waited, I reminded myself that a lot of people block this service. I had. Not everyone wants their numbers given out to everyone they call. I listened to it ring, sure I was going to hear a tinny-voiced operator telling me that my call could not be completed.

That wasn't what I heard.

What I heard was, "China Seas. Your order please?"


I called Bill's service and left a message telling him what I was going to do. Then I did it.

I wolfed down the rest of the dumplings while I looked at a Queens map. The chow fun I stuffed into the office fridge. It's good for breakfast anyway.

Out on the street I had to wait a few minutes for a cab. Waving for one reminded me how sore I was and how much I'd wanted to crawl into bed a million times today. But at the same time my skin prickled and my heart raced. Partly that was because I was getting to do something, not just waiting around.

And partly it was because meeting Bic was something I'd really wanted to do.

A cab finally swerved to a stop in front of me, and the driver wasn't even too grouchy about taking me all the way to Flushing. He was Pakistani; he probably lived there. He could stop off at home for dinner.

I thought about the voice on the phone as my cab played stop-and-go through the streets of Manhattan. I replayed the message in my head the same way I had on the machine.

"This is Bic. Grandfather Gao wants me to tell you I didn't steal any porcelains."

I knew that voice.

"This is Bic."

Why would a West Coast gangster care what Grandfather Gao wanted?

"Stay out of my way."

We arched over the Queensborough Bridge, one of those few thin, glittering threads that connect Manhattan to the rest of the world.

"Grandfather Gao."

I knew that voice.

"This is Bic."

The river, thick and inky, was behind us now.

"Stay out of my life."

I knew.

In Flushing, the cab dropped me at the end of Main Street. I walked the blocks to China Seas wondering if I should be doing this. If I was right it explained some things. Maybe if I thought about them I could get just as far without seeing Bic face to face as I could by confronting him. He didn't want to meet me and now I knew why. Maybe you should leave it alone, Lydia.

But there was still a dead boy whose mother had loved him.

And there were still Nora's porcelains.

Maybe Bic really didn't have anything to do with those things. But I wanted to ask him.

China Seas had a glowing red-lettered sign above a slick new aluminum-and-glass storefront. I checked my watch. It was twenty-five minutes since I'd left; that made it thirty-five since Bic's call. I hoped he'd called before he'd ordered dinner, and I hoped he'd been hungry.

I walked in and saw them right away, three gangsters at a table by the front window. One of them was older than the other two, though no older than me, with a nicely tailored suit where they wore leather jackets. That one had a wide, shiny scar along his left cheek, as Trouble had said, but I didn't need that.

He didn't see me come in. He didn't see me until I was standing right next to him.

"Hello, Matt," I said in a quiet voice. "Long time."

His head snapped up. For a brief, motionless moment the entire restaurant seemed to be freeze-framed. Then he leaned back in his chair, and a slow, self-possessed smile took over; but before that, before his guard was up, when he first caught sight of me, I saw a ghost of the eager joy Matt Yin and I used to bring to the times we were together, when I was fifteen.

Or maybe I felt it more than saw it. Maybe the ghost wasn't Matt's.

"Well," he said with a cool gangster smile. "I'll be damned, guys. It's Lydia." He spoke in a slow, easy drawl; I could hear the languid breezes of California in his words.

Chopsticks clinked onto plates. One of the other boys started to rise, hand snaking into his jacket, but Matt touched his arm. He smiled again, recovered now, the *dai lo* in charge. "Lydia. You're still like that, huh?" He shook his head, smiling. "You're still like that."

I wasn't completely sure what it was I was still like, but I knew I was still like that.

"Move over, Camel." Matt elbowed the boy next to him. "Let the lady sit down. This was once a special lady, guys. I used to think she was really special." He winked at the boy, who, sullen-faced, scraped his chair a few inches across the floor so I could sit.

"How long have you been back, Matt?" I asked quietly, once I was seated.

"Maybe eight months," Matt said cheerfully. "Have you had dinner? God, this lady can eat," he told the others. "You wouldn't think so to look at her, but I'd back her against either of you." He shook his head again, as though at a fond memory. His eyes met mine, and we looked at each other for a long, silent moment. Then he spoke. The smile remained, but his

164

voice came out as softly icy as a New York January night. "What the hell do you want, Lydia?"

I almost shivered in the chill, but I tried not to let it show. "Does Nora know?"

"How did you find me?" The soft voice ignored my question.

"The miracles of modern technology. Does Nora know?"

"Grandfather Gao told you."

I shook my head. "I traced your call."

"No kidding." He regarded me with raised eyebrows and an ironic smile. "You mean you're really a detective?"

"Yes."

"I thought that's what Grandfather Gao was telling me. But you know, my Chinese has gone completely to hell since I moved west." He chuckled. "So what do you think? You came looking for Bic and you found your old honey. Surprised?"

"I knew it was you."

His face fell; he frowned in mock disappointment. "So he did tell you."

"No, Matt. You did."

"Me? Oh, please explain this, great detective." He reached into his pocket for a cigarette. He lit it with a gold lighter, grinning at me as he snapped the top closed.

I realized my shoulders were rigid. I forced them to relax. "I recognized your voice, but I couldn't place it. But you said 'Grandfather Gao.' Why would a West Coast gangster say that? Even Trouble just calls him 'Old Gao.' Only a Chinatown kid would say that. When I realized that, I knew."

One of the other boys snickered. Matt shot him a narrow-eyed look, then relaxed. "Damn." He grinned. "What a smart-ass. That always was your problem, Lydia."

"What about Nora?" I asked again.

"My poor fool sister? She has no idea who I am or how lucky she is." He directed a long, thin stream of smoke well above my head.

"That's why you wanted that corner," I said. "Because of CP and Nora."

"Nora," Matt said, to the boys at the table as well as to me, "is a bleeding-heart idiot. Trouble would have eaten her alive. Her and the rest of the nerds at Chinatown Pride." The sneer in his words made the other boys laugh.

"So you took over the territory. To help?"

"Help?" He looked amazed. He flipped the top of the lighter, snapped a flame, watched it dance. "Help her waste her life? Sit around listening to a bunch of FOBs bitch and moan about how great China was and how lousy things are here? Teach them English so they can bitch in two languages, and then babysit their kids while they drop a week's pay at *fan tan* until it's time to go back and wash pots in a stinking kitchen? Give me a break, sweetheart."

I could feel the heat in my face. "Don't call me sweetheart, Matt."

"Oh? You used to like that." He ran one finger lightly over the back of my hand.

I pulled my hand away. "Then why'd you do it?"

He laughed. Leaning forward, he said in a low voice, "I'm here to stay, sweetheart. I learned a lot out west. I met a lot of people. Then—well, then it just got to be a good time to come back east." Grinning, he flicked cigarette ash onto a plate. "There's plenty of opportunity here for someone like me. I have big plans. But you've got to get respect. You've got to have face. What would it look like if I couldn't protect my own sister? She's stupid and she's wasting her life. But if she wants to do it, Bic is going to make sure nobody gets in her way."

"Does Trouble know who you are?"

"Trouble?" He snickered. "Trouble wouldn't know his own dick if he saw it in a mirror."

All three of them laughed at that. Matt narrowed his eyes at me, smiling. "Did I embarrass you? Poor sensitive Lydia."

Ignoring the comment and the flush in my cheeks, I asked, "Then what are you proving?"

"I'm proving," Matt said, squashing the cigarette into a

puddle of sauce, "what I want to prove. That Bic takes what he wants. That you don't fuck with me. And," he added, "if some meddling little snoop wants to spread it around Chinatown who I used to be." He paused, shrugged. "That'll be all right. I'm set up here now. I'm strong. The Main Street Boys will take all comers. Right, guys?"

"Fuckin-A, Bic," the one called Camel muttered. He took a long pull from a bottle of beer, then leveled a challenging stare at me, as though he was daring me to slap him for using a dirty word.

I almost laughed in his face. That made me realize just how on edge I was.

Turning my attention back to Matt, I forced myself to be calm—or at least to act it—and asked my next question. "That's why you killed Hsing Chung Wah?"

He stared at me, then laughed. They all laughed, as though I'd delivered a punchline they'd been waiting for.

"So you're really a private eye?" Matt asked. "License and everything? Little Lydia?"

I kept my voice even. "Is that why you killed Hsing Chung Wah?"

Matt lifted his teacup to his lips. He made a face, poured the tea back in the pot, signaled for more. A waiter appeared instantly with a fresh steaming pot. "And a cup for my girl-friend here," Matt told him. The waiter brought one.

"Are you going with anyone?" Matt asked me amiably. "Last time I heard from Nora—that was a while ago—you weren't."

"I want to know why you killed Hsing Chung Wah."

Camel spoke, grinning. "Sounds like she's only interested in one thing, Bic. Not the same what you're interested in."

Matt shook his head. "She was always like this. She gets something into her head and she won't stop. Lydia," he said, "sweetheart, you'll never get a man with that attitude. Lighten up." Before I could say something I might have regretted, Matt added, "I did not kill Hsing Chung Wah."

I asked casually, "One of them did?" Heart pounding, I

coolly indicated the other guys. Lydia knows the ropes. She knows how this game is played.

"Them? Gee, I don't think so. Fellas?"

The one who hadn't spoken lit a cigarette and shrugged. Camel slurped some more beer, said, "Oh, fuck her."

Matt turned back to me. "See?"

I didn't see that those reactions proved anything at all. I changed my approach a little. "But you knew him?"

"Me? I'd never even heard of him by name until he turned up dead. Next thing I knew I was telling some stupid cop where I'd been and what I'd been doing every minute for the last three days."

"You didn't know him by name. But by reputation?"

He glanced at the other boys. "See? She's not bad." He nodded approvingly.

I kept my eyes on him. "And you know he's the one who broke into Chinatown Pride and stole their porcelains? The ones Grandfather Gao was talking about?"

"I wouldn't say I *know* that." He toyed with his lighter, flicking it open, closed, open. "But," he said in an elaborately confidential tone, "that's what I heard."

"Whose idea was it for him to do that?"

"How would I know?"

"Was he working for Lee Kuan Yue?"

"You know," Matt said with a smile, "I sort of like this game. I tell you everything you want to know, and then you come home with me and we party."

"Was he working for Lee Kuan Yue?" Calm down, Lydia, I ordered myself, as anger and frustration and some other, older, sadder feeling put a tremor in my voice.

Matt looked at me for awhile. He snapped his lighter, watched the flame. Then he said, "I heard he was."

I found myself reaching for the tea he had poured me. It was bland but it was hot, and the heat seemed to prop me up.

"Hsing was a Golden Dragon," I said. "You were paying for that territory. He was poaching. You killed him for face."

"Lydia. My little hot-pants private eye. I told you I

didn't." Matt's voice had the chill in it again, a chill that, I imagined, could turn to frozen, terrifying ice in seconds.

"Then who did?" I asked, brave as could be.

"You're a detective. Detect it."

"I'm working on it."

"You sure you don't want to come home with me?"

Something inside me snapped. I wanted to slug him, to scream, to do something that would blot out the images of Trish's blood-soaked blouse, of Mrs. Hsing's desolate face, of Trouble and his boys leaning over me, images that crowded around me as I looked into Matt Yin's eyes.

I stood. In a voice that sounded harsh and strained I said, "Matt, I wouldn't go to the corner with you. But I'm going to find out what's going on here. I just hope for Nora's sake that what you said is true."

Matt stood also. I could have turned then and left, but I didn't. I stayed still as he folded his hand slowly, tightly over mine. He leaned toward me, brushed my lips with his. Their warmth was familiar, as familiar as the scent of his cologne and his cigarettes and his own skin that filled my head.

A tingle went through me. Before it had a chance to take me over I twisted my hand from his and stepped back.

His small, mocking smile was still burning in my watery eyes as I pushed through the door and escaped into the icy January night.

TWENTY-FOUR

I went back on the subway. The Orient Express, New Yorkers call this line now, the Seven that goes from Manhattan into the heart of Flushing. It's not an express, though.

It's a slow, slow train, and I stomped back and forth in the practically empty car, almost hoping that someone would try to mug me so I could beat their brains out. I knew that if that happened I would probably get killed, but it was a safe fantasy, because nobody tries to mug a wild-eyed woman stomping up and down on a moving train.

From the Seven's last stop in Manhattan—Times Square—I called Bill. He answered on the first ring.

"It's me," I said belligerently.

"Christ! Are you okay?" Relief rushed his words.

"Why shouldn't I be?"

"I was going to give you another half-hour and then come out there myself."

"A lot of good that would have done."

"Did you see him? Bic?"

"Yes. Yes, I saw him." Even I heard the choking in my voice.

"Lydia? What's wrong?"

"Dammit . . ."

"Are you all right?"

"I said I was!"

"Where are you?"

"In the subway."

"Come up here."

"Meet me downstairs," I said. "At Shorty's."

"You don't drink."

"You do."

"I can drink up here."

"I don't want to come up to your place, Bill."

"Why not?"

"I don't want you to make a pass at me. I don't think I can handle it right now."

In his silence I closed my eyes, heard the rumble of a train somewhere else in the station.

"I won't," he said quietly. "I'll meet you downstairs if you want. But if you want to come up here, you can."

"Bill?" I swallowed. "I'm sorry. I don't know—I'm not

sure what I'm doing. That was a terrible thing to say. I'm sorry."

"Come up," he said. "We'll talk about it."


The train got me to Bill's in ten minutes. He waited in the doorway as I climbed the two flights of stairs. When I got there he smiled, took my jacket, didn't kiss me hello.

"Hot water's on," he said, settling on the sofa, where a half-finished amber drink sat on the side table.

He lit a cigarette and waited while I brewed chamomille tea. Most of the teas in Bill's kitchen were left there by me at one time or another so I'd have choices I liked when I came up. That had never seemed pushy to me before, but it suddenly did now.

I took my tea to the big armchair and curled up.

Bill said, "He really got to you, this Bic."

I sipped my tea, but it was too hot. I stared into it while neither of us spoke. "I really am sorry," I told Bill finally. "I shouldn't have said what I said to you."

"Did you mean it?" His words were quiet. "Am I like that?"

"I meant it," I said. "But not because you're like that."

I lifted the steaming mug of tea to my lips. It was sweet, and it tasted like summer, but it was unconvincing.

"I saw Bic," I said. "I used to know him."

Bill said nothing, waiting.

"He's Matt Yin."

"Oh," he said softly.

I nodded. "It's been ten years since I've seen him, and longer than that since we were . . . whatever we were. But it shook me, to find it was him. I know I'm reacting badly. I don't know what's wrong with me."

"I don't either," he said. "Just because you run into an ex-boyfriend who's now a major gangster on the same night as you find someone dead, which happens to be the day after you got the shit kicked out of you, you fall apart."

Our eyes met. His had an ironic smile in them.

Mine, before I knew it, had tears.

I tried to stop them, but they made hot little streams down my face. My hands smeared them around as I turned away from Bill and bit my lip to keep from sobbing.

Bill got up and went into the bedroom. By the time he came back with a Kleenex box I'd lost the sobbing battle and was curled in the chair, crying and silently cursing myself for it. Bill set the box in my lap and perched on the edge of the seat with me, wrapping his arm around my shaking shoulders.

"It's okay," he said softly. I didn't know exactly what was okay, but he stayed where he was, not talking and not moving, and after a little while I wiped my eyes and blew my nose and soon my face was able to stop twisting up and my eyes, though I knew they were red and swollen, stopped dripping.

Bill kissed my hot, sticky cheek and smiled.

"How can you kiss someone who looks like this?" I demanded with a little hiccup.

"I closed my eyes. Oh, shit. Was that making a pass?"

"You better hope not, or I'll have to slug you." I got up, went into the bathroom, and did what I could. When I came back he was on the sofa again, with a fresh drink. He'd turned the fire on under the kettle, and it was happily spouting steam. I poured some hot water into my tea, thinking maybe I should be a kettle. Then I could spout off and be happy at the same time. That thought made me giggle weakly as I curled back up in the chair.

"What's so funny?" Bill asked.

"Your tea kettle. It's really silly."

"Remind me tomorrow, I'll go out and buy a serious tea kettle. Now that you've told me who Bic is, tell me what he said."

"Wait. There's something else first. Did Steve Bailey call you?"

"He called my service before I got back. He didn't say where he was, and he didn't say how to find him."

"Damn. Me, too. He called twice. He said he had to talk to us."

"I don't think we can do anything but wait and see if he calls again."

"I hate waiting and seeing."

Bill raised his eyebrows. "Is that right?"

"All right, stop it. If I'd waited we never would have gotten to see Bic."

"And one of us still hasn't. Are you going to tell me?"

I told him: about the well-tailored suit, the gold cigarette lighter, the voice of January ice. I didn't tell him about the kiss, or how, in the contemptuous set of Bic's shoulders, I could still see the first arms that had held me.

But I think he knew.

The questions he asked me, though, were about the case.

"Do you think it's true that he—he and the Main Street Boys—didn't kill Hsing?"

"I don't know. I got a feeling he knew something he wasn't telling me but he wouldn't mind if I found it out."

"Which means?"

"It could mean it was something useful for us to know— useful to him, I mean; he obviously doesn't give a damn whether it's useful to us—but it would look bad if it came from him. Bad for his reputation, something he'd lose face for revealing."

"Any idea what it was?"

"Uh-uh. But: he did say he'd 'heard' that Hsing had stolen the porcelains working for Lee Kuan Yue."

"That," Bill said, lighting another cigarette, "is very interesting. Lee says Hsing stole porcelains from *him*. Bic says Lee and Hsing stole porcelains from Chinatown Pride. And Lee and Franco Ciardi say Lee doesn't deal in stolen porcelains at all."

"I wish I knew whether the cup Hsing gave his mother was one of ours." I chewed on my lip with what I thought was frustration; then I realized it was hunger. "Do you have any food in this house?"

"Never. You want me to call the take-out Chinese place?" He grinned.

"That dump on the corner? You're kidding, of course."

"Of course," he agreed. "I could make you scrambled eggs."

"I can make them," I offered dubiously.

"I insist."

He made me three eggs with fresh-ground pepper, scrambled in the pan, and brought them to the table with toasted slices of sourdough bread cut from a loaf from the freezer. He had butter in a butter dish and homemade orange marmalade from a farm stand, and put everything on the table on woven straw place mats.

"I'm impressed," I said. "I didn't know this about you."

"I do a mean peanut butter sandwich, too."

Starting on the eggs, I said, "Tell me about your date. Rosie the Queen of Wherever."

"Killarney. Actually she's from Dublin, which is nowhere near Killarney."

"And I suppose you know all about her childhood and all her relatives by now, too."

"The Irish are like the Chinese. They have too many relatives to ever know all about them."

"You don't."

"I'm only half Irish."

"Oh. So: Rosie."

"Rosie. Rosie says she never saw Dr. Caldwell before about two weeks ago. He came to the house, was received cordially—Rosie remembers Mrs. Blair saying it was a pleasure to meet him, which I took as a hint they didn't know each other already—stayed for a brief visit during which Rosie was asked not to interrupt them—she thinks that was Dr. Caldwell's idea, by the way—and then he left, on what Rosie thinks was a bad note."

"No kidding." I chomped into a piece of toast, a little bit

burnt on the top, just the way I like it. "Does she have any idea what the bad note was about?"

"She says not."

"And she says she never saw Caldwell before, even though Mrs. Blair told us he and Mr. Blair consulted?"

"They must have done it outside the house."

"Mr. Blair was a recluse, I thought."

"Well, according to Rosie, he did go out, though not often. He preferred the company of his porcelains to the company of most people, except his wife. Visitors rarely came to the house, and no one ever was invited to see the collection."

"Not even Mrs. Blair's brother?"

"The elusive Lee Kuan Yue. Rosie says no."

"Well," I said, polishing off my eggs, "that's great. The Main Street Boys didn't kill Hsing Chung Wah, Lee Kuan Yue doesn't deal in stolen porcelains, Dr. Caldwell didn't know Mrs. Blair, and nobody ever saw the Blair collection. I suppose . . ." The phone rang, cutting off Bill's chance to find out what I supposed.

He got over to his desk before the second ring. "Smith. Yes. All right. Where are you?" He looked at me and nodded. I rose, listening to the urgency and the reassurance in his voice. "I can find it. Stay there. Don't leave. We'll be right there."

"Steve?" I said, as he hung up.

"Steve." He threw me my jacket, grabbed his own. "He's at a bar in the Village. He promised not to leave until we got there."

He locked up. We clattered down the stairs and into the first cab we saw.

## TWENTY-FIVE

The bar was Dusty's, one of the Greenwich Village bars along West Street that would have a great view across the Hudson River if anyone were interested in looking out. What they were interested in looking at, though, when Bill and I walked in about ten minutes later, was us. It was a shadowy place, track lights concentrating on odd oil paintings with household appliances in them and not bothering much about the darkness in the corners or the veils of cigarette smoke swaying above the tables. The hour was edging up to midnight but Rusty's was packed, techno-rock music charging out of speakers to help sweating pairs of men follow the beat on a small dance floor to the rear. I was the only woman I could see, which would have made me stand out except that my leather jacket fit right in. I thought that gave me points, but I didn't notice that anybody cared; they all seemed to find Bill much more noteworthy.

"Hel-*lo*," a man with a carefully trimmed goatee and three gold earrings in his left ear said over the music, smiling at Bill as we made our way into the room. "You're new here." He didn't look at me at all. Bill nodded noncommittally. He may have been about to say something, but a figure rose and an arm waved and Steve Bailey called, "Ms. Chin! Over here."

The man with the earrings looked disappointed as Bill and I crossed the room to join Steve in his booth near the dance floor. He stayed half-standing until we got there, as though he were afraid he'd lose sight of us. He had a beer in front of him, and he wore a leather jacket and an anxious expression.

"Where have you *been?*" He looked from one of us to the other. "I've been calling all night. Jesus. I have to talk to you. I have to tell you what happened. I—oh, god, did you go up there?" His wide eyes rested on me, and I nodded. "Did you—did you see what happened?"

"Tell us what happened, Steve," I said.

A waiter, a skinny young man with black daggers tattooed on his forearms, came to our booth. Bill ordered beers for himself and Steve and a club soda for me. I kept my eyes on Steve.

"I'm scared," he said. A thought seemed to strike him. "Did you tell anyone where I am?"

"No," I said. "Have you been here all night?"

He nodded. "I come here all the time. They know me. I guess I figured I'd be safe. Oh, god. Was that stupid?"

"Safe from what? Steve, tell us what happened. Why did you call us?"

"Safe from him." He spoke as if he were surprised I didn't know that was what he meant. "I called you—well, that's different. Wait, I don't know, maybe it's not. That's what I'm afraid of, that it was him."

"That what was him, Steve?"

"The man who—the man who—" He gulped, opened his mouth, closed it again. "The man who—" He seemed stuck, like a needle on a record. His eyes widened with alarm.

"The man who killed Trish?" Bill asked calmly, as though it were a natural thing to say.

Steve turned to him, nodded slowly. The tattooed waiter came and went, leaving our drinks. Steve looked into his, quickly gulped some of it, put it down and spoke. "He came this morning. That's why I called you. He was looking for stolen porcelains. I mean, I guessed that was why you came, even though the Director didn't tell us. He acted like it was confidential. Well, he should. I mean, he shouldn't go around telling secret things if they're secret. But you *were* private investigators and you were interested in porcelains and so was he and he said he was looking for stolen ones so I figured so

177

were you probably and then after I talked to Trish I thought—I thought—"

"Steve," I said, "slow down." He sounded like a train about to roar off the tracks. "Who was this man, the one who came this morning?"

"He was a private detective. His name was Jim Johnson. He wanted to see the Director, but he was out, so he talked to me and Trish." Steve gulped some more beer, then went on. "He said he was looking for some stolen porcelains and wanted to know if we knew of any on the market—you know, if the museum had been offered any. He described some of them. Trish is the—was the—was the porcelain person, not me, and she said no, we hadn't been offered anything recently, but she'd look out for them. He said he'd be in touch. Then he left."

"What did he look like?"

"Just sort of average. A little taller than me, but not as tall as you," nodding to Bill. "Brown hair. I guess maybe brown eyes, too. I didn't really look. I'm sorry."

"Did he see Dr. Caldwell?"

"No."

"And that's why you called us? Because of his visit?"

"Almost. I mean, I might have anyway, but after I talked to Trish . . . ," he stalled out.

"After you talked about what, Steve?" I asked, to keep him moving.

"The pieces. The pieces Jim Johnson asked about. Well, one of them really." He drank some more beer, and then blurted, as though confessing a transgression he really needed to get off his chest, "It was ours."

"Yours?" Bill and I exchanged glances. "It belonged to the Kurtz?"

Steve nodded miserably. "It did. I'm sure it did. But Trish said no, I was wrong. But I thought about it, and I looked. I'm not wrong."

"If Trish was the Kurtz's porcelain expert, why do you know about this piece?"

"She wasn't really our porcelain expert," he corrected me, sounding distracted. "I mean, porcelains were her field, but the Director is the real expert. Oh, but anyway, that doesn't matter," he said, impatient with himself. "The thing is, Trish and I help each other pack and unpack. When shipments come in or go out. Gifts and loans and stuff. Things come and go from museums all the time, you know."

"I didn't know. But go on."

"Well, anyway, we do. Help each other." He swallowed. "Did." He picked up his beer, then put it down without drinking any. "That piece came about a year ago. It was a covered dish, small, like for cooked fruit or something. I remember it because it had a dog's head knob on the lid, and dogs painted on it, and they weren't Chinese dogs. They were spotted terrier kinds of dogs, which meant they must have been copied from the customer's sketch. They did that all the time. But I remember it because I had a dog that looked just like that when I was a kid."

"Could there be another dish like it?"

"Oh, sure there could. That wouldn't be strange. There could have been a whole set. What was strange was Trish telling me I was wrong. You know how I am. I mean, I'm not subtle. I always make too much noise. I got excited to see Spike on a museum dish, and I went on about it. She thought it was funny, and she agreed he was a cute little dog, and I told her about the tricks he used to do. But then yesterday she told me I was wrong, and we'd never had a dish like that."

"Did Jim Johnson know you recognized the dish?"

"I said, 'Oh, that sounds like that one we have, remember, Trish?' and she said, 'No, we never had anything like that,' and she gave me this sort of look which means, 'Shut up, Steve.' So I shut up because I thought she didn't want him to know for some reason. But when he left and I asked her she acted as though we *really* never had that dish. And I know we did."

"All right," I said. "Tell us the rest. How do you know about Trish?"

"About Trish." His soft blue eyes blinked. "I went up

179

there," he said. "To meet you. We close at four-thirty, and I went out to do some errands. Trish was still there when I left, but she said she was leaving soon, and when I got back the museum was dark. I went in—"

"You have a key?"

"Sure. We all do, Trish and the Director and me."

"What about the alarm system?" Bill wanted to know.

"That was a little weird. It was off. But sometimes, like if someone's just running out to pick up a sandwich, like if you're working late, we don't put it on, because it's complicated and if you screw it up the security company gets mad and sometimes the cops come. In fact it worried me a little that it was off. I was afraid the Director or Trish might be coming back, and they'd be there when you got there. But there wasn't anything I could do about it, and anyway it was dark, so I went up, and I got to the office, and I turned on the light . . . and there she was. Blood, and papers, and the computers all smashed . . . all this blood . . ." He looked away from us, his face gray-white in the smokey, packed room. The pounding of the rock music had increased steadily while we talked, so that we'd been leaning close, focussing tightly on each other's loud voices. Steve stared into the gyrating crowd, holding his lips squashed shut. I wondered if he was going to be sick.

He suddenly turned back to us. "I think it was him."

"Jim Johnson?" I asked.

He nodded.

"You think he killed Trish?"

He nodded again. "Doesn't it make sense?"

"Not really," I said gently. "Why would he do that?"

"Oh," Steve said, blinking. "Oh. I didn't tell you the other thing."

"What other thing?"

"He called. He called back later."

"Johnson?"

"Uh-huh. I was in the Director's office, filing something, but I heard Trish talk to him. She told him I wasn't there. I guess he must have wanted to ask me about the dish. But then

180

she talked to him some more. She said she wanted to meet him, that she might be able to help him, maybe."

"Did they arrange to meet?"

"I think so, but I couldn't hear where. But it could have been there, after work."

Bill tapped the ash from his cigarette. "Steve," he said, "why did you want us to come up to the museum? Why didn't you arrange to meet us somewhere else, where there wasn't any chance of running into anyone?"

"I wanted to show you. In the computer. I was right."

"About the dish?" I said.

"I looked it up. Later, when Trish went to the bathroom. I called it up in the computer, in the Acquisitions file. It's there. That stupid dish. It's there."

## TWENTY-SIX

The music continued to pound, and the air had grown so smokey and thickly warm that I was beginning to long for the wind-blown January streets.

"Steve," I said, "the police are looking for you. Did you know that?"

"The police?" He turned even paler, if that was possible. "Me? Why?"

"You had a key to the museum. You were supposed to meet us there. You weren't there when we got there, and Trish was dead."

"Wait—they think I killed her?" He said it as though it were a totally new idea. "That's crazy. Why would I do that?"

"They look at everybody," I said. "They have to. You have to go see them, Steve."

"I have to go to the police? But what if he finds me?"

"Who, Johnson?"

He nodded rapidly. "What if whatever reason he killed Trish for, he thinks I know about it too?"

"Tell the police about him. Tell them that's why you haven't called them."

"Will you come with me?"

I looked to Bill.

"It might be a good idea," he said. "They're going to want to check his story with us anyway. And ours with him. If we don't come in with him they'll wonder why."

So the three of us inched our way through the throbbing music and the now shoulder-to-shoulder crowd of leather-jacketed men until we reached the door. West Street, when we hit it, seemed to me more like the vast, empty, quiet reaches of an Alaskan glacier than it probably ever had to anyone before.

Glacier or not, we found a cab right away, and after a wordless ride uptown presented ourselves at the Nineteenth Precinct. Outside, it looks like the building that's been there for more than a hundred years, but the inside is all new and shiny and fluorescent-lit, reflecting modern police operations in a city where crime and cops never sleep.

After midnight, though, the cops get a little chip on their shoulders about it.

At the main desk, which is up on a platform so even people like Bill aren't taller than the cop in charge, we asked for Detective Bernstein. The desk sergeant made a phone call, and a uniformed cop took us up in an elevator. In the squad room Bernstein was leaning back in a desk chair, watching for our entrance. When we made it, he didn't get up.

"I knew I should've left ten minutes ago. What do you people want?"

"We can come back if this isn't a convenient time," I offered cooperatively.

"I already told you, don't get smart with me," Bernstein said without particular hostility. "Who's this?"

"Steve Bailey," I told him, since Steve didn't answer.

"Oh ho, no shit." Bernstein showed a glimmer of interest. "Where've you been, Mr. Bailey?"

Steve swallowed, and then looked at me, and then told Bernstein where he'd been.

Then came a period when Steve, Bill, and I were all talking to different cops in different rooms, so they could make sure the where-Steve-had-been-all-evening stories matched. Then the cop talking to me left and was replaced, after the required period of leaving me alone with my thoughts—presumably so my conscience would start to gnaw at me and I'd confess—by Bernstein.

"It's so nice to see you again, Miss Chin," Bernstein said, not too weary to be sarcastic. He tugged at his trouser legs and plopped his bulk into a molded plastic chair. "Especially in the company of a material witness—maybe even a suspect—who I've been looking for all night."

"I'm happy to help, Detective."

"Let's talk about porcelains. The theft you're investigating for the client you won't name."

"That's right."

"What if I told you Bailey already named them?"

"He doesn't know who my client is. No one at the Kurtz does, or did."

"Ah, what the hell. I didn't think it would work." He rubbed his upper lip and regarded me thoughtfully. "You still going to try to tell me your case has nothing to do with this?"

"I really don't know," I said. "I'm not sure what Steve's story even means. Or if it's true. If it is, this Jim Johnson seems kind of important."

"If he exists."

"I think he does," I said slowly. "But that's probably not his name."

"Oh?"

I told him what Franco Ciardi had told us. "And Mr. Ciardi says he checked with the State Board, and there's no Jim Johnson with a p.i. license in New York," I finished.

Bernstein nodded. "Well, at least that's true."

"You know that?"

"I just ran him, after I heard Bailey's story."

"Steve's afraid of him. He's afraid he's next."

"If he exists," Bernstein said again.

"If he does, Steve could be in danger."

"Yeah. And if he doesn't, Bailey could be full of crap. Come to think of it, even if he does, Bailey could be full of crap. Don't get your shorts in a knot." He waved his hand as I was about to speak. "We're sticking him in a hotel with a cop in the hall, at least for tonight."

"Not in jail?"

"It'd make me happier," he admitted. "But I don't have a motive and I can't link him to the weapon, except that it came from his desk. That's not enough to indict, so why bother? This way at least I'll know where he is while I'm looking. And just in case he's right, maybe I'll be a hero and save his life, too. You know, Miss Chin, it would be awfully nice if you told me who your client was."

His sudden change of topic threw me. My confusion made me realize how exhausted I was. I shook my head. "I can't do that, Detective. Trish's death may have nothing to do with them. Steve found the door open. Maybe so did someone else. Someone came in to rob the place, was surprised by Trish, and panicked."

"On the third floor?"

I shrugged. "Trish's murder isn't my case. The stolen porcelains are my case."

Bernstein stood abruptly. "All right. Look. I've had it, I'm leaving. I'm giving you twenty-four hours. Maybe I'll find Johnson, maybe Bailey'll confess. Maybe *you'll* confess. If I don't have somebody in the tank by tomorrow night, I'm going to pick you up as a material witness and hold you until you give me all the details. Good night, Miss Chin."

He turned his broad back on me and strode out, leaving the door open.

I took the hint and left too.

*    *    *

This time it was my turn to head north. The desk sergeant wouldn't tell me whether Bill or Steve were still being questioned. I could get a lawyer, and demand to know, and spend all night doing this; or, knowing that Steve—according to Bernstein—was taken care of, I could wait awhile for Bill, who could take care of himself. If he didn't show, I could go home, sleep, and find him in the morning. The worst that could have happened was that he'd irritated some cop enough that he'd be spending the night in jail.

It wouldn't be the first time, after all.

Two blocks up Third the windows of an all-night coffee shop spilled hard-edged blocks of light out into the street. One cup of tea, I promised myself, and then I'd go. I ordered the tea and a carrot-raisin muffin from a skinny Greek teenager who looked sleepier than I felt. He passed my order in Greek to the T-shirted man behind the counter. So tired I was bone-cold, I kept my jacket zipped and slumped into the corner of a padded booth, listening to the to-me meaningless, guttural rhythms of their casual conversation.

We were on to something. This Jim Johnson meant something, I knew that. The dish with Steve Bailey's childhood dog on it meant something, and the fact that someone else—even someone who made my gut clench the way Matt Yin did—had connected Hsing Chung Wah with Lee Kuan Yue meant something.

Something, something, something. What a silly-sounding word. It ought to be spelled with a "p" in the middle. Sumpthing. Okay, Lydia, go home. Drink your tea so you don't fall asleep in the cab, and then go home.

I nibbled my muffin, drank my tea. I watched the door, asked for more hot water, forced my eyes to stay open. I gave up, asked for my check, and stood.

Bill walked in as the skinny kid handed me my change at the cash register.

"Gee," he said. "I waited for you before."

"I knew you were about to walk in, so I paid so we wouldn't waste time."

"What about my coffee?"

I bought him a cup of black coffee to go and we went.

In the cab on the way home we talked but it didn't do us any good. I told Bill that Bernstein had Steve packed away, and Bill told me that Bernstein hadn't had much to say to him beyond the usual warnings.

"He's going to lock me up tomorrow if he doesn't get anybody else to lock up," I said.

"Me too."

"Well, that'll be cozy."

We talked some more. Bill had the same sense I did, that we were getting close, but he didn't know, either, what we were getting close to.

I looked out the window while he drank his coffee. I wondered if everyone else I saw moving under streetlights and in the darkness of the city shadows was as cold and exhausted as I was. I felt sorry for everyone who wasn't in a warm cab on their way home.

"Bill?" I said.

"Hmmm?" he answered through a sip of coffee.

"Were you surprised to find Steve at a place like Dusty's?"

"You mean a gay bar in the Village?"

"Yes."

"No."

"Me either. I almost expected it, just from the way he acted when we met him that one time."

"You're getting at something."

Something. That dumb word again. "I told you what Dr. Caldwell said about not knowing whether Steve and Trish had a romantic relationship. It just strikes me as sort of weird that Caldwell didn't know Steve was gay."

"Maybe he did know. Maybe he was trying to do Steve a

favor by not bringing it up. To guys Caldwell's age being out isn't automatic."

"But still . . ."

"Still what?"

"I don't know. The way he said it. He made saying Steve couldn't have done it sound like . . . like he was lying for Steve, or something." Something. Leave me alone, you stupid word.

"Is it possible he was trying to help Steve by confusing things?"

"That's not very smart."

"People don't necessarily think very well when they're in shock."

I didn't answer.

"I think we just have to sleep on it," Bill said, finishing his coffee. "That's not a pass, by the way."

"Yes it is," I murmured, my eyes already closed, my head lolling against the cab's back seat. "It's just not a very good one."

The cab rolled across Canal into Chinatown. Chinatown's not a late-night place. All the corrugated shutters were locked down and the neon signs were dark. The streetlights cast a wide, lonely glow on near-empty streets. When the cab stopped at my building I turned automatically to Bill, to kiss him good night, but I got suddenly confused. Since I'd been so obnoxious about his making a pass at me, maybe it wasn't fair of me to kiss him. And maybe he wouldn't want me to. And maybe I was too tired to think about it.

Bill solved the problem by leaning over and kissing my cheek.

"Call me," he said. "As soon as you're up."

I watched the cab pull away. Then, taking out my single key, I climbed the flights to my own front door.


I fell asleep immediately, probably before I actually lay down. But somewhere around four I woke, with a nagging feeling that there was something I needed to do. "Go back to sleep?" I suggested to myself, but that wasn't it. I lay blankly on my pillows waiting for inspiration. It didn't come, but the slightly guilty thought that I'd gone to bed without my cup of Mr. Gao's unpleasant tea did.

Since I wasn't sleeping, I got up. I tiptoed through our silent apartment to the kitchen to make my tea. At the living room window I stopped to watch the clouds blow away over the rooftops of Chinatown. The moon, close to full, glinted icily. Today had been gray; tomorrow, it seemed, was going to be clear.

As I turned from the window a gleam of moonlight fell on the cabinet where my mother keeps the little mud figures of scholars and horses and carp for longevity that my father used to collect. One of the gods—the one who stuffs evil spirits into a wine barrel—glared at me with his mock-fierce expression, the face that had always made me laugh as a child when my father imitated it.

"Yeah," I whispered to the figure, so I wouldn't wake my mother, "you're about as tough as I am. You don't scare me."

He snarled all the harder, as though scaring me was the point. The colored glazes of his robes threw little glittering stars of moonlight into the room. I turned to walk past him. One step, and then I stopped. I turned back, staring at him and his companions.

"Oh," I whispered. "Oh oh oh oh oh."

As I dashed back to my room to call Bill the wine barrel god's glare had taken on a triumphant air.

The phone rang twice. "Smith," Bill muttered, then coughed a smoker's cough.

"Wake up. It's me."

"What's wrong?" he demanded, and from his voice I knew a jolt of adrenaline had wakened him fully.

"Nothing's wrong. Mrs. Hsing's cup. I know where we saw it before."

I told him the wine barrel god's inspiration.

"He's a genius," Bill said, when I was done.

"What about me?" I asked indignantly.

"You're a good medium. All right, go back to bed. Nothing's going to happen now. We'll go in the morning."

I knew he was right, but I said, "You have to be kidding. I can't sleep now."

"Sure you can. The sleep of the righteous."

"Me?"

"Try it."

He was right. I slept soundly for the next couple of hours. But before I tried, I went back to the kitchen and brewed Mr. Gao's tea. While it was steeping I tiptoed back to the living room, lit three sticks of incense, and stuck them in my mother's little altar to burn down. I wasn't really sure of the right way to do this, but I figured the wine barrel god would know it was for him.

## TWENTY-SEVEN

In the morning I woke all stiff. I stumbled into the bathroom, dumped a package of Mr. Gao's herbs into a steaming tub of water, and sat there feeling my muscles melt. I deep-breathed the fragrance of the floating twigs and petals. It cleared my head.

When, softened and passably supple, I wrapped myself in my thick robe and padded into the kitchen, I found my mother hanging the shirt and pants I had worn the night before on the creaky clothesline that runs outside our kitchen window. The frigid January air blasted in as she leaned, clothespins in mouth, out over the windowsill.

"Ma, what are you doing?" I objected. "I'll take them to the laundry."

"They smell terrible," she scolded me, mumbling through the clothespins. "Stale smoke and sweat. I'd be too ashamed to let the laundry have them until they've aired out. They won't be clean but at least they'll smell like it. You must have been in a very unhealthy place last night, Ling Wan-ju."

More than one, I thought. For more than one reason.

When I left it was still early, not yet eight-thirty. The day was clear, as the night had promised, and seemed a little warmer than the one before it. I took a cab to Bill's. We jumped in the rush-hour subway and sped uptown.

Bill had suggested a cab uptown, too, if I wasn't feeling up to being jostled by crowds, but at that hour it doesn't pay to try to drive, and the subways are frequent and fast.

And it never pays to admit you're not up to something.

We arrived at the brown brick building off West End twenty minutes after we left Bill's. The doorman remembered us, and called upstairs. Soon we were in the wheezing elevator, and then walking the worn carpet, and then knocking on Dr. Browning's door.

The door opened part way, and Dr. Browning's wide eyes and thick glasses peered out. His head moved slowly back and forth from Bill to me, as though he were comparing us to photographs he thought he might have seen once.

"Well," he said. He smiled the little shy smile. "Ms. Chin. And Mr. Smith. This is an unexpected pleasure. What can I do for you?"

"There's something we'd like to ask you about," I told him. "May we come in?"

"Oh. Oh, my, of course." Dr. Browning stood aside in the doorway, and we came in.

The dimness, the paper snowdrifts, the musty smell were the same, and if anything had been moved since we were here last, I wouldn't be the one to be able to prove it.

"Would you like to sit?" Dr. Browning asked with bashful pride. He gestured at the spaces Bill had cleared on the small sofa and the chair at our last visit. They were still clear, and their cushions still showed the imprints of us. The piles

Bill had moved to the floor were still where he'd put them, and would probably stay there, I thought, until some other force of nature put them somewhere else.

I'd seen Bill's eyes, when we first came in, search out what we'd come to see, although, when he'd found it, his expression hadn't changed. Now he smiled, thanked Dr. Browning, and sat, his jacket loosely open, his whole demeanor casual and friendly.

I didn't sit, although I smiled also. I wandered over to the china cabinet on the wall, the one glittering thing in this dusty room, the one place where, instead of disappearing into the shadows like a footfall into carpet, light bounced and played and shot little piercing sparks into the dimness of years.

Just like the wine barrel god's cabinet in my own living room.

"They are lovely," I murmured. "Your collection."

"Oh," Dr. Browning blushed. "Well, they're so small, but they're quite special. Each of them really is wonderful, in its way. Thank you for noticing."

I turned to him, some part of me already apologizing silently for what I was about to say. "You might not thank me, Dr. Browning, for what I noticed. Would you take one of them out for me?"

"Take one of them out? One of my little ones? Why— why would you want me to do that?" He moved protectively toward the cabinet.

I looked from him to the small, shiny porcelains on the shelves, and I caught Bill's eye. "Well," I said, "I suppose that may not be necessary." I studied the shelves again, and then navigated the paper hillocks to the small sofa. "But I think you know which piece we've come to talk about."

Dr. Browning remained standing, his owl-eyes regarding me through their thick lenses. Neither Bill nor I spoke; we waited. The silence was as thick and old as the dust that was everywhere. Slowly, Dr. Browning's thin, stooped form seemed to deflate; he sank into the desk chair as though his legs were finally too weak to support their burden.

When he spoke, his words were so soft that I had to lean forward to hear him.

"The truth is," he whispered, with a small, sad smile I didn't understand, "that I don't. Although I might hazard a guess."

"I beg your pardon?" I said, more because I wasn't sure I'd heard him than because I expected him to explain himself.

"They're all . . . my little ones are all . . ." He trailed off, hands twisted in his lap, head bowed.

I glanced at Bill, then spoke again. "The cup." I tried to make my words gentle. "The tiger cup with the tiger on the lid. It's from the Blair collection, isn't it?"

Dr. Browning nodded, eyes still on the floor. "I thought that must be the one you meant." Suddenly he looked up. "I could tell you it isn't." That was offered in the tone of a hopeful suggestion, but before I could respond he folded in on himself again. "Oh, I'm no good at that," he sighed. "I always knew my only luck would be not to be found out. And it lasted such a long time, too, my luck. But I always knew this would happen one day, and there'd be nothing I could do about it. I'm no good at the bold-faced lie."

"Dr. Browning," I asked, "what are you saying?"

The great owl-eyes blinked at me. "Stolen," he said. "All of them. My little ones are all stolen."

The thick silence covered the room again.

Bill and I looked at each other; then my glance went back to the cabinet, all the proud little pieces standing to attention.

"All?" I said lamely. "All of them?"

He nodded again. "On an assistant professor's salary," he said, as though it were an explanation. "An assistant art history professor, in a field so unglamorous. I could never have collected. Not even my little ones."

He rose, shuffled over to the cabinet. From his trouser pocket he pulled a long gold keychain, hand over hand the way you'd draw a bucket up from a well. With the gold key on the end he unlocked the cabinet. The door opened silently on well-oiled hinges. Dr. Browning removed the tiger cup, held it in both hands while he regarded it. Then he locked the cabinet and, walking slowly to the small sofa, handed the cup to me.

"I knew this would happen," he said, seating himself again. "It was bound to. I was never a very good thief. But I'm glad it's you, Ms. Chin. And Mr. Smith," he added politely. "I am. I like you, you see." He blushed furiously, his eyes fixed firmly on the dark patterns in the carpet.

I held the delicate, translucent cup to what gray light had managed to make its way through the windows' grime. The red tiger shimmered, and its eyes glowed. It seemed alive, about to flick its tail, about to spring into fierce flight across the room.

"I'm not sure I understand," I said. "All these pieces are stolen? Stolen from where?"

"From so many places," was his answer. "Wherever I found them. So many dark places."

The meaning of that was not clear to me. I tried to find another direction to come at this from. "The platter we saw at the Kurtz? That one too?"

Dr. Browning smiled as if in fond memory. "Oh, my, yes, such a beautiful piece. Quite unique in the height of the lip on its rim, for the time. From the Harwood House Museum," he added. "In Concord, Illinois."

"You stole it?" I asked, trying to make sense of this. "You stole it from one museum and gave it away to another?"

"Well, yes," Dr. Browning answered. "Of course. I donate all the large pieces. I can't possibly display them here." He gestured around the shadowy room, with its paper mountains and bookcase crags, showing me what I must have unaccountably forgotten.

"Displaying them?" Bill asked in a soft voice, speaking for the first time. "That's the point?"

Dr. Browning nodded vigorously. "Yes, of course. So they can be seen. Why else would I take them?"

"Some people," I suggested, "steal for money."

"Money?" He looked horrified. "You mean, sell them? Try to . . ." he paused, seeming to search for a word, ". . . *fence* them?" He blushed again. "I? Ms. Chin, I wouldn't have the first idea of how to go about that. Nor any reason to. Whatever untoward profit these pieces might bring me, were I to follow the path you suggest, with it would come a degree of guilt that I'm sure would be unbearable. The guilt I already suffer is, I assure you, quite difficult enough to carry."

"Then why do you do it?" I asked.

"As Mr. Smith has suggested," he answered patiently. "In order that they might be seen."

"Dr. Browning," I began; but he continued on his own, in a slow but steady rhythm, as though a gate had been opened and what had been locked inside could not now be prevented from marching out.

"The little ones," he said, "the little ones, you see, are so rarely displayed. Even when most of the collection is out, the little ones are often left behind. In the basement, or in a stuffy attic. In dark boxes, where no one sees them from one year to the next. Think of that, snow to spring to summer, and still no one to admire them. Except the occasional dried-up scholar, who'll unpack them, turning them in his hand looking for the brushstroke or chop that will prove his pet theory, then pack them away again, for years and years . . . No, Ms. Chin. It's simply unacceptable."

I thought of myself in the basement of the Kurtz, the melancholy feeling I'd had at the thought of all those bright objects shut in all those dark boxes.

"The occasional scholar?" I asked. "That was you?"

He blushed again, as though at a compliment. "It's been my privilege to have studied most of the major collections of export porcelains over the years. And many smaller ones also," he added, keeping the record straight.

"And you stole from them? While you were studying them?" I was trying to keep my voice matter-of-fact. Lydia Chin comes across this sort of thing every day.

"Yes, indeed. Though rarely anything large," he said earnestly. "Certain items, like the Harwood Platter . . . well, they weren't going to display it, you see. They hadn't the space. They received their porcelains in a bequest from a local gentleman who'd been fond of the place. But they know little about porcelains, and their staff, bless them, are overworked as it is."

"So you took it," I said. "And no one noticed?"

"Why, they never do, do they? Remember, Ms. Chin, these are the pieces no one unpacks from year's end to year's end."

"The Blair collection cup." Bill spoke up from the dimness of the large armchair. "Why did you take that?"

Dr. Browning turned to him. "For the same reason, of course. Nora was not going to display it."

"How do you know that?" Bill asked.

"They have such little space in that tiny museum. And, after all, there were two."

"There *were* two!" I burst out. Dr. Browning gave a little jump in his chair. "There were! The other one *was* ours, then!"

"I'm so sorry?" Dr. Browning's apologetic voice was tentative. He fixed his worried eyes on the tiger cup I was still holding. He seemed ready to charge to its rescue if I did anything else loud or sudden. "I don't understand."

I placed the cup gently on the top of the bookcase beside me before I spoke. "I saw another cup yesterday," I said. "Exactly like this one. There are good reasons to believe it was stolen. If it was, it was stolen from CP with the rest of the things from the Blair collection, wasn't it?"

Dr. Browning kept his eyes warily on me as he answered. "Most likely," he said. "There may be others like it, of course. But there was one in the Blair collection crates that are now gone."

"You didn't tell us about it," I said. "It wasn't in your photographs or on your list."

"Well, I hardly could, could I? You were sitting right here questioning me about the collection, right here with my little cabinet. I was terrified, even so, that somehow you'd know about it, that you'd see my cup and my secret would be out. I've always been afraid like that, you see." He smiled a sweet smile. "I'm rather glad it's over."

The question of what was and wasn't over for Dr. Brown-

195

ing was, I suspected, more complicated than he thought. I left it for another time.

"That cup," I asked. "Had you photographed it?"

"Yes, of course. That was part of the task with which Nora charged me."

"Where's the photograph now?"

"I destroyed it. I'm sorry," he added anxiously when I frowned, although my frown was more in thought than in anger.

"Professor," Bill said, in an easy, friendly manner, "you weren't quite truthful with us about the photographs. May I take it that you were less than candid about other things, too?"

I wasn't quite sure what he was getting at, but Dr. Browning nodded as though he had been expecting the question.

"Mr. Blair's inventory lists," Bill went on. "They're more complete than you led us to believe."

"Yes," Dr. Browning agreed. "Mr. Blair was a thorough man."

He lifted the battered briefcase, stood it on his knees, extracted a file, and replaced the briefcase on the carpet. A small cloud of dust arose to cheer its return.

Dr. Browning opened the file. "I couldn't let you see this, because my—acquisition—was on it. And I honestly didn't believe it could help you locate the thief." He blushed, dropping his eyes to the floor, smiling the shy smile again. "The other thief."

"Dr. Browning," I said, more because I felt I had to than because I wanted to, "there *is* another thief, isn't there?"

"Another . . ." His round eyes widened as he realized what I was saying. "Oh, my. Yes. Oh, my. You don't think I stole all those pieces? From Nora? Oh, I never could have done that. How terrible! What you must think of me! Oh, Miss Chin, never. Only my little ones. Only so that they can be admired. Never in quantity! From a friend? Oh, never."

He sat hunched in his chair, deflated to the point where I thought he might collapse. His mouth quivered. I was afraid his great round eyes would fill with tears. Before that could happen, I said, "I'm sorry, Dr. Browning." Apologizing to a thief for thinking he might have stolen something? What are you coming to, Lydia? "I did have to ask."

"Yes, I quite understand." Dr. Browning withdrew a handkerchief from his pocket and blew his nose. He took a determined breath, replaced the handkerchief, and returned to the file on his lap. "Shall I?" he asked with dignity.

"Please," I said.

He opened the folder, extracted a sheet of yellow legal pad paper. It was a list in fine fountain pen ink, written in a firm, legible hand. "I still don't see what good it could do you," he said. "But in the spirit of—I believe it's called 'coming clean'?—I'm happy to give it to you."

He handed Bill the list. I stood and peered over Bill's shoulder. Nine pieces were described briefly, with dates listed beside them. A group of letters—either ASR, PKM, or SG—stood next to each date. Two of the pieces were a pair; they were the tiger cups.

"What is this exactly?" I asked.

"It seems to be Mr. Blair's record of the new acquisitions. He fell ill, apparently, before he was able to complete his records in a formal manner. Nevertheless, all the information is there."

"The descriptions of the pieces?"

"And their acquisition dates and provenance."

"Provenance?" I wasn't entirely sure of what the word meant, and I didn't see anything on the list that looked like it might mean that.

"The source from which they were acquired. Somewhere among Mr. Blair's papers I'm sure Mrs. Blair, by now, will have found bills of sale and other formal documentation, although she hadn't at the point when she made her donation to the museum. In any case, Mr. Blair recorded for himself the source of each piece."

"These letters next to the dates?"

"Yes, exactly. If I may?" Dr. Browning reached for the paper, which Bill passed him. "These two, you see, were acquired from private collectors. ASR, that would be Dr. Arthur Reid, in Indiana. A lovely man. And SG is a Mrs. Grunewald in Boston. I've not met her, but I've no doubt this is she. The remainder of the new acquisitions seem to have come at one time from one source. You see? PKM. That would be right here in New York: the Peter Kurtz Museum."

My heart took a leap into my throat. Dr. Browning, looking pleased and cooperative, handed the list back to Bill. Pushing the words out around my heart, I said, "The Kurtz? He got the stolen pieces from the Kurtz?"

Dr. Browning turned his attention to me. "Why, yes. I expect they were deacquisitioning. Their collection is quite extensive. You've seen it, have you not?"

"Yes, we were there." More than once, I thought. For more than one reason. "Dr. Browning," I said, "we showed your photographs to Dr. Caldwell. He didn't give any sign of having ever seen those pieces before."

"Dr. Caldwell?" he asked. "You did? He didn't?"

Bill asked, "Could PKM mean anything else? Maybe another collector?"

"Oh, I don't think so," Dr. Browning said. "The attribution appears elsewhere in Mr. Blair's collection, and in fact it's rather commonly used in the profession to refer to the Kurtz Museum."

"Then why didn't Dr. Caldwell admit to knowing those pieces?" I asked.

"I—I wouldn't know."

I watched him. He watched the folded hands nervously twitching in his lap.

"No," I said. "But you know something, don't you?"

"I?" he said without looking up. "Oh, no. About what would I know anything?"

I glanced at Bill, who behind his friendly manner was watching Dr. Browning as intently as I was. I asked him a question with my eyes and he, with his, suggested I go ahead.

"Dr. Browning, this whole situation is more serious than I think you know." Dr. Browning didn't look up when I spoke, but focussed more intensely on his own twined fingers. "There have been two homicides possibly connected with this case. One occurred at the Kurtz Museum, last night."

Now he looked up, with a startled movement. "Homicides?" he whispered. "People have been killed? At the Kurtz?"

"One at the Kurtz. Trish Atherton, one of Dr. Caldwell's assistants. A porcelain expert."

"Oh, my. Oh, my. The poor girl. Who killed her?"

"The police are investigating, but so far they don't know. Dr. Browning, I can't help thinking that something you know is relevant to the stolen porcelains, and therefore possibly to these killings."

"Oh, my. Oh, I hope not. I can't see—" He broke off as if struck by a new thought. Slowly, he said, "But then, I don't know why I should expect to see. I'm not the expert in these matters."

"No," I said. "Maybe you should tell us whatever it is, and let us judge."

He looked back into his lap, as if to make sure his hands hadn't done anything while he wasn't watching. "Yes," he sighed. "Very well." He cleared his throat. "I don't even know, you understand, why I'm reluctant. I'm not sure whom I'm protecting. But I suppose both as an art professional, and as a . . . as a thief, I've felt this was something in the way of dirty laundry, not to be aired in public."

"Well," I said, trying to sound encouraging and patient, as opposed to jumping out of my skin, "maybe if you tell us . . . ?"

"Yes." He reorganized himself in his chair, realigning his feet to be precisely parallel and as tight to each other as possible, refolding his hands. "Well. It's about the records at the Kurtz. They're wrong, you see."

"The records?" I said.

"Yes. They're wrong."

"Wrong in what way?"

"Inaccurate. Incorrect."

"Professor," Bill broke in, probably to keep the top of my head from blowing off, "could you give us an example?"

Dr. Browning turned to him, then to the china cabinet. "Do you see," he said, his eyes and voice softening, "my lovely salt cellar? Not the larger one. The petite one on the top shelf. With the lotus blossom and the silver spoon."

In the gloom it was hard to pick out details on the individual pieces, but with the help of a gleam of stray light I found a finely painted blue lotus flower on a miniature bowl.

"Yes," Bill and I said together.

"It is from the collection of a gentleman in Canterbury."

"Canterbury, England?" Bill asked.

"Yes. One gets the occasional grant, you see. It's quite possible to travel and stay inexpensively in England and on the Continent, and there are so many important collections."

Bill said, "So you were in Canterbury studying this gentleman's collection, and you came home with this piece?"

"Yes, I suppose that's rather what happened." Dr. Browning's voice held a small note of wonder. "The gentleman had inherited his porcelains from a great-uncle, and had very little interest in or knowledge of them. I was studying them for a monograph I was writing. The gentleman was pleased that someone thought them worthy of study. He kept them packed away, you see."

"Tell us about the relationship between this piece and the Kurtz," I suggested as mildly as I could.

"Well. My trip to England took place four years ago. Not quite two years ago I had occasion to study some pieces in the Kurtz collection, for a similar monograph. I was given access to all the Kurtz porcelains, those in storage as well as those on display. I believe it was Ms. Atherton who made my arrangements, in fact."

"And you found . . . ?"

"To my surprise, I found a number of pieces from the collection of the gentleman in Canterbury."

Bill and I exchanged glances. "Why is that surprising?" I asked. "Couldn't he have sold them to the Kurtz? Dr. Caldwell goes to Europe on acquisition trips at least twice a year, from what I understand."

"Oh, yes, certainly. I would have felt nothing more than the pleasure of seeing old friends again," he said, without a trace of self-consciousness, "were it not for the records."

"What was wrong with them?" Oh, please, I thought, please just tell us.

"As I say, I had been in England two years previous to the period of my study at the Kurtz, and I had seen those pieces at the time. But the records at the museum listed those same pieces as having been acquired nine years before, under the previous Director, from a dealer in Belgium."

"I don't get it," I said. "The acquisition dates were false?"

"Yes, indeed," Dr. Browning said emphatically.

"Could you be mistaken? Could these be different pieces with the same design, or something?"

In answer, Dr. Browning gave me a brief pitying look, then rose and made his way to the china cabinet once again. He performed the ritual with key and lock, lifted out the salt cellar, and held it in the palm of his hand with the lotus blossom facing him. On the other side was a tiny painting of a house with six chimneys.

"This is the residence of the five-times-great-grandfather of the great-uncle of the gentleman in Canterbury. It was he who ordered the set from Canton in 1783. This house appears on all the set's pieces. There exist—in Canterbury—very clear records of the set's contents. Of certain items, platters and tureens for example, there was only one in any given shape and size. The set was compete when I studied it in Canterbury. There is no question of a mistake."

He carefully replaced the salt cellar and relocked the cabinet. He glanced longingly at the tiger cup, on the bookcase beside me, but said nothing as he returned to his seat.

"The dates are false," I said, as if by repetition this fact would reveal its own meaning. "But the pieces are genuine?"

"Oh, quite."

"Did you check with the gentleman in Canterbury, to see

if he had all his pieces?" Dr. Browning's eyes went to his salt cellar at the same time mine did. "No," I said. "I suppose you didn't."

"I had no reason to," he murmured by way of apology. "My monograph, after all, concerned the pieces, not their provenance."

"And so you decided it was none of your business?"

"Well, it wasn't. Was it?" His voice had an anxious quaver.

"You weren't just a little curious? You didn't ask Dr. Caldwell about it, as one professional to another?"

"Dr. Caldwell was abroad at the time. I'm not even sure he knew I was studying his collection. I did begin to mention to Ms. Atherton that I was uncomfortable with some of the Kurtz's provenance attributions and suggested she confirm them if she had the opportunity. The scholar in me demanded that. Then I'm afraid I rather backed down. The—the other part of me realized that it would be unfortunate if Ms. Atherton were to do anything that would alert the Canterbury gentleman that something was amiss in his collection."

"Dr. Browning," Bill asked, "could those pieces be fakes? A mistake of the previous Director's, something he was duped into buying?"

"It would be immensely difficult to fake a piece like those I saw," Dr. Browning assured Bill. "And immensely costly, also. I don't believe it would be worth it, for financial advantage."

"What about some other kind of advantage?" Bill asked. "Prestige, for example?"

"I can't see where such prestige would arise. One couldn't display a . . . a 'forged' piece of porcelain. We are, as I've said, a small fraternity. Such a piece might easily be recognized by someone who'd seen the genuine article the week before in its actual home. In any case, I did study them. As I say, I'm quite satisfied the Canterbury pieces I saw at the Kurtz were authentic."

Dr. Browning offered that comment half-apologetically,

as though his expertise in his field, while not to be questioned, were as much a source of embarrassment as pride.

Bill reached into his jacket with an automatic motion and lifted his pack of cigarettes halfway out of his shirt pocket. He always says a cigarette helps him think. Then he looked around, at the closed windows and the dusty carpet, the musty drapes. He pushed the pack back down.

Good thing, too, I thought, frustration making me short-tempered. All this room needs is a little cigarette smoke. We'd all end up smelling like my clothes from last night, the clothes my mother was too ashamed to send to the laundry.

A sudden vision of my mother, clothespins in her pursed mouth, burst like a roman candle in the room and was gone. Her scolding voice, though, rebuking me through clothespins, lingered.

"They won't be clean," mumbled the stale air. "But at least they'll smell like it."

"Laundry," I said.

Dr. Browning's great eyes widened. "I beg your pardon?"

Bill was more to the point. "What?"

"Laundry," I repeated, almost as surprised as they were. "The Kurtz. It's an art laundry."

The stuffy room was suddenly electric. "Go on," Bill said swiftly, straightening in the armchair. "Stolen art?"

"Stolen in Europe, bought cheap on Dr. Caldwell's 'acquisition' trips." I spoke as fast as I was thinking, and as disjointedly. "Maybe commissioned, maybe Caldwell just drops by to see what's in stock with a few people he knows, whenever he goes over. Brought here, given an earlier acquisition date and a provenance. Kept in storage awhile, years maybe, until it cools off. Then sold. 'Deacquisitioned.' Sold for what it's worth, because it's genuine. And bought probably for peanuts, because there's not much of a market in stolen porcelains. And I'll bet not silver or any other of those sorts of things. The sorts of things they have at the Kurtz. Am I right, Dr. Browning?"

"Decorative arts," Dr. Browning said after a moment, in a breathy voice, as if he'd gotten winded following me. "No, I don't suppose there is. Decorative objects tend to be bulky and breakable, or at least capable of being damaged: scratched or dented or mildewed. Unlike fine art paintings and drawings, which, once removed from their frames, are light and simple to transport. And the value of the objects is rarely high enough, one would think, to be worth the risk."

"So Caldwell buys low, because he's the only buyer. And sells high, because he's got the real goods," Bill said. "Is that our theory?"

"And because the goods have such a good provenance," I said. "They come from the collection at the Kurtz, after all."

"And as long as he never gets greedy," Bill said, "never tries to move too many pieces at once or asks too high a price, he can go on like this forever."

"Unless the pieces are recognized by someone and known to be stolen."

"And that would depend on the buyer."

"You mean, that the buyer would recognize them?"

"That might not be a problem. Maybe the buyer already knows and doesn't care. But you want to avoid too many people seeing them after the buyer buys them."

"So you don't sell, for example, to other museums."

"No." Bill said it before I could: "You sell to private collectors. The more private, the better."

We stared at each other. "Wow," I breathed. "He must have been a godsend, Mr. Blair."

"A reclusive collector. A man who loves to acquire and hates to have people around him. The perfect customer for stolen art."

"Dr. Browning?" I turned to the wide-eyed professor. "Is it possible? Could it have happened like that?"

Dr. Browning sat with his lips pressed tightly shut, his eyes glittering, a very strange expression on his face. Suddenly his lips burst apart. He threw his head back and let out a high-pitched bray and then collapsed into cackling peals of laughter.

"Dr. Browning?" I asked, slightly alarmed. "Are you all right?"

He started to speak. His words got caught in his chortles and they fell out of his mouth together. "A thief," he gasped with delight. "Roger Caldwell! A bigger thief than I am! Oh, my. Oh, my. Oh, my." He wiped his eyes, composed himself, then was struck by another fit of giggles. "Oh," he breathed, when that was spent. "My! Well, you never do know, do you?" He beamed at me and at Bill, with a smile that corrugated his cheeks like layers of soft clay.

"No," I said. "You never do."

## TWENTY-EIGHT

And we still don't," Bill pointed out, as we made our way through the world where the sun shone and the air moved, outside the dim stillness of Dr. Browning's apartment. "It's a theory. We may be way off."

"Uh-huh," I said happily. My mood couldn't be wet-blanketed that easily. "But at least now there's something we're way off *of.*"

We had left Dr. Browning's abruptly, trading vows of silence with him. He would tell no one what the scenario was that we'd sketched in his dusty air; in return, we would not speak of his little ones and how he'd come by them. This stand-off would continue until Bill and I had made the moves we wanted to make now. Then we'd think about Dr. Browning's future.

Dr. Browning, seized equally, it seemed to me, by confusion, penitence, anxiety, and the unfamiliar thrill of being a co-conspirator, had agreed to this.

"But I have to take the tiger cup," I told him. "I'm being paid to recover the Blair collection porcelains, and this is the only one I've found so far."

"Must you?" He looked stricken.

"Yes," I said. "I'm sorry. Perhaps you'd like to pack it up for me?"

He seemed almost grateful to me for the offer. Now, under my arm, as both evidence and insurance, I carried the cup, wrapped by Dr. Browning in two boxes and more layers of protective cloth than you'd swaddle a baby in.

Bill had lit a cigarette as soon as we'd hit the street. He'd finished it by the time we'd come to the crowded diner where we were now, following the path the laundry theory led us down.

The reason for the suddenness of our exit from Dr. Browning's had as much to do with what I didn't want him to focus on as with my eagerness to get moving now that we had somewhere to move. Over coffee, tea, and drippingly buttered bagels, Bill and I focussed on those things now.

"Caldwell," Bill said, thinking out loud for both of us. "He's laundering stolen art through the Kurtz. He sells it to private collectors like, for example, Blair, on whom he's recently unloaded a number of pieces. Everything's fine until Blair dies and his widow, having no idea, donates the collection to another museum."

"That's what the scene at the house was about," said I, struck by a thought. "That Rosie O'Malley told you about. It was Caldwell back from Europe, hearing that Blair had died, coming to make a gentlemanly pitch for the Blair collection. He'll buy it back, he's thinking, and no one will have to know. Or maybe she'll even donate it. Wouldn't that be a coup? Only it was already gone."

"No wonder he left on a bad note. So then he stole it back?"

"He sort of had to, if Dr. Browning is right. He couldn't risk anyone seeing those pieces."

"So he finds Hsing Chung Wah, renegade Golden Dragon, to do it for him," Bill went on. "How does he do that?"

I thought about that question, but couldn't find the answer. "I don't know. But," I said, struck by yet another thought, "maybe that's how Lee Kuan Yue gets into this."

"What's how Lee Kuan Yue gets into this?"

"Damage control. He finds out that the porcelains are gone and that Hsing Chung Wah took them. He's not really closely tied in to the Chinatown organized crime network, but he does what he can to recover the stolen porcelains, for his sister."

Bill drained his coffee cup. "Could be. Seems to fit." Then he asked the question we'd both been skirting. "And what about Trish Atherton?"

I didn't answer at first, sitting quietly at our little table island, surrounded by a storm of waiters swirling plates of pancakes and omelettes and homefries through the air around us. Then I gave him the answer we both knew. "Caldwell killed her. She found out, and he found out that she found out, and he killed her."

"How did she find out?"

He asked that not because he couldn't come up with half a dozen theories of his own, probably the same as mine, or different but as good. He asked it because this is the point when you can't just make it up anymore, when you have to talk it all out and poke holes in each other's theories until you find ones you can't poke holes in. This is the point when you're talking about people's lives. This is when you have to be right.

"The other p.i.," I said, breaking off a piece of bagel. "Jim Johnson, whoever he is and wherever he came from. His questions made her suspicious, and she started to look."

"And who is he, and where did he come from?"

"I wish I knew." I sighed. "If he did start her thinking and she ended up dead, he's got something to answer for."

"And she found . . . ?"

"Well, she found something, because she made plans to meet Johnson later on, according to Steve."

"Why did she act so strangely about the bowl with Steve's dog on it?" Bill wondered.

Licking butter off my fingers, I was hit by a thought. My

eyes met Bill's, and I realized he'd been hit too. I said it first: "Because she already knew."

"She was part of it," Bill said. "She would have to have been. She acquisitioned the porcelains."

I could almost hear the clink as pieces dropped into place.

"She was part of the laundry," I said, my words tumbling fast. "She didn't want to admit to the dog bowl for the same reason Dr. Browning didn't tell us about the tiger cup. So no one would find out it had been stolen twice." I gulped some tea and started up again. "But she panicked after Johnson came. She was afraid it would all fall apart. She wasn't worried when we were there because she didn't know why we'd come. But after Johnson, she was ready to get out. I'll bet she was going to sell information to him and split."

"Sell Caldwell, you mean," Bill said.

"Exactly. Only Caldwell showed up before Johnson, found out what was going on, and took care of her."

"Her, and the computers too, at the same time."

"Destroyed the records!" I said. "Damn. You're right. So now his little scheme is in the clear. We can't prove it. We can't prove anything."

Something else occurred to me. "That rat," I said. "That's why he didn't say anything about Steve being gay when Bernstein had that stupid idea about a romance between Steve and Trish. It's not that he didn't know or wanted to protect Steve's privacy. He was just figuring the more suspects, the merrier."

We looked at each other. I felt deflated and frustrated. Finally Bill said, "What do we do now?"

"You mean," I filled in, "do we go to the police?"

"It's homicide. It's Bernstein's case."

"It's just a theory. We have no proof."

"It's his job to find proof."

"If he doesn't tell us to go to hell."

"That's his job, too."

"I know," I said reluctantly. "It's just . . ."

Bill settled back in his chair to finish his coffee. He said,

"It's just that you'd like to keep Dr. Browning out of it if you can."

"For Nora," I said. "Because of Matt. She cares so much, and she works so hard, and this is going to be such a mess. If there were some way we could get Caldwell to trip over himself, then maybe at least Dr. Browning wouldn't have to get involved with the police. Then whatever had to happen would just be between himself and his conscience."

"Uh-huh," Bill said. "And also maybe then Bernstein wouldn't tell us to go to hell."

"Well, there's that," I admitted.

"And that," Bill grinned, "is what I love about you."

"What? My competitiveness? My fighting spirit? My eagerness to show the world that Lydia Chin does so know what she's doing?"

"No," he said. "Your absolute obviousness."

We ordered more coffee and tea, and after the waiter-shaped storm cloud had descended on our table and whirled away again we worked out our plan of action: not an elaborate plan, a let's-try-this-and-see plan.

My favorite kind.

"But," I said, after we'd gotten ourselves organized, "I have to call Nora. Don't I?"

Bill didn't answer. The conflict was mine; the resolution would have to be mine, too.

I hadn't spoken to Nora since I'd seen Matt. I hadn't told her about Matt, because I hadn't been able to think of a way. Your brother's a gangster, I could have said, your very own gangster, right here on this corner. The good news is, he didn't steal your porcelains. The bad news is, he probably killed the boy who did.

Now, added to that, was this other news: Your favorite professor is a thief.

But if Bill and I were going to go ahead with what we wanted to go ahead with, Nora, the client, would have to be in on it.

My conversation with Nora, carried on through the grace of a pocket full of change—Bill's pocket—on a pay phone where I had to keep pressing myself against the wall to accommodate the turbulent stream of waiters, was short and ultimately satisfactory. I didn't tell her about the tiger cup, or about Dr. Browning's little ones; that was the deal, and anyway as far as I was concerned the later in her life Nora learned those things the better. I didn't tell her about Matt, either, though I knew that sooner or later—and probably soon, though I'd be told it was already late—I'd have to tell Mary, and then Nora and the rest of Chinatown would know.

But right now, I had a case to solve for Nora, and all I told her about was that.

She was silent on the other end of the phone when I finished my outline.

"Dr. Caldwell?" she finally said, incredulity ringing in her voice. "Roger Caldwell? I can't believe it. I can't believe this, Lydia. I've known him for years."

You think that's a surprise, I said silently, wait until I tell you about some other people you've known for years. "Well, it's possible we're completely wrong. But if my sources are right about the faked dates and provenances, it all leads right to him."

"But murder," she said, her voice still shocked. "How could he do that, kill someone to protect his reputation?"

I felt such a pang of guilt when she said that that I had to fight an urge to hang up the phone. "People do," I said gently. "But listen: The point is this. We can't prove any of this yet. We'll have to tell the police, soon, so you'd better be prepared for that. But first, I want your permission to try something else."

"Try something else? What else?"

"We want to go to Mrs. Blair and get her to help trap Dr. Caldwell."

"You mean, without the police? Absolutely not. If he's a killer we have to tell the police right away."

"They won't be able to prove it either. All the computer records at the Kurtz are destroyed; we need some kind of evidence."

"It's dangerous."

"Not the way we're going to set it up. If she agrees we'll bring the police in on whatever we're going to do."

I stepped aside for a barrelling waiter, traded a few more sentences with Nora, and hung up the phone. Back at the table I didn't even sit down. "Okay," I said, grabbing up the check and the tiger cup's box. Bill had already left the tip money under the salt shaker. "Let's go."

"All systems?"

I nodded. He stood. We swam upstream to the front counter, paid the check, and strode out into the bright, cold, promising day.

## TWENTY-NINE

We took a cab to the Upper East Side. Wind tossed the bare branches of the Central Park trees and the sun sparkled on everything. The cab dropped us at Eighty-second and Park; we walked the block to Mrs. Blair's.

Rosie O'Malley, answering the door, gave Bill a big smile.

"My," she said, "I didn't expect to be seeing you so soon."

Does that mean you expected to see him later? I found myself asking silently, my eyes narrowing; but then I told myself sternly that that was none of my business and besides, we had work to do.

"We'd like to see Mrs. Blair," I announced, before Bill said anything.

I thought Rosie O'Malley lifted her eyebrows slightly before she smiled politely and said, "I'll just go see if she's in."

Rosie O'Malley showed us into the parlor with the satin-striped furniture and the gauzy sunlight. As we had the first time, Bill and I both remained standing after she left, looking around at the small, polished objects displayed in their well-chosen places. I examined the portrait of the younger Mrs. Blair, proud and aristocratic, gazing steadily out from the canvas. I was watching her eyes, those portrait eyes that seem to be seeing you back, when Bill said, "What's wrong with this picture?"

"Nothing," I said. "It looks just like her."

"Not that one," he said. "The one that isn't there."

I looked where he was pointing. He was right.

The silver-framed photo of Mr. Blair, the fishing picture, wasn't there.

"Well," I said. Then: "Maybe she broke the glass?"

Bill didn't get a chance to answer. The front hall echoed with high-heeled steps, and Mrs. Blair opened the parlor door.

"Ms. Chin." Dressed in a severe, elegantly simple navy wool dress, she gave us a smile of greeting. "Mr. Smith. Good morning. Please, sit down."

We thanked her and sat. Arranging herself with not an extraneous movement on the chair with the delicate arms, Mrs. Blair asked, "I assume you've come about the case?"

"We have," I acknowledged. "It's a little delicate. We need your help."

"Of course." She nodded. "I'll do whatever I can. Delicate in what way?"

"We've found the man who stole your husband's porcelains," I said. From habit, I watched her closely as I spoke. It seemed to me her eyes widened a bare fraction and the tiniest of frown lines appeared and then disappeared instantly on her brow.

"We think we know why, and something about how," I went on. "But we're going to need your help proving it."

"You've found him?" Her voice was controlled, shadowing something that might have been excitement. "Who is he?"

"Roger Caldwell."

She missed a beat before she spoke. "Roger Caldwell?" She seemed to hold confusion in her voice. "From the Kurtz? Why would—what makes you think it was he?"

I was about to launch into the whole explanation—keeping my sources anonymous—when it suddenly struck me that Mrs. Blair probably knew nothing about the status of the porcelains her husband had bought from Dr. Caldwell. To find out that Mr. Blair had been duped, at the end of his life, into merrily purchasing an armload of stolen goods would be a shock to her, and, I realized, a disappointment I'd like to spare her. Well, but what are you going to do, Lydia? Make up a story? Or say, trust me, just do what I tell you, don't ask questions? Bill and Mrs. Blair both sat, saying nothing, while the gauzy curtains swayed almost imperceptibly in the heat rising from the bronze grille on the floor.

Oh, go ahead, Lydia, I growled at myself. Just do it.

But tell her the worst part first.

"Have you heard," I asked carefully, "about what happened at the Kurtz last night?"

"No," she answered. "I don't believe so."

"There was what seemed to be a break-in," I said. "The office records were destroyed and a woman was killed."

"Killed?" Her face went completely pale, but she didn't move. "Someone was killed?"

I nodded. "I'm sorry. Yes. Trish Atherton, a young woman who was one of Dr. Caldwell's assistants. She seems to have been killed by the person who destroyed the records. Mrs. Blair, I'm sorry to tell you this, but we have reason to believe that that person was Dr. Caldwell."

"Roger Caldwell? He killed her?" Her hand went slowly to her mouth. She sat completely still for a moment, moving nothing, not even her eyes; then she lowered her hand to her lap again, laying it carefully over the other. Seeming to have won a battle within herself, she said sternly and with complete control, "Ms. Chin, that is a very serious accusation. I assume you have something you regard as proof when you say things like that."

"Mrs. Blair, believe me, I don't say things like that often. And we don't have proof. We have what we think is a very convincing explanation for a set of facts. But it's circumstantial. That's why we need your help."

Her black eyes, cold and appraising now, caught and held mine. All the intimidating Chinese women of my youth—my mother; my grandmother; my mother's unmarried older sister, who came from China, speaking no English, to live with us when her hair was already white and her back bent—were in that look.

Breathing in my best controlled manner, I forced myself into the same self-possession she had, though mine was only, like beauty, skin-deep. I returned her gaze.

"Very well," she finally said. "Tell me what you have in mind. We'll decide then how to proceed."

I forced myself not to breathe a sigh of relief. Okay, that's the first hurdle, Lydia. Now tell her the rest.

"Thank you." I recrossed my legs, keeping my posture as straight as I could make it, and began. "Dr. Caldwell wasn't happy when he found out you'd given your husband's porcelains to the Chinatown Pride Museum, was he?"

"No," she said evenly. "He was not."

"Did he tell you why?"

"He said he'd hoped to acquire them for the Kurtz."

"Were you aware that a number of them had come from the Kurtz just recently? That that's where your husband got them?"

"Not until Dr. Caldwell came to see me. He told me."

She said that with no change of manner, with the same steady gaze. I wasn't sure what to make of it.

"Didn't it seem strange to you that he'd want back pieces he'd just sold to your husband?"

"Perhaps it was the rest of my husband's collection in which he was interested, and he would have sold again the pieces my husband had recently acquired."

"Perhaps. Or perhaps it was those pieces he was interested in."

"Please make your meaning clear, Ms. Chin."

Oh, go on, Lydia. You'll only break the woman's heart. It's no worse than a swan dive into the Hudson in January.

I took a breath. "Those pieces, Mrs. Blair. The ones your husband bought from the Kurtz. Those are the ones you called the 'new acquisitions,' the ones that were in the crates stolen from Chinatown Pride. The point is, we think the thief chose them on purpose. And we think that's not the first time they were stolen."

For a moment she just watched me. Then she said, "What are you saying? Stolen from whom? Under what circumstances?"

Such self-possession, I thought. Learn from this, Lydia. No indignation, no righteous anger. Just the facts, ma'am.

"We're not certain of the circumstances, Mrs. Blair. But these pieces' provenances seem to have been deliberately misattributed, and the pieces were never exhibited. Instead, they were sold to Mr. Blair, who was known to keep his collection very private."

"Are you insinuating," she said, ice on her words, "that my husband was involved in some sort of shady transaction?"

"Not deliberately," I answered quickly. "Not at all. But if he'd inadvertently bought pieces that were stolen, and you gave them away to somewhere where they'd be exhibited, the whole scheme could have unraveled. So the person whose scheme it was had to get them back. So he stole them."

"And you believe that was Dr. Caldwell?"

"Yes."

"How would he have done it?" Skepticism, and something else I couldn't identify, filled her voice. "The alarm system at the Chinatown Pride building was disabled, Nora said. Surely a man such as Dr. Caldwell hasn't the skills for that sort of activity."

"We believe a boy from the Golden Dragons gang was hired for the actual theft." I paused, then continued, "Mrs. Blair, that boy is dead now too. His death is probably related to this theft."

Her brows knit together in a puzzled frown. "Dead?" she said tonelessly, after a moment. "Another death?"

"I'm sorry," I said. "I know all this must be hard for you to hear."

Mrs. Blair didn't answer that. She let her eyes wander the room, but in a curiously vacant way, as though she already knew she wasn't going to find what she was looking for.

She came back to me. "And the death of the young woman?"

"We think she was involved in the misattributions. Bill and I hadn't told her about the theft from Chinatown Pride, but someone else seems to have. She may have decided that it was time to get out, but she never got the chance. We think Dr. Caldwell killed her to keep her quiet. He destroyed the records at the same time."

Mrs. Blair was silent for a long time. The sunlight through the swaying curtains was as diffuse as fog and all the street noises were muted. I caught Bill's eye, but all I got for it was a briefly raised eyebrow.

Then Mrs. Blair stood abruptly, strode to the parlor door, and called—without raising her voice, quite a skill—for Rosie. When Rosie appeared, Mrs. Blair asked her to bring coffee. Rosie turned one way and Mrs. Blair turned the other, came back, sat.

"What is it you want me to do?" she asked.

I exchanged glances with Bill, then said, "The police are investigating the death of Trish Atherton. Everything we've just told you is theory: Now that the records at the Kurtz have been destroyed, there's no proof. We want to be able to give the police a motive, something that will tie Dr. Caldwell to Trish's murder."

"And how are you planning to do that?"

"With your help," I answered, "we'd like to try to set Dr. Caldwell up. We think if you told him you'd found records Mr. Blair had kept, and suggested that they implicate someone—but it's not clear who—at the Kurtz in this sort of laundering scheme, his reaction and the moves he makes might give him away."

"Is that what this is called?" she asked. " 'Laundering'? Such a homely, domestic word for something so distasteful."

Although she was looking at me as she said that, she seemed to be almost brooding, speaking to herself. I hesitated, uncertain whether to continue to outline the plan Bill and I had worked out, or to wait a little.

Into my pause the parlor door opened, and Rosie O'Malley entered, carrying a silver tray that held graceful silver pots and a plate of sugar cookies and flared porcelain cups with tiny flowers painted on them. She set the tray down with a quick sidelong smile at Bill and left. Mrs. Blair poured coffee from one pot for herself and Bill, and tea from the other pot for me. Until the refreshments came, she'd never asked us which we wanted, or whether we wanted anything; that would have put the burden on us, as guests, to insist that she not go to any trouble. Take lessons, Lydia, I thought.

We clinked the delicate cups in their saucers and passed the plate of cookies around. I sipped some tea, strong but not bitter, and replaced the cup on my saucer, nudging my cookie over. Nobody was saying anything, so I figured it was time to get back to it.

"What we need," I began, "is to make Dr. Caldwell think that he didn't get away as cleanly as he thought when he stole the porcelains fro.n Chinatown Pride. We need to connect him to that. From there the police will be able to connect him to the murder of Trish Atherton. And," I added, to be inspirational, "we may be able to recover Mr. Blair's porcelains. Or at least settle the question of what happened to them."

Mrs. Blair ignored that. She asked, "And the other murder? The gang boy?"

"We don't think Dr. Caldwell was responsible for that. It probably had to do with the theft, but it seems to have been a gang territory dispute more than anything else." I think, I added silently. And dammit.

Mrs. Blair finished her coffee with two elegant sips. She replaced her cup and saucer on the polished table beside her, regarded me without speaking.

"Bill and I have this worked out pretty carefully, Mrs. Blair," I said, wondering what was on her mind. "If you agree, we'll bring the police in before we start. I don't think there's any danger to you."

"Danger can mean many different things, Ms. Chin," she answered. I heard the sudden, unexpected echo of Mr. Gao's voice in my head, saying almost the same thing. "The sort of danger you're talking about is not something that concerns me."

She stood, paced the room slowly to the marble fireplace mantel. There, after glancing at the likeness of her younger self, and, it seemed to me, at the spot where her husband's photo no longer stood, she turned back to face us.

"Roger Caldwell may well have killed that young woman. He is quite capable of an act like that, I believe. If he did so, it may have been to protect whatever 'laundering' scheme, as you call it, he had created at the Kurtz. If there is a way to prove that he did, and if I can help in that, I would consider it my duty to do so.

"However, if you intend to prove that he committed that crime by connecting him with the Chinatown Pride theft, you will fail at that."

The certainty of her words knocked me off balance. I looked at Bill; he seemed as at sea as I was.

"Why do you say that?" I asked.

"Because Roger Caldwell did not steal my husband's porcelains from the basement of Chinatown Pride," she said in a tone of calm control. "I did."

# THIRTY

I felt like a department store dummy, a figure in one of those scenes where the action is frozen in the middle of a situation that's unexplained. Nothing had changed from the second before Mrs. Blair spoke until now, except that the room seemed stuck in time, no one able to move, no sounds able to penetrate from outside.

Bill recovered before I did. "Mrs. Blair," he said, gently placing his coffee cup on the table beside him, sounding as calm as she was, "would you explain that, please?"

She looked as though she had been waiting for an indication that we were ready for her to proceed.

"Everything you've just told me about the laundering scheme at the Kurtz," she said, remaining standing by the mantelpiece, "I already knew. Except its name. May I assume that, since it has a name, such things go on all the time?"

"Usually with money," I managed, staring at her. "I've never heard about it with art before."

"It's possible, I suppose, that Roger Caldwell invented it, or adapted the standard procedures of such schemes to his profession," she said thoughtfully, and with what sounded to me like bitterness. "In any case, I apologize for putting you through the process of explaining to me the entire situation and your theories regarding it, but it seemed important to me to find out exactly how much you knew. I suppose I thought—or hoped, rather—that the possibility still existed that my act could remain undiscovered. And I confess to being shocked at what you told me that I did not know: about the two deaths connected with this case."

She looked down, her lips pursed. Then she raised her head and began again.

"Ms. Chin, Mr. Smith: What you have surmised is correct, but only partially. My husband did, indeed, purchase stolen porcelains through the Kurtz. I knew nothing about it until Dr. Caldwell returned from Europe, was informed of my husband's passing, and came here inquiring as to the disposition of his collection.

"I had not met Dr. Caldwell before this, but I did know that he was one of the few people that, toward the end of his life, Hamilton was willing to leave the house to see. That had inspired in me a gratitude toward Dr. Caldwell that, I see now, was extremely ill-founded. In any case, thinking his interest solely professional, I received him and informed him I had donated the collection to Chinatown Pride, on the advice of Dr. Browning.

"I was prepared for a certain disappointment, but not for his reaction. He became extremely agitated. He told me this was impossible, and that I must retract the gift. That, of course, was out of the question. Imagine making a donation and then retracting it! It's simply not done. I refused, of course."

Mrs. Blair stopped, and the parlor was heavy with silence again. Looking no less in control than ever, but suddenly weary, she crossed the room to her seat on the satin chair. She arranged her skirt and, her back ramrod-straight, continued.

"He told me then about the stolen pieces, the six new pieces that Hamilton had bought from the Kurtz in the months before his death.

"I reacted with furious anger that he had cheated my husband in such a way.

"And he told me he hadn't."

She looked down as she said that, for the first time seeming unwilling to meet anyone's eyes.

I said, "You mean, Caldwell said it wasn't him?"

"No," she said, looking up again with her steady gaze. "I mean, he said there was no cheat."

I caught her meaning just before she explained it, but I still felt the chill of disappointment, a ghost of what she must herself have felt, as she said, "Hamilton, according to Dr. Caldwell, knew exactly what he was buying."

"Oh," I said weakly. "Oh, dear."

"Are you sure that's true?" Bill spoke up, a deep, calm voice of reason. "He could have said it just to apply pressure."

Mrs. Blair gave Bill a small, grateful smile, and shook her head. "He claimed Hamilton had wanted certain pieces for many years, pieces he had been unable to obtain. My husband was a patient man, but he was growing weaker and progressively unwell. According to Dr. Caldwell, those particular pieces were stolen on Hamilton's instructions. He claimed to be able to prove that."

"And you believed him?" Bill asked.

"I felt I couldn't take the chance. My husband was a well-respected man, both in his profession and among those who shared his love of porcelains. It was unacceptable that his reputation and good name should be destroyed after his death. Even," she said steadily, "by accusations based in truth."

"So Roger Caldwell blackmailed you into stealing your own porcelains back from CP?" I asked, still getting this organized in my head.

"No. I told Dr. Caldwell that I could not tolerate such a man as he in my house and requested that he leave at once. I said that, for my husband's sake, I would find a way to ensure that their mutual crime not be brought to light. I did not tell him what I was planning; at that time I did not know myself. He called me a number of times over the next few days, but I refused to speak to him. He didn't know what I had done until you and Mr. Smith showed him the photographs of the stolen pieces. He came to me not knowing it was I who had arranged the theft. He was greatly worried that those pieces would reappear on the market.

"I told him I could assure him that there was no question of that, that I had arranged for the solution to the problem, and that I would appreciate it if he did not contact me again."

"So you risked your own name and reputation to commission the theft?" I said.

"If my husband's reputation were ruined, would not mine be in any case?" She shrugged. "I had nothing to lose."

"Your brother," I suddenly said. Oh, good morning, Lydia! "Lee Kuan Yue. He's the one who actually made the arrangements, the one who hired Hsing Chung Wah to commit the theft."

"I wish I could deny that," she said. "I don't know how you found out about his involvement, and I must admit my heart sank when you mentioned his name to me. I'm ashamed to have entangled Kuan Yue in this, but after I had demanded that Roger Caldwell leave my house I didn't know where to turn. Kuan Yue and I have always looked out for each other."

"That's why he claimed Hsing had stolen the cup from him," I said, still following this path, thinking out loud, "but he didn't respond when I offered him hot porcelains. I thought he was lying when he said he didn't deal in antiquities, but then everyone else also said he wasn't in the stolen-art business. And he isn't, is he? Except for that one time."

"No, he isn't." Mrs. Blair shook her head slowly. "Although I'm not sure what offer you mean . . . ?"

"Never mind," I said. "An investigator trick. It didn't work, anyhow."

Mrs. Blair's look was doubtful, but she continued. "As I say, I'm ashamed to have involved my brother, but it was necessary. I have no contact with the class of person who could commit a theft. Any Chinatown merchant, however, knows, at a minimum, those gang members to whom he pays protection money. I knew Kuan Yue could find someone to arrange things. I could not retract the gift without considerable damage to my own reputation, and the gossip that would be engendered in collecting circles if I did might bring to light, eventually, exactly what I was trying to hide.

"The loss of the collection would also be a blow to Chinatown Pride. If those particular pieces could be retrieved, however, my husband's reputation would remain intact, and the rest of the collection could remain at Chinatown Pride. The standing of their museum would be—will be—greatly enhanced by their ownership of the Blair collection, and they would not feel the loss of those pieces."

"You weren't afraid of being caught?"

"There was a risk, but once the actual theft was successfully accomplished, it was small. Nora, I felt, would be unwilling to involve the police in an investigation, for the sake of Chinatown Pride's reputation, and could be persuaded to take another path."

"And we were that path. Because you didn't think we could do it." My blood was beginning to boil, but my voice was steady. After all, she'd almost been right.

"Ms. Chin, please don't take offense. No criticism of your professionalism was implied. I felt that, because your resources were more limited than the authorities', and because these pieces were not going to reappear on the market, you would be less likely to come close to the truth. I had not counted on your ingenuity, nor Mr. Smith's. In a way I must congratulate you."

I looked to Bill. He was smiling a small, polite, ironic smile.

"However," Mrs. Blair went on, in stronger, clipped tones, "the situation has changed entirely. If it's true, as you tell me, that two young people have died, then one's reputation no longer has much meaning, has it? You will not need the deception you were planning in order to unveil Dr. Caldwell. I am prepared to go to the police and tell them everything I have just told you."

Her calm and her self-possession filled the room as completely as the soft sunlight filtering through the curtains. My anger faded, and it occurred to me as I looked at her that I'd never met a more courageous person. The thought surprised me, and I put it away for later. "I think," I said slowly, "that that's the right thing to do. And I can imagine how difficult it will be, considering the reasons you did all this."

"Well," she said, "I suppose there will be some satisfaction for me in this, if it results in the apprehension of Roger

Caldwell. I do blame him for tempting a weakening, aging man into an act that, in his final few months, largely cancelled the virtue with which he had struggled to live the lifetime that preceded it."

"I'm not sure that's how it works," Bill said. "I don't think virtue at the end cancels a lifetime of corruption, and I don't think it works the other way either."

Mrs. Blair smiled at him in thanks, but didn't answer.

"Is that why you removed his photograph?" I asked gently. "Because you're angry at him?"

She returned her gaze to me and waited before she spoke. "That's part of the reason," she said. "I felt increasingly uncomfortable each time I looked at that photograph, until finally I felt I must do something. Partly it was because I was angry with him, yes. For his weakness. And for his lack of trust in me, that he told me nothing of this when he was alive. And partly, after what I had done—and entangled my brother in—I felt he must be angry with me."

The ghosts, I thought. Like my mother, she's living with the ghosts. Active presences, real beings who demand room in your life. Are we all like that, Chinese women? Are the ghosts demanding my attention too, and I'm refusing to notice?

The room suddenly seemed alive to me, the diffuse light moving with the not-quite-visible spirits of Hamilton Blair, of Hsing Chung Wah and Trish Atherton, even of my father and my mother's sister. Not all of them wishing us well, and all complaining, in voices I could almost but not quite hear, of neglect, of abandonment, of loneliness.

Stop it, Lydia. I shook myself mentally. Get a grip. This is theft and murder and cops we're talking about, not seances. Make a plan. Talk to the woman.

Before I could, however, the parlor door opened. The ghosts vanished, whisking away to corners and shadows as the solid form of Rosie O'Malley appeared, stopping at a respectful distance just inside the room.

"I'm sorry to disturb you, ma'am," she said, "but there's a

telephone call. I told him you were engaged, but he says it's important."

"Thank you, Rosie. Who is it?"

Rosie O'Malley gave Bill a lightning-fast glance and a tiny secret smile before she said, "The gentleman from the museum, ma'am. Dr. Roger Caldwell."

"Tell him I can't speak to him." The anger in Mrs. Blair's voice was faint—one tried, I supposed, not to display such strong emotions in front of the servants—but definitely there.

Rosie turned to go.

"No," I said. "Wait. Mrs. Blair, talk to him. If you can. See what he wants. It might help."

Her look was all reluctance and distaste.

"I'll get on the extension," Bill said, standing. "Be non-committal. Just let him talk."

Mrs. Blair looked at him, then stood. "Very well," she said, smoothing her skirt. "If you think it's important. I'll take it in the study, Rosie. Show Mr. Smith to the hall telephone."

The study was the back room, opening off the parlor. I stood and followed Mrs. Blair into it, trying to establish myself close enough to hear but far enough away that I wouldn't make her nervous. The small room, dim and wood-panelled, held a desk, a few large framed paintings, and alcoves whose glass-doored shelves were empty. The collection room, I realized.

Mrs. Blair picked up the receiver. "Dr. Caldwell." Frost hung on her words. She waited.

"Yes," she said. A pause. "Yes, I know them." Another pause. "No, I don't think so." More pause. I tried to hold my frustration in check. "I don't see—" Silence as he evidently cut her off. "You cannot possibly be serious." About what? I demanded silently. "That is unthinkable. I cannot—" I clutched an easy chair so I wouldn't run over to the desk and grab the phone. "You wouldn't do that," she breathed, in apparent disbelief. "There is not—you cannot prove—" Another pause. Involuntarily I stamped my foot. Mrs. Blair looked up. I held up my hands in apology. She went back to the phone. "Even if

225

I were willing, I would not know—no, it is *not* the same. I have—" A long silence, during which I almost exploded. When she spoke again the disgust in her voice was obvious. "Very well. I will consider what you say. You will hear from me." Without a good-bye, Mrs. Blair hung up.

Sitting at her husband's desk, her hand on the phone, she regarded me with a curious look.

"Well?" I said, trying to sound professional and at least a little bit disinterested. "What did he want?"

I heard the parlor door open. Bill crossed the parlor, entered the study as Mrs. Blair answered me.

"He wants me to have you killed."


T H I R T Y - O N E

I felt my jaw want to drop, but I refused to let it. "Me? Killed?"

"And Mr. Smith," Mrs. Blair told me, with an equanimity born, I suspected, of breeding and not of the emotions of the moment.

"Roger Caldwell does? He wants us killed?"

Bill and I looked at each other; he shrugged. Then he smiled.

I realized I was grinning from ear to ear.

"Mrs. Blair," Bill said, "do you mind if I smoke?"

Mrs. Blair, looking very confused, waved away the question distractedly. "No, go right ahead. Ms. Chin, what on earth is there to smile about?"

"This is good," I said, trying to collapse the smile and cut off the adrenaline flow that had sparked it. "This is very good. Tell me what he said."

Bill struck a match, lit up a cigarette that I imagined he'd been wanting for some time now.

Mrs. Blair, still looking confused and now a bit impatient, said, "He asked if I knew who you both were. I said I did. He then said that you had information that, if made public, would put him in such a bad position that it was worth his while to take rather radical measures to insure that your silence was maintained. Further, he said, your information would surely reveal my own participation in the theft from Chinatown Pride, and my husband's crime also. For this reason he was prepared to offer me the following choice: either he would turn himself in to the police, making the best deal he could by offering evidence against my husband and myself, which, he said, would result in my going to jail and the loss of my husband's good name.

"Or I could arrange to have you two 'taken care of' as I had arranged to solve the earlier problem."

"Did he actually say to kill us?" I asked, looking from her to Bill. "Did he say that?"

Bill shook his head as Mrs. Blair answered, "No, not in so many words. But he said that any solution I devised must be permanent and foolproof. He said he himself could think of only one such solution, and he was sure I could envision the same one. He said he was looking forward to reading the morning *Times.*"

I looked at Bill. He shrugged. "He'll be disappointed," he said. "Guys like me don't get *Times* obits. You?"

"Twenty-eight-year-old female p.i.s? Are you kidding?" I said.

"One question is why, if he did Trish himself, he wants to hire us out."

My mind went back to the night before, to the gum-chewing black woman cop escorting Roger Caldwell into his own office, past the body of Trish Atherton lying dead on the floor.

"You didn't see him," I said. "He looked like he was going to be sick, and I don't think he's much of an actor. Whatever happened between them, I'd bet anything he hadn't planned to kill her. I don't think he could do it again with his own two hands. Anyway," I said, unwilling to dwell on the question when I had a much more interesting one to think about, "we'll just have to ask him, won't we? Okay. So what are we going to do about this?"

Mrs. Blair stood up from her husband's desk chair. "What are you going to do? Can you even ask that? We'll go to the police at once, of course. Mr. Smith and I both heard the conversation. There can be no question as to his intentions. Roger Caldwell must be arrested immediately."

Bill and I were looking into each other's eyes, and I could see by the glint in his that he was thinking along the same lines I was.

"Yes," I said to Mrs. Blair. "We'll bring the police in. But I think we should go through with this."

"Ms. Chin, what are you saying?"

"The contract hit," I explained. "I think you should do it. And I know just the contractor."

I called Mary.

"Lydia? For Pete's sake, where have you been?" she demanded, after some yelling across the Fifth Precinct squad room had brought her to the phone. "I've been worried about you."

"Why? Has anything new happened? Between the Main Street Boys and the Golden Dragons?" A sudden fear that I hated to admit to clutched my stomach, dampened the sizzle put in my spine by the plan Bill and I, to Mrs. Blair's astonishment and disapproval, had worked out.

"No. Nothing. I just don't trust you when things are too quiet."

"Ummm." The good news was that that meant she hadn't heard about the murder of Trish Atherton and my being mixed up in it. The bad news was that I was going to have

228

to tell her. "Now, listen," I began. "And don't yell until I'm done, okay? There's a really good idea at the end of this."

"I don't like the beginning already," she said in a cold cop voice. "What's wrong?"

"Nothing. I'm about to hand you Trouble on a platter."

"Oh, thanks. That's just what I need, a platterful of trouble. Or do you mean Trouble, like in the Golden Dragons?"

"That's what I mean. You want him?"

"What's he going to cost me?"

"Nothing. It's a great collar. You'll be famous. You'll get a promotion."

"You're trying to talk me into something."

"It's too good to pass up."

"If it were that good you wouldn't be trying to sell it to me before you even tell me what it is."

Touché. "Okay, here it comes."

I started to lay it out for her, what we wanted to do. I began with Roger Caldwell and the death of Trish Atherton, which got me the reaction I expected.

"A homicide? And you didn't tell me? What the hell's the matter with you, Lydia? You're turning into the worst kind of cowboy. What are you thinking? What—"

"Mary, come on. We called the cops right away. This guy Bernstein caught the case. He's a detective. He did all the right things. You know him?"

"No. And I don't care. That's not the point. When you get to where there are two bodies involved in the same case you're working on, get out, Lydia! What's wrong with you? And don't give me the thing about this could all be coincidence. I want to know what you're working on, who it is, what it's about."

"I can't, Mary. But I can give you something better. Let me finish?"

"Lydia—"

"Please?"

She breathed out a sharp, exasperated breath. "Okay, finish. But it won't do you any good."

So I went on. I told her about the art laundry scheme, skated cleverly around the relationship of Mrs. Blair and her brother to the situation by saying that Dr. Caldwell knew the Blairs through Mr. Blair's collection, which anyway was true. I managed not to mention Chinatown Pride and my original reason for being part of this case. I spoke fast, and was eloquent, reasonable, thorough, and persuasive.

"No," she said, when I was done.

"Mary, think about it. You can take him off the street. Keep the thing from starting between the Golden Dragons and the Main Street Boys. Isn't that worth a little risk?"

"No."

"What can go wrong?"

"Besides him killing you?"

"He won't. You won't give him the chance. I won't go anyplace you guys didn't get the chance to get there first." Damn, I thought. There goes my English grammar again, and Tim's not even in the room.

"Lydia, you're *nuts*. Most people disappear when they hear there's a contract out on them. You two want to help organize it." She was silent for a minute, a good sign. "Why not just let Bernstein pick up Caldwell based on the phone call? He could squeeze him and take the Atherton case off the books, anyway. We'll deal with Trouble some other way."

"Caldwell's not the problem now. Bernstein can get him any time. But the Golden Dragons and the Main Street Boys: It's going to happen unless we stop it, Mary. You know what it'll be like if it does. We can't let it." I added the other thing I was thinking. "And I want Trouble, Mary. This is my chance. And it's yours, too. You could make Second Grade over this."

"Or get busted to night paperwork. I think it's crazy, Lydia."

Now we were really getting somewhere: "I think it's crazy," instead of "It's crazy."

"You might get some of the others, too." I tried to

230

sweeten the deal as much as I could. "For illegal weapons, anyway. You'll have probable cause to search them."

"Don't use cop terms when you're trying to sell me something. It makes me suspicious."

"Sorry." I held my breath. If Mary weren't my good, good friend, she wouldn't be yelling at me for wanting to do something this risky. But if she weren't an ambitious cop, she wouldn't have made detective this early in her career. I asked, "Will you do it?"

"I don't want to."

"Will you?"

"I'll have to run it by my C.O."

I stopped myself from cheering. "Go ahead. Call me back." I gave her Mrs. Blair's number, hung up, gave Bill and Mrs. Blair a big grin and a thumbs-up. Bill returned the grin. All Mrs. Blair had for us was a disbelieving stare.


THIRTY-TWO


M ary called back. There was a lot of arranging back and forth. Mrs. Blair, still both amazed and reluctant, called Lee Kuan Yue and asked him to come uptown. When he got there he had the same reaction to the plan as she had had, but he was finally persuaded that it was a good idea, good for Chinatown and good for all of us.

So he made his phone call and went back downtown.

And we waited.

While we waited, Mrs. Blair, her breeding impeccable even in a situation as absurd as this, had Rosie O'Malley prepare lunch. We ate in the dining room, around a table so polished—probably by Rosie—that I could see my reflection in my own eyes.

Eating sliced chicken on very curly lettuce, with a fine-crumbed white bread, butter, and pickled green beans, we talked about Hong Kong, which Bill had seen in the Navy and where Mrs. Blair grew up. We talked about my childhood in Chinatown, and about Bill's, in Kentucky and then on Army bases all over the world. It was polite conversation, the kind people have at the dining table in a dining room where family portraits watch you eat. I'd never been watched by family portraits before.

As we were finishing our coffee and tea, Rosie came to announce that Mr. Lee was on the telephone. The electricity in the room, so civilly veiled as we'd waited and conversed, jumped to life. I felt it fly through me, sparking off the table and the portraits and the glinting silverware.

We all gathered around the telephone in the hall, where Mrs. Blair briefly spoke to her brother. She replaced the receiver softly in its cradle and turned to us. "It's arranged," she said. "Kuan Yue doesn't know exactly what will happen next."

"He's not supposed to. He's out of it now. Now it's up to us."

"And what is it that's up to you? What are you going to do?"

"We're going to go downtown," I said. "And wait some more."

Which is how Bill and I came to be hanging twitchily around my office, staring at the silent phone, listening to the radiator hiss. Bill smoked endless cigarettes, I drank endless cups of tea. We sat, stood, paced, sat again, stood some more, and talked about nothing.

The only argument we were thinking about having we got out of the way early.

"There's no *point* in your being there," I objected, for the third time. "It would be better if you were with the cops."

"It wouldn't be better." Bill knocked ash off his hundred and fourth cigarette. "It would only make you feel better, because if you got killed I wouldn't get killed too. Although allow me to point out that if you get killed you won't care whether I get killed or not."

"Only in your cynical white person theology. In reality, I'm being particularly unselfish in not insisting that you do get killed with me so I could have someone I know with me on the other side."

"Baloney. You want me to live if you die, so you can come back and haunt me. I'm just trying to avoid that."

"I wouldn't haunt you."

"You do anyway, and you're still alive."

"That's not my fault."

"That you're alive, or that you haunt me?"

I glared.

"Anyway," he said, "it is. Your tall alabaster body with its long tanned limbs, your flowing mane of golden curls, the clear pale blue of your eyes . . ."

"You're not making sense."

"I'm nervous. A Chinese gangster half my age is planning to kill me and he doesn't call, he doesn't write . . . Besides, the vests are mine."

He waved his cigarette at the Kevlar body armor piled on my desk.

"I thought you were going to give me one for Christmas."

"I didn't, did I?"

"Bill—"

"Forget it. This is a crazy idea, and the only possible way I'm going to let you do it is if I'm there."

"What do you mean, 'let me'? Just how do you think you could stop me?"

"Not by physical means, clearly. But I have enormous moral authority in your life. You know that's true."

"God," I said. "If I say you can come, will you shut up?"

"Uh-huh."

So Bill won the argument. I felt guilty, but secretly I was glad.

Then came the babbling about nothing, folded in with short silences in which the radiator hissed and Bill and I each thought our own thoughts. Maybe the radiator thought thoughts, too.

It was close to two hours before the phone rang. Although that was the one thing we'd been waiting for, the sudden shrilling of the bell froze us both. I didn't grab it up until the third ring.

"Chin Investigative Services. Lydia Chin speaking." I tried not to let my words trip over themselves the way my heart was flopping around in my chest.

"So, little private eye really got office." The sneering, taunting voice was the one I'd hoped to hear.

"What do you want?" As if I didn't know. I nodded to Bill.

"How you feel? Hurt a little?" the voice asked me with mock concern.

"Go to hell."

"Mustn't talk like that," he scolded. "Not good for woman, use bad words. Little private eye still looking for porcelains?"

"Why? You have some?"

"Might. Want to talk about it?"

"Last time I talked to you I was sorry."

"Last time, because you snooping. This time Trouble inviting you."

"Where?"

"Someplace private. Better for business."

"I don't like your kind of business. Where?"

"End of pier, Christopher Street. Nice breeze, nice view. Tonight. Eight o'clock maybe."

"The end of the Christopher Street pier?" I repeated, looking at Bill. He shook his head, pulling his hands toward his chest in a way that meant "come closer." "You've got to be kidding," I said to Trouble. "You expect me to go to the end of the pier in January? At night? To meet you? Forget it."

"Little private eye want porcelains, better come."

234

"The pier, but not the end. The parking strip in front." I raised my eyebrows at Bill. He nodded.

"Hmm," Trouble said. "Okay, sure. Parking strip." It was easy to see what he was thinking: that Lydia Chin was dumb enough to think that a fifty-foot-wide block-long strip beside the highway, inhabited by stumbling junkies and the cardboard-housed homeless, was a safe place.

"It's more public," I told him. "Easier to get away from."

And, I didn't tell him, easier to fill with cops hiding behind things.

"Okay," he said. "Eight o'clock. See you, little private eye."

"One more thing. I'm bringing my partner. I'm not talking to you alone again."

"Sure, no problem," Trouble agreed easily. "Like to meet him anyway."

I hung up with no good-bye.

"What did he say?" Bill asked. "I wish you had an extension, by the way."

"Where would I put it, in the bathroom? Buy me one for Christmas. He said he wanted to meet you."

"Most people do. It's the price of fame."

"The parking strip in front of the pier? Does that sound good?"

"Terrific. What time?"

"Eight."

"He'll be early, to plant his guys."

"So Mary will just have to be earlier."

Mary, at the station house, answered the phone before the first ring was over. "Where the hell have you been?" she barked.

"You're getting repetitive. I've been in my office waiting for Trouble to call, just like I was supposed to be."

"And?"

"He called. He wants to get together." I told Mary what Trouble and I had arranged.

"Nuts. You're nuts."

"Mary, think 'collar.' Think, 'Second Grade.' "

"Think 'funeral.' "

"Think 'we've already set this in motion, it's too late to stop it now.' "

"I know. I never should have let that happen. I'm having serious second thoughts."

"I'm sorry. But even if we wanted to stop now, we really can't. Trouble thinks he's got a contract on me and Bill. He'd get suspicious if Lee suddenly told him don't bother. That could be dangerous for Lee. Unless you want him actually to go through with it, we have to do this. This way at least you'll have the situation under control, and end up with Trouble on a plate."

"Nothing you're ever involved in is under control, Lydia."

"Mary, don't shake my confidence right now, okay? Let's fight later, when it's all over."

"I just hope we get the chance."

From then on our talk was all business, going over the plan. Mary drilled me on alternative moves for different scenarios. There really weren't many alternatives: Basically, Bill and I were supposed to drop to the ground when the action started and not come up until it was over.

"Don't pull a gun," she said. "And tell your cowboy boyfriend the same thing."

"He's not my boyfriend, and he's not a cowboy."

Bill made a face of wounded pride.

"Let us do the shooting," Mary went on, ignoring me. I decided not to press the point, under the circumstances. "We're going to be all over them the first weapon we see. That's all we're going to wait for."

"Okay," I said.

"He'll get there early." Mary repeated what Bill had said. "To spot his boys around. We'll be there earlier. Don't worry."

"You're the one who's worrying."

"Someone has to."

"You just said not to."

"I'll see you later. You have your vests?"

"Yes."

"Goodbye. Lydia?" she said, as I was about to hang up. "Good luck."

"I don't need it. I have you."

She hung up, instead.


The next few hours were excruciating, just a long bridge, a causeway to be sped over as fast as possible connecting now and later. Because there was the possibility, small as it was, that the appointment had only been to throw us off guard and Trouble could be planning an ambush, Bill and I had decided to stay together and out of sight. We left my office as soon as I hung up with Mary and took a cab to Bill's place. No Golden Dragons were in sight and no one followed us.

At his apartment Bill put on music. We started with something relaxing and soothing—Chopin Ballades, he told me—but that didn't work, so we moved to jumpy, fast-moving works, by Bartok and Scriabin (names I knew) and then Sessions and Pärt (names I didn't). We read the *Times*. Bill, who works out of his house, did paperwork. At six we called Shorty downstairs and asked him to send up chili for Bill and a spinach salad for me. We ate, cleaned up, put the *Times* on the recycle pile.

We looked at each other.

I asked, "Can I say, 'let's roll'?"

"Just once."

"Let's roll."

We Velcroed ourselves into the vests, me ouching as mine pressed on the bruises left from my last meeting with Trouble. Bill checked his .38, which we both knew was loaded and antiseptically clean, and slung his shoulder holster over his vest. I checked my .22 and put it in my jacket pocket.

"You're going out there with that?"

"That creep stole my .38, I told you that. One of the

237

many things I have against him. This is the only other weapon I have a license for besides a slingshot."

"You might be better off with a slingshot."

"Mary says we're not supposed to use them, anyway. She specifically said to tell you that."

"I don't intend to have to. Isn't that the plan?"

It was. And it was a good plan, too.

And it almost worked.

## T H I R T Y - T H R E E

Shouldered with concrete barriers and filled with frozen puddles, the broken pavement of the parking strip at the end of the Christopher Street pier spread itself four car lengths wide on the river side of the West Side Highway. There was one way in, off the highway from the north, and one way out, onto the highway from the south.

A hard breeze was pushing in off the water as Bill and I drove in. Black choppy waves roughened the river's surface, dulling the reflections of the lights that glinted from the New Jersey waterfront. As we rolled slowly down the length of the strip, I thought that the river's other shore had never seemed so far away.

The tree-lined streets and intimate restaurants of Greenwich Village beckoned coyly from across six lanes of traffic; here, with the whoosh of cars on one side and the lapping of the river on the other, the most picturesque objects were a few parked cars, some abandoned ones, and a jettisoned supermarket cart.

On the strip's north end, hard up against the wet, rough timbers that formed the river-side edge, three figures hunched around a fire built in a steel drum. Cinders flew into the air, thrashed wildly in the wind, and blinked out.

Other scattered people could be seen in this freezing no-man's land. Leaning on the burned-out hulk of a car, a pair of black men waved their hands in jerky, slow-motion emphasis to whatever drugged-out discussion they were having. A figure so swaddled in coats and hats that I couldn't tell its sex or age snored, legs spread, back against a wooden piling, an empty bottle of Thunderbird by its knee. Others, shadowy, moving little, huddled in the darkness near the cars, or in the meager protection of the windowless cars themselves.

Bill pulled halfway down the strip and parked against the timbers, as we had arranged with Mary. He let the car idle for a few seconds longer than he usually does; then he turned it off.

We looked at each other.

He said, "You take me to the nicest places."

I tried to think of a wise-guy comeback, but I didn't have one.

Bill leaned toward me, kissed me softly. His kiss was warm and the touch of his hand on my hair was warm and I knew the night outside, on this rubble strip between the black river and the mindless headlights of the highway, was icily cold. For the first time I ever remember, Bill was the one, in the end, who moved away.

"Ready?" he asked.

"No."

"Want to wait awhile?"

"Uh-huh. How about until June?"

"Sure," he said. He grinned.

I grinned back, wondering if his felt, from the inside, as shaky as mine.

There was no signal, and no more words, but it was time. We opened our doors.

Another glance at each other.

We got out.

This was the scariest part. My heart pounded a fast staccato beat against the walls of my chest.

I had Trouble pegged as a guy who'd want to gloat, who'd want to be in his victim's face, taunting and laughing, before he pulled a trigger. We were counting on that.

But I could be wrong. Maybe he'd decided to just wait until we were exposed and, from cover, blow us away. Even with the vests, flying bullets were a thing you wanted to avoid: They could hit you in the head, and you'd die. Or the knee, or the hand, and your life would never be good again.

With jerky glances I scanned the parking strip. I seized on the wavering of a shadow. I jumped at a paper bag tumbling across the pavement. I bit my lip, waiting for the explosive burst of gunfire, snapping my head around when a piling cracked against the pier.

I realized I was holding my breath.

Let go, Lydia, I told myself. It looks like it isn't going to happen.

And nothing happened. Over the roof of the car, Bill's eyes met mine. We closed our separate doors, not slamming them, just pressing them shut. We walked around to the trunk, met there, and waited.

"How many of these guys do you think are ours?" Bill muttered, gazing across the asphalt at the zombie figures, half-seen in the darkness and shadows.

I thought, suddenly, about my mother's ghosts, and Mrs. Blair's. And my own.

I said, "I hope all of them."

The tide was in; even this far up, the Hudson reeked like the ocean, salty and smelling of distance. On the highway, cars that didn't know we were even here raced by in both directions. Eerie yellow light from the towering streetlights made all the shadows sharp, but didn't let me see if anything was moving in them.

And something was.

"Little private eye!" A shout; three figures, sauntering out of the shadows, ambling easily toward our car, toward us.

"Christ!" Bill said, under his breath, but he didn't move. "That's him?"

"Sure as hell," I said.

Beside me, Bill lifted an eyebrow.

I never swear.

"Little private eye!" Trouble repeated. "And look, big private eye too." Stopping about six feet from us, he grinned at Bill. "Hi. Name is Trouble."

"I know that," Bill answered steadily. "I'm Smith."

"Okay," said Trouble.

I looked at the boys with Trouble, standing one on each side, wearing identical leather jackets and identical sneers. The boy on Trouble's left was greasy-handed Jimmy, from the time in the courtyard. I didn't know the other.

"So," I said briskly, "you have something to sell?"

Trouble grinned. "No."

"No?" I made myself sound indignant. "Then why'd you bring us all the way out here? I thought you were selling something."

"Not sell," said Trouble, still grinning. "Give away."

"You said porcelains. You're giving away porcelains?"

"You know," Trouble said thoughtfully, "porcelains making trouble for Trouble since you first come talking them. Fucking porcelains bad for Trouble, bad for face. Maybe now, people stops."

"Stops what?" Dammit, Lydia, speak English.

"Stops looking," Trouble said. "Last time, private matter, for face. Everyone doesn't knows. Now, everyone will knowing. People gets killed because porcelains, maybe other people stops."

"Killed?" The conversation was going more or less according to plan, but my heart didn't want any part of it. It was trying to escape from my chest. It took a few seconds before Trouble's words really registered.

When they did, I realized that I actually wasn't sure what was going on.

" 'Last time'?" I asked. "What does that mean, 'last time'?"

Trouble chuckled. So did Jimmy. The other boy was busy looking around nervously; he must have missed the joke.

" 'Last time'?" I repeated.

Then the light dawned.

I suddenly felt lighthearted and happy, an unacceptable sensation when you're standing in the icy wind in zombie-land with three guys who've come to kill you. "Hsing Chung Wah," I marvelled.

Bill cut me a look; I saw the light dawn on him, too.

Trouble grinned, but he didn't answer.

I nodded to myself. "That's the way it was, isn't it? The Golden Dragons killed Hsing Chung Wah yourselves. Not Bic." Not Bic. Life was good. "Not the Main Street Boys. They didn't kill anybody."

"Oh, little private eye getting so smart." Trouble applauded me sarcatically.

"For face." Bill picked it up. "Lydia's right, isn't she? You had an arrangement with the Main Street Boys, and Hsing broke it. You didn't know anyone had stolen porcelains from Chinatown Pride until Lydia came to see you. It pissed you off, didn't it? Made you look bad, a guy who can't stick to a deal. So you had to find out who it was. That probably wasn't hard. Maybe Hsing even bragged about it. To embarrass you. To make you lose face. I'll bet he did, didn't he?"

"Hsing Chung Wah." Trouble stopped grinning; he spat on the pavement. "Little stupid boy. Thinks can be big shot, *dai lo*, big maybe as Main Street Boys, even big as Trouble. Bullshit little boy."

"Yes," I said. "But you had to do something about it."

"That's right," Bill said, his eyes on Trouble. "That's why there was no payback, why the Golden Dragons never came for the Main Street Boys. What Hsing did was bad for the Dragons' face. It made Trouble look like he couldn't control his own crew. Trouble couldn't let that happen, so he had one of his boys blow him away. Right?"

"Not boys!" Trouble snarled. "Trouble doesn't needing

boys, give him face! Trouble does everythings Golden Dragons needs!"

Stepping sharply in, Trouble shoved Bill back against the
car.

Bill, caught off balance, seemed to stumble. Then his fist
drove forward, caught Trouble under the ribs. Trouble
grunted. He grabbed for Bill's throat. Greasy-handed Jimmy
whipped a gun from under his jacket to hold on me in case I
had any ideas about wanting to help.

All right, Mary! I thought. Look, a gun. Come out, come
out, wherever you are.

As Bill broke Trouble's hold, the lounging black junkies
from the burned-out car sprang into action. "Police! Don't
move!" one yelled. They charged across the broken asphalt.

More shouts. The three guys from the steel-drum fire
raced down the pavement in our direction.

Trouble spun around, forgetting about Bill. He whipped
out a gun, aimed at one of the racing cops.

Jimmy, next to him, did the same.

The other kid, wild-eyed, didn't seem to know where to
turn. He had his gun out too, waving it while he stared frantically around as though he were looking for something.

Then a car screeched onto the parking strip from the
highway. It burned rubber to reach us. Rocking and fishtailing
as the driver slammed the brakes, it swerved to a stop between
us and the cops.

The passenger-side door flew open. A figure stepped half
out, one foot on the pavement, one still in the car.

"Hey, asshole!" a familiar voice bellowed. My blood went
cold. "Trouble! Asshole! There are some people you don't
touch!"

"No! Don't!" I yelled, my words flying into the freezing
wind. But it was already too late, before I spoke.

I heard the chatter and whine of automatic fire.

Something slammed into me, knocking me to the ground.
It was Bill, who pressed me to the pavement as Matt Yin, with

the AK-47 he hugged against his hip, blew Trouble and Jimmy away.

The other Golden Dragon flew toward the car, yanked open the rear door. I thought Matt was going to shoot him too, but he didn't. The kid flew in and the door slammed behind him.

Tires screeched again. The car plowed straight on. Cops dove for cover, shooting after it.

It didn't stop.

## THIRTY-FOUR

It took a long, long time to get things straightened out at the Fifth Precinct, a long time before Mary let me go home.

In fact it was a long time before she even came to speak to me in the stuffy interview room where the uniforms who'd hauled us down to the station house had stuck me. One rough-voiced cop had opened the door after some interminable length of time and asked if I wanted coffee. When I shook my head he didn't give me a chance to ask for tea, just said, "Suit yourself," and shut the door again.

Except for him, I was alone for over an hour, trying to breathe and meditate and find some way to chase from my mind Matt's hard smile, and the wink he'd given me as our eyes met in the second before the car sped off.

Even in the dry, overheated room I still felt cold. It was a cold that came partly from hunger, partly from standing in the shivering wind off the river for a time that felt like forever. The EMS and the Crime Scene Unit and the Medical Examiner's man had raced onto the parking strip, squealing their tires, screaming their sirens, flashing their lights. Numb, I'd watched as the medics and the cops did what they do, moved around and over and between the blood and the bodies. Radios had chattered and squawked, and horns had honked impatiently as the highway traffic had slowed so the drivers could gawk.

I'd mumbled answers to some questions, though I had a feeling more had been asked than I had really heard. Mary, finally, sounding more disgusted and angry than I'd ever known her, told someone to take me and Bill downtown, and stalked off without looking at me. Trouble's blood was freezing into crusted pools on the broken pavement by the time I was led away.

Now, staring at the grimy mustard-yellow wall of the interrogation room, I sank my hands deeper into my jacket pockets, hunched my shoulders up further, tried to stop thinking, tried to be warm.

When Mary pushed through the door carrying two steaming styrofoam cups of tea I was almost glad to see her.

She put the tea on the gouged wooden table and stood there, hard-faced. I just looked at her, unsure what to say.

"Well?" she finally asked. "Well? What the hell was that?" When I didn't answer, she gestured shortly to the tea. Then she yanked out a chair for herself across the table.

Sitting, she said again, "What the hell was that?"

I reached for a cup, held it in both hands. The tea was dark and bitter and the styrofoam squeaked. My hands trembled, no matter how hard I tried to make them behave.

I sipped at the tea, until I thought maybe I could talk.

"I don't know, Mary." My words were scratchy in my throat. "I didn't know about any of that."

"You didn't know Matt Yin was Bic? You didn't know the Main Street Boys had an informer on the Golden Dragons?"

She almost yelled her questions at me. "You didn't know who killed Hsing Chung Wah? Don't lie to me, Lydia! You're in enough trouble already."

"I only knew . . ." Those words didn't sound like words at all. I cleared my throat and tried again. "I knew about Matt. But not any of the other things. What was supposed to happen tonight—what was supposed to happen was what we set up. Trouble was supposed to think he was ambushing me and Bill, and you were supposed to ambush him. Really, Mary. That's really what I thought."

"And Matt? When were you going to tell me about that?"

"I . . . I don't know. I don't know why I didn't."

"I know why. Because you know everything. You know better than anyone, and you're going to solve everybody's problems and be everyone's hero."

She reached for the other cup of tea. "So now Matt's killed two people," she said. "So they wouldn't kill you." She looked up from the tea. I felt like she'd punched me. "And we can't find him. Do you know where he is?"

I shook my head. I offered weakly, "There's a restaurant in Flushing . . ."

"China Seas. We've been there. We picked up two of his boys. That's how we know about the informer and what was on Matt's mind. Are you lying to me now, Lydia? Do you know where he is?"

I shook my head some more. "I never lied to you. Really. I didn't tell you everything, because I wanted to protect some people, but I never lied."

"Protect. Who the hell are you to protect anyone? Protect who? Matt?"

"No. Well, maybe." My confusion must have been as obvious to Mary as it was to me, because she shoved her chair back from the table and began to pace the room behind me. "Nora," I said, before she spoke.

"Nora? Nora Yin? What do you mean, so she wouldn't know her brother was a gangster?"

"Yes. But not only that. I thought he'd killed Hsing Chung Wah. For her."

"What do you mean, for her?"

"He was protecting her too." That thought struck me as funny. I swallowed some tea so I wouldn't start to giggle. Matt was protecting Nora. Lee Kuan Yue was taking care of Mrs. Blair. Brothers making a mess all over New York, taking care of their sisters. I started to giggle anyway, tried to hide it in a cough. Oh, please don't get hysterical, Lydia, I begged myself. Chew on your styrofoam, but please don't get hysterical.

It seemed to be a losing battle. I sputtered as I swallowed some tea. All those brothers. The Five Chinese Brothers. One of them had an iron neck, one could swallow the sea.

Then a thought, like a big black wave of icy Hudson water, broke over me.

I sobered up instantly.

"Lydia?"

I was startled back to the mustard-colored room by Mary's voice.

"Lydia, what's wrong with you? Don't zone out on me. There's no room for that. There's too much going on now."

"No," I said. "No, I'm all right." Which wasn't true. I had an answer now to a question I'd almost forgotten, and the anger that had suddenly exploded in me was enough to bounce me off the walls.

Instead, I sat where I was, drank the rest of my tea, and told Mary about the case. I guessed it didn't matter, now. I heard myself talking, about Nora, about Chinatown Pride, about Bic and Trouble and Dr. Caldwell—who had been picked up by Bernstein from the 19th on a conspiracy-to-murder charge an hour ago, according to Mary—as if I were a long way away, as if all this were some story that might or might not have actually happened, but in any case hadn't happened to me.

As I talked, the anger burnt itself out rapidly, like a fire you can start but just can't keep lit. The numbness took over

247

again. I knew I was way beyond the end of my strength, running on fumes and habit. And the need to be tough.

Mary waited until I was through. Then she asked questions and I answered them. She went away, came back, asked some more questions. She went away again, for a long time.

Finally, she came back. "You can go home," she said.

"I can?"

"It doesn't make anybody happy, but nobody can think up a reason to hold you. Get out of here before someone does."

I started to stand. As soon as I moved I realized I was badly stiff and sore and, I found, dizzy enough to grab onto the table.

"You going to be all right?" Mary asked, concern peeking out grudgingly around the edges of her voice.

"I'm fine." I stood on my own two feet, and didn't fall down, so that must have been the truth. "What about Bill?" I asked her.

"He has a different problem."

"What problem?"

"He wouldn't tell us anything. He kept saying it was your case, it was up to you. He made my lieutenant mad. They booked him for obstructing an investigation."

"Oh, Mary, come on! I told you what you wanted to know. What's the point?"

"Gives the guys something to do."

"You're really going to make him spend the night down there? I have to call his lawyer and everything?"

Reluctantly, she said, "I'll call over and see what I can do."

"Thanks."

"Not that I feel like doing either of you any favors right now. You made me look pretty stupid. We could have lost people. There's going to be an investigation. This whole business is going to be trouble for a long time."

"I thought it was a good idea." I was too exhausted to defend myself. "You thought so too, didn't you?"

"No. I let you talk me into it."

"I'm sorry, Mary. I really didn't know."

"No," she said. "You really didn't think."

## THIRTY-FIVE

I stumbled home through the empty streets of Chinatown. Shutters were down, gates were locked, boxes of rotting rejects from the fish and vegetable sellers cluttered the sidewalks. At least in this season they didn't stink.

It wasn't late, not really. Just past eleven. My mother would be watching the news on the Chinese cable channel. I could have a bath, steam up the tiled room with Mr. Gao's mountain herbs. I could sink down into the hot, hot water, listen to the silence, look at nothing. It was achingly tempting, though I knew that it really wouldn't work. I knew what I'd be seeing would be Matt Yin's hard smile, and what I'd hear would be Mr. Gao, telling me that danger can mean different things to different people, and that I should keep away from Bic.

The high nasal voice of the Chinese newscaster pierced through the door as I turned my key in my mother's multiple locks. It was a little loud, and anyway it was what I expected to hear. Until I was actually through the door I didn't hear the other conversation going on inside, the one being carried out in quieter, more casual tones, as befits a discussion between mother and son.

"Ling Wan-ju!" my mother called out, as I shut the door behind me. "Come say hello to your brother. He stayed late waiting for you."

I stood frozen for a moment in the little vestibule. I felt

like a piece of machinery whose gears wouldn't catch. Then the reserve fuel tank kicked in, and anger shot fireworks through my system again.

I stepped out of my shoes, stalked into the living room without bothering with my slippers. Standing in my leather jacket and formerly decent black pants, now streaked with parking strip mud and dust, I stared down at my mother and Tim, side by side on the flowered couch.

My mother, unperturbed, barely looked up from her mending. "Why are you so late?" she asked, and broke a thread with her teeth.

"I was working."

"Hmm." Tim cleared his throat, shifting a little in his seat. Or maybe he was squirming. Good, you creep, I thought. Squirm. "That's really what I wanted to talk to you about, Lydia," he said, in a lawyer voice. "That's why I came over. We've decided it's gone far enough, this detective thing—"

"Investigator," I said in English. "Licensed private investigator."

"Whatever." Tim switched to English too. "We really think you have to stop this, Lydia."

"Who's 'we'?"

"The family. Ted, and Ma—"

"Andrew? Elliot?"

"It's not as though we had a meeting or anything," he hedged. "But you know how everyone feels."

"No. I know how *you* feel. And boy, do I know all about that, Tim."

"I want you children to speak Chinese," my mother interjected crossly. She'd been watching us like a spectator at a ping-pong match.

"I think this is better done in English, Ma," I told her in Chinese. "As a matter of fact I think it would be better in private. Come on," I said in English to Tim, and started to head for my room.

"Absolutely not!" My mother's tone was the one you

didn't argue with. "Anything you have to say to your brother you can say in front of me. In Chinese," she added.

"Is that how you want it?" I asked Tim. In Chinese.

"I . . ." He looked uncomfortable, but he said, "Sure. Why not?"

Chinese then. "Because this is about you. This is about how little you trusted me. This is about how you were so worried that I was going to screw up and make you look bad that you hired someone to watch me! A white p.i., a guy who called himself Jim Johnson while he was messing around in my case but I'll bet his name is something else. He's not very good. But I'm sure he has a license and I'm sure he's experienced because fancy uptown lawyers don't hire just anyone, do they?"

I was sputtering and I knew it and it made me even angrier. I could feel my cheeks burning. Tim just sat there stony-faced, probably the face he used across the negotiating table from an opponent he disliked but whose case was stronger than his. He looked like he was trying to think up a strategy.

"Lydia, I—"

"Don't bother!" I cut him off savagely. "You had him following me. That's how you knew I'd met with Trouble, isn't it? He reported to you on every move I made."

My mother said, "Trouble? The *dai lo* of the Golden Dragons? Ling Wan-ju, what a terrible thing to do!"

"Don't worry, Ma," I said bitterly. "He won't be a problem to anyone anymore." I said to Tim, "When I caught on, your guy stopped following me, but he kept popping up in all sorts of other places involved with this case. What was he supposed to be doing, keeping an eye on me? Or solving the case so it would go away?"

Tim stared at me for a moment before he answered. My mother was mercifully silent.

"Both," Tim finally said. "In the beginning he was supposed to follow you, see what you were up to and use whatever you found to solve the case himself. After you spotted him I told him to keep working on the case but to keep away from you so you wouldn't get lucky again. He has a lot of experience, Lydia. Much more than you have."

" 'Lucky'?" I could have punched his pompous face. "And you thought that would make a huge difference? How much experience he had?"

"Lydia, you're just a kid! You're—"

"I'm two years younger than you and I've been in this business six years! How long have you been a lawyer? Do you know this experienced guy of yours got someone killed?"

That stopped him. It stopped my mother too, who my antennae told me had been on the verge of cutting in. There was no sound in the apartment except the Chinese newscaster, giving us the market closings on Taiwan.

Tim broke the silence, one weak word.

"What?"

I told him about Jim Johnson, about his visit being enough to inspire Trish Atherton to try to sell out Roger Caldwell, and about the end of Trish Atherton's life on the floor of the office in the darkened museum.

When I finished, the room flooded with silence again. I was suddenly exhausted: empty and tired and disappointed and almost too weak to stay on my feet.

Finally my mother spoke.

"Ridiculous," she said.

"What?" I echoed Tim. I had no idea what her meaning was.

"It's ridiculous that anyone your brother hired could be held responsible for such a thing. If this happened it's because the girl was greedy. I'm not at all surprised, with the sort of people you associate with. It's because of the profession you're in, Ling Wan-ju. Your brothers wouldn't have to look after you if you were more sensible. And more obedient," she added. "Your brother was trying to protect you. You should be grateful to him."

She began to fold her sewing, with deliberate, satisfied movements. Tim said nothing. He sat on the couch next to our mother, looking defiant and uncomfortable, but not looking wrong.

"I'm going to bed," I said, and turned and walked away from them.

I locked the door to my room, something I've almost never done since the last of my brothers moved out. Dropping my clothes in a heap, I crawled under the covers, curled up tightly, and worked on not crying myself to sleep.

## THIRTY-SIX

When I woke up in the morning Tim was gone. I had my hot bath, the one with the mountain herbs, and I soaked in it a long, long time. I heard my mother bustling around, and I let the sounds rattle in my head. They were reassuring sounds. She was my mother. Lots of people didn't have mothers. Bill didn't have one anymore. I'd never heard the story, but I knew that for many years they hadn't spoken, and they'd never really reconciled. I'd always thought how sad that was.

When I was ready, when I felt soft and limp and warm, and finally, in some way, clean, I got out, dried, dressed, and went to talk to my mother.

The table was set, breakfast for one. There were two steamed dumplings, a bowl of congee with tiny pieces of pickled radish, rice sticks, sweetened milk. On one of my mother's best dishes, one her older sister had brought from China when she came to live with us in America, an orange cut in eighths spread itself like a blossoming flower.

My mother just happened to wander from the kitchen

into the living room with a pot of hot tea as soon as I entered from the other direction.

"Sit down," she ordered me. "Everything will get cold." She poured my tea.

"Okay, Ma," I said as I pulled my chair up to the table. "Do you want to talk about it?"

"I don't know what you mean. Eat your breakfast."

I picked up a rice stick, dipped it in the milk, and talked about it anyway. "I appreciate that you love me. I appreciate that you're worried about me. I'm even willing to admit it's barely possible those are Tim's motivations too. But this is what I do. I'm not going to stop just because you make me *dim sum*."

She stood with the teapot in her hand, her lips a narrow line. "Always talking," she said. "Always knowing best. If you don't eat you'll get so thin finding a husband for you will be even harder."

She turned and disappeared into the kitchen with the teapot.

"You know, you solved the case for me, Ma," I called behind her.

"What are you talking about?" she muttered, as if she didn't care much what I answered.

"Something you said the other day. It came back to me just at the right time and gave me an idea. It was absolutely perfect. It solved the case."

"Well, then." She turned the water on in the sink and started making domestic noises with pots and pans. "If you listened to your mother more often you would solve many more cases."

I picked up a dumpling in my chopsticks. That was practically permission, I thought, as I dipped it in scallion sauce and took a bite. From a Chinese mother, that was just about carte blanche.

\* \* \*

254

I called Bill after breakfast. On the sixth ring I was about to hang up, but he answered.

"Smith." His voice was deep and rumbly.

"You sound like you're asleep," I told him.

"I was," he said groggily. "Are you okay?"

"Better than you. I didn't spend the night in jail."

"I didn't either. Only half of it."

"I'm sorry about that. I really am. Nobody ever went to jail for me before."

"That you know about," he corrected me. "Anyway, it wasn't so bad. They had me in a holding cell with two unlicensed Senegalese street vendors. I learned half a dozen words of Waloof."

"Tell them to me."

"There's only one I'd repeat without being afraid you'd punch me."

"I wouldn't punch you. You have too much credit with me right now."

"Come over and let me earn some more. I have a present for you."

"No kidding, really?"

"Well, I don't have it. But I could go out and get it and be back by the time you get here."

"I have to go see Nora first."

"Oh." He paused; I could hear him striking a match, pulling on a cigarette. "Want me to come along?"

"No. I need to do this by myself."

"Okay. Call me when you're done?"

"Definitely."

Before I went over to Chinatown Pride I called the Fifth Precinct. Mary wasn't in yet, they told me; she'd had a late night.

I called her at home.

"I have a peace offering," I said.

"It's going to take more than that."

"Can it be a beginning?"

"What is it?"

"The other p.i. The one who called himself Jim Johnson."

"You know who he is?"

"No. But I know someone who does."

"Who?"

"My brother Tim."

"*What?*"

I told her what.

When I finished, Mary said, "I don't believe he did that." She sounded almost sympathetic.

"He thinks I'm a jerk. He was afraid I'd make him look like a jerk."

"He looks like a jerk to me already."

That was definitely sympathetic. "Thanks, I appreciate that. Anyway, go tell Tim the NYPD is interested in talking to Johnson. It'll help make the case against Caldwell."

"Caldwell's not doing so well already. His lawyer is looking to bargain and he hasn't even been indicted. Why hasn't Johnson called us? He must know he's a material witness."

"Because he's not a public-spirited, cooperative type of p.i., unlike some other people."

"Don't push it."

"Sorry," I said quickly. "Can I ask you one more thing, and then I'll get off the phone so you don't get tired of me?"

"What's that thing?"

"Is there any chance you found my gun?"

"Your gun? You'll be lucky if I don't pull your license! Anyway, no, we didn't find it in Trouble's place or the gang apartment. It was just a .38 revolver, right?"

"But mine."

"Well, not anymore. That's not a fancy enough piece for these boys to be seen with. They probably sold it the day they stole it."

"Damn. Well, thanks anyway. Listen, Mary?"

"I thought you were hanging up."

"I am. It's just that when you go see Tim, try to keep a low profile, okay?"

"You mean don't embarrass him? I can't believe you care, after what he did."

"Well, he wouldn't have done it if it weren't really important to him. I'd like to take him outside and slug him, but I'd rather he not lose face in front of the people in his office."

"You're unbelievable. I'll call you later."

I hung up, overjoyed that she'd ended this call the way we'd been ending calls to each other all our lives.

I didn't call Nora. I just went straight over. This was going to be hard enough, but doing it on the phone would have been impossible.

In the surly door, up past the peeling paint. I knocked on the open door of Nora's office. She looked up from the paperwork cluttering her desk. Her pen stopped in her hand.

"Hi," I said.

"Hi." Her look was serious. I stepped into the office and closed the door.

"Mary was here last night," she said, before I said anything.

"She told you about Matt?"

"Why didn't you tell me, Lydia?"

"I would have, Nora. I just wanted to solve the case for you first, so I could give you good news at the same time as the bad news."

One corner of her mouth lifted ironically. "That's not such good news either, is it?"

"No. Mary told you about that too?"

"Yes, and then Mrs. Blair called this morning. She said as long as it was going to come out she wanted to tell me herself."

"What's going to happen?"

"You mean, about the theft? Nothing. If we don't file a complaint there's no crime. The boy who actually broke in here is dead, I understand. We're certainly not going to prosecute Mrs. Blair and Lee Kuan Yue. I wish she'd just *asked*. Just

257

taken her gift back. So it would have looked strange. How bad would that really have been?"

"That's what this was all about, on all sides, wasn't it? Face. Reputation. People desperate to protect their good names."

"And other peoples'." Nora shrugged. "Well, it's over. We're not going to do anything at all, now. Especially since there's nothing to recover anyway."

I didn't understand. "Nothing to recover?"

"The porcelains." She gave me a strange look. "Mrs. Blair destroyed them. Didn't you know?"

"She *what?*"

"So that they wouldn't be a threat any more to her husband's reputation."

"My god." I felt a little sick. I flashed to the silver-framed photograph of Hamilton Blair that Mrs. Blair had removed from her mantel, because she was angry with him and because she thought he must be angry with her.

It hadn't occurred to me at all to wonder what he was supposed to be angry with her about. I'd thought she meant the theft.

"But they weren't hers," I said. "I mean, they weren't his. They were *stolen*, Nora; that was the whole point. You can't just destroy stolen goods."

"The records at the Kurtz are gone," Nora pointed out. "Now the porcelains are gone. Now it's over."

I frowned. I didn't like it, but she was right.

"How did you find out?" Nora asked me. "That Mrs. Blair was responsible?"

"Did she say I did?"

"She was very impressed with you and your partner, she said. She congratulated me on hiring you. She said you reminded her of herself when she was young, except you were braver."

I sat up a little straighter and tried to keep my chest from swelling. "She's being very generous. Anyway, we didn't figure it out. We were close but on the wrong track. Once we knew about the laundered porcelains it started to come together, but I'm not sure we'd have gotten it if she hadn't come out and said it."

"How did you know about the laundering?"

"Dr. Browning." I thought of Dr. Browning, his anxious solicitude for his little ones, their gleaming small presences in his dim, musty room. I thought about the reason Hamilton Blair's ghost was angry with Mrs. Blair. I made a decision. "He remembered something he'd forgotten about the Kurtz museum. It tied things together for us."

"Poor Dr. Browning," she said. "It'll break his heart when he hears that those pieces were destroyed."

"It will," I agreed. And cause him to treasure the tiger cup I still had in my office safe even more deeply, when I gave it back.

Almost as deeply as Mrs. Hsing would treasure hers.

"You should have told me about Matt," Nora said then, her eyes on mine. "I could have helped him."

"He thought he was helping you."

"And you. And you thought you were helping both of us. And now look."

"Has . . ." I hesitated to ask, but I did anyway. "Have they found him?"

She shook her head. "He's completely disappeared. I think he may have headed back West. He has a lot of friends out there, in all sorts of places." I was silent, not wanting to ask the next question, not feeling I had any right to the answer. Nora answered it anyway. "I told Mary all the ones I knew. But I think he has a lot of friends I don't know about."

"You sort of hope it, right?" I asked quietly.

"I don't know what to hope. I don't know how to think about this at all."

I didn't either, know what to hope or what to think.

Nora got up, turned on the electric kettle. We sat in silence until it boiled. Spooning jasmine tea into a creamy white pot, Nora said, "There's going to be a major investigation at the Kurtz. One of the Board members called me this morning about being on the outside committee."

"Are you going to do it?"

"Probably. The more credentials we acquire in the outside world the better it is for CP."

"Caldwell's other assistant," I said. "Steve Bailey? I don't think he knew anything about it. It would be good if you could clear him. He loves this work. It would be a shame if he came out looking bad and couldn't work in this field anymore."

"That's one of the things we'll try to do, then. But I don't know anything about investigating."

She handed me one of the thick cups. I tasted the tea. It took me a minute to understand what she was saying to me.

"Nora? You want me to be involved?"

"We'll need a professional investigator. You already know about this case."

"I can't believe you ever want to work with me again."

"You're pushy and headstrong."

"That's what my mother says."

She smiled. "But no one can say you're not discreet." Her face got serious again. "You just have to learn to trust other people, Lydia."

"Uh-huh," I said, sipping my jasmine tea. "I'm working on it."


When I left Chinatown Pride I called Bill. He was home, so I went over. I walked along Canal Street through the sunny, cold day, stopping to glance at the earrings and scarves, the electronics parts and the leather jackets the shopping crowds were pawing through. Two tall black men were selling Rolex knockoffs from a stand set up on a pair of cardboard boxes. I watched them stamp their feet and blow puffs of steam out with each breath. I wondered if they were the Senegalese vendors Bill had spent the night with, and what Waloof sounded like.

At a Korean fruit stand a few blocks from his place I

stopped and bought flowers. He buzzed me in and held the apartment door open while I came up the steps.

At the top I handed him the bouquet.

He kissed my cheek. "You brought me flowers?"

"The etiquette book says always bring flowers to people who spend the night in jail for you." I unzipped my jacket. "You didn't have to do that, you know."

"I had no idea how much you wanted to tell them. I thought it was safest just to keep my mouth shut. You would've done it if it'd been my case."

"Oh, you think so?" I flung my jacket and hat on the sofa.

"I know it. That's why I bought you a present."

He lifted a ribbon-tied shoebox from his desk.

"Wait," I said. "I want to tell you some stuff first, that you probably don't know."

"This must be important stuff. I've never seen you turn down a present before."

"I'm not turning it down. I'm saving it."

"Okay. Sit down, and tell me the stuff."

I started with Matt's disappearance. He already knew; he'd called a friend in the NYPD and asked him to check on the situation.

"I don't know how I feel," I said. "He gunned down two people in cold blood. I saw him do it. I ought to want him caught."

"But you don't."

"I don't know," I said again, helplessly.

"You don't have to want anything. The police are going to do what they do and they're going to find him or not. You can't stop them and you can't help, can you?"

I shook my head.

"Then you don't have to decide how you feel."

I looked into his deep brown eyes, just looked for awhile. "You know," I said, "sometimes you're particularly smart."

"Don't spread it, you'll blow my cover. Open your present."

"No, there's still something else."

"What's that?"

"Jim Johnson."

"You're kidding. You smoked him out?"

"Not exactly. I found out who he was working for."

"Who?"

I told him who, and why, and what the scene with Tim had been like.

"My mother thinks he was worried about me. But that wasn't it. And it's not the point anyway," I said at the end. "Even if he *was* worried about me, it's because he thinks I'm no good at what I do. Otherwise he wouldn't think I'd screw up. Is he right?"

My question caught Bill off guard. "Is Tim right? About what?"

"Me being an incompetent, lousy detective."

Bill lit a cigarette, shook out the match, looked at me with an expression I wasn't sure how to read.

Finally he said, "Open your present."

"Don't change the subject."

"It's the same subject."

He reached for the shoebox and handed it to me. I took it; it was surprisingly heavy.

"Lead Nikes?" I asked doubtfully, weighing it in my hands. I untied the ribbon and lifted the lid.

Under one layer of crumpled red tissue paper and nestled on another was a Smith & Wesson Model 10 .38 revolver.

I lifted it out, broke it open. It was empty, so I took aim, fired, let the hammer click. It fit my hand perfectly. I opened my mouth to say something and realized there was a lump in my throat. Oh, come on, Lydia! I thought. You're getting choked up about a *gun*.

"I didn't like you running around with a .22," Bill said. He was grinning. "I asked Mike when I called about Matt Yin whether there was any word that they'd found guns anywhere they'd searched. He told me no, so I figured your .38 was gone. So I got you a new one."

"You can't do that," I stammered.

"Why not?"

"Well, for one thing, you can't *do* that. You can't just buy me a gun and give it to me in a shoebox. There's paperwork. There's all sorts of things, i.d. and things—"

"I know. We have to go do the paperwork. The guy who runs the gun shop where I got it is a friend of mine. I promised I'd bring you in this afternoon. We'd better go or he'll kill me. And we need to get all that done in time for dinner."

"Dinner?"

"Doesn't the etiquette book say you have to take your employee to dinner at the end of a case?"

"Oh, I'm taking you?"

"There's a clam house in Hoboken where they make linguini with calamari that's been haunting my dreams."

"I thought I haunted your dreams."

"No. You haunt my every waking moment. My dreams are still my own. But I'll tell them to you if you want."

I put the gun carefully in the box, put the box carefully on the coffee table. I got up, walked over, and kissed him. The kiss made me think of another, on a bench by Central Park under the glow of a streetlight.

"You know," I said, "I think someday I might want you to do that. But not now."

I stood up and straightened my shirt. "Right now, I think we should go do the paperwork. Then maybe I'll take you to dinner. There's this clam house in Hoboken where I hear they make great linguini."

I picked up the gun in the shoebox. We put our jackets on and we locked up Bill's place. Sunshine glowed off glass and chrome and the cloudless blue sky seemed huge, endless, and full of possibility as we walked out onto the New York streets.